D0174284

DARK
MIRROR

DARK MIRROR

M. J. Putney

St. Martin's Griffin ⚘ New York

This is a work of fiction. All of the characters, organizations, and events portrayed in this novel are either products of the author's imagination or are used fictitiously.

DARK MIRROR. Copyright © 2011 by Mary Jo Putney, Inc. All rights reserved. Printed in the United States of America. For information, address St. Martin's Press, 175 Fifth Avenue, New York, N.Y. 10010.

www.stmartins.com

Library of Congress Cataloging-in-Publication Data

Putney, Mary Jo.
    Dark mirror / M. J. Putney.—1st ed.
        p. cm.
    ISBN 978-0-312-62284-8
    1. Young women—Fiction.   2. Magic—Fiction.   3. Boarding schools—
England—Fiction.   4. Aristocracy (Social class)—England—Fiction.
5. London (England)—Fiction.   I. Title.
    PS3566.U83D37 2011
    813'.54—dc22

                                                        2010040374

First Edition: March 2011

10 9 8 7 6 5 4 3 2 1

To all the brave people who came together at Dunkirk to rescue an army,
which was the first essential step toward saving Western Europe.
Your courage will never be forgotten.

ACKNOWLEDGMENTS

My thanks to all the usual suspects, most especially Pat Rice and Susan King for helping me bat this around, and to John, who is terrific at the warrior stuff.

A special thanks to two most excellent editors: Betsy Mitchell, who suggested I write YA, an idea that immediately seemed absolutely right. And to Sara Goodman, who had the brilliance and exquisite taste to fall in love with Tory and her friends.

I mustn't forget the amazing Robin Rue, an agent who is willing to let her authors follow their mad particular stars, and also thanks to her assistant, Beth Miller, who was a great help as I shaped *Dark Mirror.*

Nicola Cornick and Elspeth Cornick generously offered to help make my prose properly British and accurate to the period. I'm grateful for your help. Any errors are mine.

Many thanks also to John Tough, archivist of the Association of Dunkirk Little Ships, who helped me as I struggled to make the evacuation as accurate as I could.

PROLOGUE

London, late seventeenth century

"Be damned to all mages!" the earl snarled as he stormed into the coffeehouse.

Sally Rainford, the proprietress, rolled her eyes silently. There were more than a thousand coffeehouses in London, but hers, the King's Cup on Saint James Street, had the most aristocratic patrons. And most, like this earl, were a plaguey nuisance.

The earl gestured to Sally to bring coffee, then claimed a seat at the communal table occupied by a dozen or so of his fellow aristocrats. "We must make the practice of magic illegal in England!"

Make magic illegal? How could they ban something so natural? Keeping her thoughts to herself, Sally assembled a tray with coffee, a small pot of cream, and little bowls of shaved chocolate, cinnamon flakes, and chipped sugar.

The cool viscount sitting opposite the earl arched his brows. "That's rather extreme, my dear fellow. What happened?"

Sally carried her carefully prepared tray to the earl. She'd rather pour the coffee on his head, but that would be bad for business.

"A poxy mage used his power and almost seduced my youngest daughter." The earl stirred a spoonful of chocolate shavings into his coffee with angry jabs. "I've made sure the brute won't seduce any more wellborn young girls, but if it hadn't been for his magic, he would never have dared try."

Sally stifled a snort. Maybe it made the earl feel better to blame a mage, but young girls often had roving eyes.

"Was it Hollinghurst? That young beast has used magic to seduce other women," a tight-lipped baron said.

The earl gave a sharp nod. "But seduction is not the only trouble mages cause. We should ban the lot of them!"

"Lord Weebley uses magic to cheat at cards," another man growled. "I'm sure of it, but I've never had proof. Bloody impossible to prove magical cheating."

The scowling baron stirred sugar chips into his coffee. "Magic is a tool of the devil, and it's time we banned it. Who hasn't suffered at the hands of mages who use their vile powers to cheat and manipulate? I say it's time we start to burn witches again!"

Disturbed, Sally pressed a hand to her belly. It was too soon for the babe to show, but her husband, Nicodemus, came of a Kentish family known for magical ability. Likely this child would be a mage, too, since Sally was a talented hearth witch. That was why her coffee was the best in London.

It hadn't been all that long since witch hunts were common, but these days, most people had come to see the value of magic. Plus, witches had started calling themselves mages, which didn't sound so wicked.

Sally didn't think that the bad old days would come again now that magic was so widely accepted. But far too often she heard patrons of the King's Cup make angry comments like these. Friends who worked in great houses reported similar remarks. Maybe in time the fancy folk would disdain all magic and leave the benefits to commoners like her.

A tall, lean man whose dark wig cascaded past his shoulders had been lounging by the fire. Raising his voice to carry through the coffeehouse, he said, "A total ban would never work. Most Englishmen like magic. They celebrate if their children show strong gifts since such talents can be profitable." He stroked his thin moustache idly. "No point in passing a law no one will obey."

Sally gave thanks that the most important man in the room was showing his usual good sense. His opinion encouraged others to speak up. A duke said thoughtfully, "A total ban wouldn't be in our best interests. I almost lost my wife and son in childbirth, but a mage healer saved them both."

"Can't afford to get rid of weather mages, either," a gruff northerner said. "As wet as it is in Westmoreland, most years my tenants' crops would rot in the fields if I didn't employ a good local mage to send half the rain away."

Sally nodded approval. The Rainfords were best known for their weather magic, and it was men like the northerner who kept them prosperous. Her husband's earnings had enabled them to start the King's Cup.

The tall, dark-haired man drawled, "Perhaps social censure might serve you better than a law. The aristocracy is small compared to the great mass of Englishmen. Though it's not feasible to ban magic throughout England, influential gentlemen like you should be able to drive magic out of the nobility. Leave it to the lower orders."

There was a pause while all the lords in the room considered the words. The angry earl said slowly, "We should speak out about how unsporting and vulgar magic is."

"We can give the cut direct to mages. Involve our wives, since they rule the social world." The cool viscount gave a faint smile. "My lady recently complained about a mage duchess who uses power to enhance her beauty. My wife was furious. She and her friends will gladly use their influence to make magic unfashionable."

"My mistress has strong illusion magic, and she can change her appearance to look like any woman I fancy," another lord said. "It's like having a harem of the most beautiful women in England!"

There was a burst of laughter from the other men. The viscount said, "I foresee a world where people of our sort are above magic, but we benefit by how commoners use it." He smiled slyly. "My mistress has very similar talents."

Sally sniffed but kept her gaze down while the lords raved about all the ways they could demonize magic among their own kind. Mostly the lords didn't notice her unless they wanted more coffee, but if someone saw the expression of contempt on her face, there might be trouble. These men had power, and it was best not to offend them. Wiser to concentrate on shaving chocolate and nipping loaf sugar into small pieces.

Sally set a pan of coffee beans to roast, thinking the viscount was right. Foolish aristocrats would drive the mages from their ranks. She touched her stomach again. Her babe would have magic. When it was born, its talents would be welcomed, and that was as it should be.

But she felt sorry for those poor doomed magelings who would be born to the nobility.

CHAPTER 1

England, 1803

Lady Victoria Mansfield flew high, high over her family's estate. Arms and legs outstretched, long skirts fluttering around her knees as she gloried in her freedom and in the soft scented wind.

She laughed with delight as she saw the familiar Somersetshire hills from above. Here was the vast stone length of her home, Fairmount Hall, there the beautiful gardens that ran to the bluffs. Waves crashed far below, and gulls soared at Tory's height, their cries haunting.

She swooped down to investigate the round stone dovecote. Doves squawked in protest when she flew inside. Startled, she almost plunged to the ground.

Concentrate on staying aloft. With a giddy rush, Tory swooped up again, soaring through the door of the dovecote and into the sky. Perhaps she should fly to the nearby estate of the

Harford family. The Honorable Edmund Harford was the eldest son and heir to his father's title and property.

She'd always admired Edmund. He was back from university for the summer and she wanted him to see that she had grown. Perhaps he'd think she was almost as pretty as her older sister, Sarah.

Tory banked into the wind and turned east toward the Harford estate.

A horrified cry shocked her awake.

Jolted from sleep, Tory realized she was floating a yard above her rumpled bed, terrifyingly unsupported. Her mother, the Countess of Fairmont, stood in the doorway, her expression horrified. "Victoria," she breathed. "Oh, please, *no!*"

Tory glanced up into the canopy above her head. A spider had spun a web in the corner, and the ugly creature was looking right at her.

She shrieked and crashed down on the bed, her breath whooshing out as she flopped onto her stomach. Shaken and afraid, she pushed herself up with her arms. She couldn't really have been flying! "What . . . what happened?"

"You were flying." Her mother closed the door, her white-knuckled hand locked around the knob. "Don't ever do that again!" she said, voice shaking. "You know how society feels about mages. How . . . how your father feels about them."

"I can't be a mage!" Tory gasped, shocked by the impossibility of her mother's words. "I'm a Mansfield. We're not magical!"

At least not that Tory had ever heard. Seeing the countess's guilty expression caused her to ask incredulously, "Mama, have there been mages in our family?"

Such a thing wasn't possible. It just *wasn't!* Magic corrupted, and she wasn't corrupt. Yes, she'd felt herself changing as she grew to womanhood. Strange dreams, new desires. But those were just growing pains. Not *magic*!

Tory refused to believe her mother could be a mage. Lady Fairmount was considered the greatest lady in the county, an example to all wellborn young ladies.

And yet . . . guilt was written as plain as day on the countess's lovely face. When the countess refused to reply, Tory's world began to crack beneath her.

"Do *you* have magical ability?" she said, shocked and desperately unwilling to believe such a thing. Yet looking back . . . "You always knew what we were doing. Geoff and Sarah and I thought you had eyes in the back of your head."

"There were rumors," her mother whispered, tears shining in her eyes. "About my Russian grandmother, Viktoria Ivanova. The one you're named for. She died when I was very small, so I didn't really know her, but . . . it's possible she brought mage blood into the family."

Tory's namesake had poisoned the blue-blooded Mansfield family with magic? And Tory might suffer for that? It wasn't *fair*!

Feeling utterly betrayed, she cried, "How could you not warn me? If I'd known I might have magic, I could have guarded against it!"

"I thought you children had escaped the taint! I have very little power. Scarcely any at all. It seemed better not to worry you about such an unlikely possibility." Lady Fairmount was literally wringing her hands. "But . . . you look rather like Viktoria Ivanova. You must have inherited some of her talent."

Tory wanted to howl. Voice breaking, she said, "I've never floated like this before. It's just a freak, something that will never happen again, I swear it!"

The countess looked deeply sad. "Magic appears when boys and girls grow to adulthood. It's hard to suppress, but you must try,

Victoria. If your father finds out, he'll certainly send you to Lackland."

Tory gasped in disbelief. Though children of the nobility who had magic were often sent to the prisonlike school called Lackland Abbey, surely *she* wouldn't be forced to leave her friends and family! "You've managed to hide your power from everyone, and so can I. I'm another whole generation away from Viktoria Ivanova." Tory drew a shaky breath. "No one will ever know about me, either."

"The ability to fly is not minor magic," her mother said, expression worried. "You may find it harder to hide your abilities than I have."

"I wasn't flying!" Tory protested. "I always toss and turn when I'm sleeping." Knowing how feeble that sounded, she continued. "If I am cursed with magic, I'll learn to control it. You always said I was more stubborn than Geoffrey and Sarah put together."

"I hope you succeed," her mother said sadly. "If your ability becomes known, I don't think I'll be able to save you from Lackland Abbey. God keep you, my child." Silent tears fell unchecked as she backed from the room, closing the door behind her.

Leaving her daughter alone in a shattered world.

Tory struggled not to panic. She *couldn't* go to Lackland Abbey. Even when students were cured and sent home, they were considered tainted, like the madmen at Bedlam Hospital.

Uneasily she remembered a story whispered by her best friend, Louisa Fisk. The daughter of a baron from nearby Devon had been sent to Lackland after her family discovered she was a mageling. The girl had been betrothed from birth to the son of a family friend, but the betrothal had been broken immediately.

When the girl finally left Lackland, she'd been forced to become a governess. A year later, she walked off a cliff.

Tory's bedside candle cast enough light to reveal her dim reflection in the mirror opposite her bed. The rest of the family was tall and blond, while Tory was petite and dark-haired. The countess always said her dark hair, slim build, and slightly tilted eyes had come from her Russian grandmother. Tory rather liked her exotic looks. It was horrible to know they might have come with despicable magical ability.

But the magic didn't show. With her wide eyes and a glossy night braid falling over the shoulder of her lace-trimmed white nightgown, she looked like any normal, harmless schoolroom girl.

Her gaze traveled around her bedroom. Her beautiful, grown-up room, redecorated as a present for her sixteenth birthday because Mama had said she was a young lady, and a lady's room might make her less of a tomboy.

Tory loved the rich moldings, the elegant rose-patterned brocade upholstery, the carved walnut posts that supported the matching brocade canopy of her bed. It was the bedroom of a young lady who would soon be presented to society and would have her pick of the most eligible young men in England.

Her mother had given her this beautiful room but failed to warn her that she might be cursed with magic. It was *damnable*!

Tory shivered, wanting nothing more than to crawl into bed and pull the covers over her head. But she must discover if she truly did carry the taint of magic.

She sat on the edge of her bed and imagined herself flying as she had in her dream. She felt a fluttering in her midriff, but to her relief, nothing happened. She remained solidly on the bed.

But was she trying hard enough? She closed her eyes and thought of herself floating in the air. She concentrated so hard that her head began to ache. Still nothing.

She wasn't a mage. It was some kind of misunderstanding!

Then the inner fluttering stabilized with a silent click. Dizziness— and Tory shrieked as her head bumped a yielding surface. Her eyes snapped open and she saw that her head was pushing into the bed's brocade canopy.

Shocked, she fell, bouncing from the edge of the mattress onto the soft Chinese carpet. Knees bruised, she got to her feet and tested herself again. This time she kept her eyes open as she consciously sought that inner change.

Click! She rose from the carpet with alarming speed. Too fast!

With the thought, her movement slowed and she floated gently up to the ceiling. She felt light and no longer afraid as the air supported her as softly as a feather mattress.

For an instant, excitement blazed through her. She could fly!

Her pleasure vanished instantly. Wielding magic was vulgar. Dishonorable, even. Noble families like Tory's were the descendants of kings and warriors. Mages were mere tradesmen like blacksmiths and seamstresses. A Mansfield would rather starve than go into trade.

Yet the pulse of magic that held her in the air felt so *good*. How could it be evil?

Her lips tightened. Teachers and vicars invariably said that feeling good was the mark of sin. She must never fly like this again.

But before she put magic away forever, Tory wanted to explore her amazing, appalling new ability. She tried to swoop across the room as she'd done in her dream, but the best she could manage was drifting a little faster.

She looked down onto the top of her bed's canopy. Ugh! Dead bugs. She'd tell a maid to take the canopy down for cleaning.

Tory drifted along a wall until she reached one of the carved angels set in each corner of the room. This close, she saw patches where the gilding had peeled away from the wood. The bare spots weren't visible from floor level.

She wasn't really flying, she decided. Not like a bird, not like a Turk on a flying carpet. But she could float safely and control her direction and speed if she concentrated.

Her new ability wasn't very useful, apart from allowing her to get books from the top shelves in her father's library. Tiring, Tory descended too fast and banged hard on the carpet.

She winced as she rubbed the stinging sole of her right foot. She must take more care in the future. . . .

No! She would never fly—float—again. Doing so was *wrong,* and exhausting as well. Tory could barely manage to climb the steps up into her bed.

Tory rolled into a ball under the covers, shivering despite the warm night. It was impossible to deny the truth. She, Lady Victoria Mansfield, youngest of the Earl of Fairmount's three children, had been cursed with magic from her unknown great grandmother.

But she wouldn't let it ruin her life. She *wouldn't!*

CHAPTER 2

"Tory!"

The annual Fairmount summer fete was in full roar. Tory could barely hear her best friend calling over all the happy chatter. Every person of consequence in western Somersetshire was on the Fairmount lawn today. Bright banners flew from canvas pavilions while a string quartet brought all the way from London filled the air with music.

Tory cut through the crowd to meet Louisa Fisk outside the sprawling food pavilion. As they hugged, Louisa exclaimed, "What a lovely day! I was afraid all the rain we've had this week would ruin the fete, but today there's not a cloud in the sky."

"The weather is always fine for our lawn fete." Tory grinned. "My mother will not permit rain and cold to ruin it."

"Does your father hire a weather mage every year?" Louisa asked.

"No, we're just lucky." Tory's words were light, but a sobering thought struck her. Though Mama concealed her magic, she hadn't said she never used it. Might the very proper Countess of Fairmount create lovely sunny days for her entertainments?

In the fortnight since she'd learned of her magical ability, Tory spent all her spare time learning how to suppress it. She'd found a slim volume in her father's library called *Controlling Magic* by An Anonymous Lady. She'd read through the book three times and practiced the exercises daily. According to the Anonymous Lady, control was mostly a matter of will, and Tory had plenty of will.

Louisa said teasingly, "Lord Harford's carriage wasn't far behind us, so your Edmund will be here soon."

"He's not my Edmund." Tory looked down, blushing. "But . . . I shall be glad to see him. Do you think he'll notice how I've grown?"

"He'll notice!" Her friend scanned the crowd. "Has Mr. Mason arrived?"

Tory nodded toward a small group of young gentleman standing at the far edge of the lawn. "He's over there with my brother. It would be most polite to go and offer your greetings. One smile and Mr. Mason will be dazzled."

"I hope so!" Louisa adjusted her flowered bonnet, then headed purposefully toward her quarry.

Tory silently wished her friend luck. Louisa and Tory had shared tutors, dreams, and gossip over the years. Though Louisa's father was a vicar and had only a modest fortune, the Fisks were well connected—Louisa's mother was second cousin to a duke. Since Louisa was also pretty, intelligent, and charming, she would marry well. Frederick Mason was a fine choice, both pleasant and in line to inherit a handsome manor nearby.

Tory collected an apple tart from the food pavilion, then glanced toward the house to see if Edmund Harford and his family had arrived. Not yet.

She loved this annual gathering. Her brother, Geoffrey, Viscount Smithson and heir to the earldom, was visiting with his wife and their adorable two-year-old son. Her big, good-natured brother had moved to an estate in Shropshire when he married, and she missed him dreadfully.

It was Geoffrey who had taught her to ride, patiently leading her pony around the ring as she learned how to keep her balance and control her mount. He'd taught her how to fall, too, because riding meant falling.

Her sister, Sarah, eight years older than Tory, was to be married before Christmas, and her fiancé had come for the fete. As a small child, Tory had followed her big sister around like a puppy. Sarah had been remarkably patient.

Tory looked again toward the house to see if Edmund Harford and his parents had appeared. Not yet.

She was finishing her apple tart when Sarah and her fiancé, Lord Roger Hawthorne, joined her. "You're looking very grown-up, Tory," Lord Roger said with a smile. "Soon you'll be as pretty as your sister."

"Never that," Tory said with regret. Sarah had inherited her mother's height and lush blond good looks, unlike Tory.

"Prettier." Sarah took Roger's arm with the confidence of a woman who knew she was loved. "She's like a fairy sprite. With her dark hair and bewitching blue eyes, Tory will have every eligible young man in London at her feet when she's presented."

"I hope you're right!" Tory said with a laugh. She watched a little enviously as the couple strolled away. They had what Tory wanted— not just a "good marriage," but a love match. Lord Roger was kind, witty, and handsome, and he had a promising career in Parliament. Sarah would enjoy being a political wife, and the two doted on each other. What more could any girl want?

"Tory, Tory, Tory!"

She turned barely in time to catch her nephew before he could cannon into her. "How's Jamie?" she said, brushing her hand over his soft blond curls. "Are you being a perfect little cherub today?"

Cecilia, Geoffrey's pretty, fair-haired wife, laughed. "Definitely not a cherub, but we're enjoying ourselves." She scooped Jamie up. He was getting to be quite an armful. "It's almost time for his nap."

A pleasant male voice said, "Good day, ladies. You're both in fine looks."

Despite all her watching, Tory hadn't seen Edmund coming. She blushed at the compliment as she turned to greet him. University life must have suited Edmund. He'd always been a good-looking boy. Now he had the easy confidence of a man.

Luckily her sprigged muslin dress was new and the sapphire blue ribbon trim brought out the color of her eyes. "Edmund!" she said gaily. "You look well also. I want to hear all about Cambridge."

Edmund offered his arm to Tory. "Shall we admire the sea while I tell you tales of university life? But I can't tell you *all*. Your mother wouldn't approve!"

Laughing, she took his arm and they moved toward the cliff that bounded the far edge of the gardens. There was definite admiration in Edmund's eyes. Sensing that he found her attractive was a heady sensation. Fluttery and breathless, like when she experimented with flying.

She *mustn't* think about that. Magic was just an odd kick in her gallop, of no importance to her life. Edmund was real.

Tory felt a pang of envy as she listened to Edmund's stories. "Your classes sound so interesting," she observed. "It's a pity females can't attend. My godmother thinks there should be colleges for girls."

"Cambridge is no place for females." He smiled down at her. "You are much too pretty to bury yourself in dusty books, Lady Victoria."

He said she was pretty! Though she loved learning about history and other countries, being thought pretty was so delightful she was willing to overlook his foolish belief that girls and books didn't go together.

They reached the path that edged the cliff and turned right. As the wind whipped Tory's skirts, she drew Edmund farther from the brink. "Stay away from the edge. The rain has made the ground soft, and bits of cliff fall off regularly."

He obligingly moved away from the ragged edge. "I was glad today dawned so bright and clear. I've been looking forward to the Fairmount fete all summer."

Her pleasure in his words was undercut by worry that her mother might have invoked the fine weather. If Mama was discovered doing such a thing, her reputation would be ruined.

Would Papa set her aside as his wife? Tory didn't think so, but— she wasn't sure. Papa took his dignity and his responsibilities very seriously. He would lose his influence in the House of Lords if the other peers knew his countess was a mage.

The pair strolled along the cliff. Tory never tired of watching the sea, and seeing it with Edmund was even better.

When the path ended at a hedge that divided the gardens from the pasture, they turned to retrace their steps. Edmund said, "I must return to Cambridge for the Michaelmas term, but I'll be home at Christmas." He looked down into her eyes, his gaze lingering. "I hope to see you then."

Trying not to sound breathless, she replied, "I shall look forward to seeing you." She was acutely aware of his strong arm under her hand. Would he prove to be *the one* for her? Perhaps, but she must be presented in London before making a final choice of husband.

Others were also enjoying the cliff path. A hundred yards ahead, her brother walked with some of his particular friends. Tory grinned as she saw her nephew running toward his father, chubby legs churning with delight because he'd escaped his mother.

"Papa, Papa!" Jamie called happily. He swerved onto the cliff path.

Tory's smile froze with shock as the earth crumbled away under his pounding feet. The small blond head vanished and he fell from the cliff, still shrieking, *"Papa!"*

Cecilia, who had been following her son at a brisk walk, stopped dead, horrified. Then she raised her skirts and raced screaming to the cliff. "Jamie! *Jamie!*"

Geoffrey bolted from his friends and caught up with his wife at the edge where Jamie had fallen. More of the cliff crumbled under Cecilia's feet.

Geoffrey grabbed his wife, jerking her back with a hoarse cry. "Cecilia!"

They tumbled to safety on solid ground, but Cecilia immediately jerked loose from her husband and began to crawl toward the cliff on hands and knees. "He was only out of my sight for a moment!" she cried, agonized.

Tory launched herself toward them but was stopped in her tracks when Edmund caught her arm. "The fewer people there, the better," he said grimly. "That whole section is unstable."

She bit her lip, knowing he was right. Several years back during the winter rains, a chunk the size of the Fairmount drawing room had crashed into the sea.

"Get back!" Waving his friends back, Geoffrey lay on his belly and inched forward to look over the edge. After a moment, he exclaimed, "Thank God! Jamie is caught in a clump of shrubs halfway down. Jamie, lad, can you hear me?"

"I'm sorry, Papa," a plaintive voice called over the wind. "I didn't mean to fall."

"We'll bring you up safely," his father promised. Geoffrey's voice was calm, but there was terror on his face.

Tory dropped to all fours and crept toward the edge so she could see. Edmund grabbed at her ankle. "Stop! The cliff is too dangerous."

She kicked his hand away and kept crawling. "He's my nephew! I have to see," she retorted. "It will be all right. I don't weigh much."

The ground was soft under her hands and knees, and she felt a worrying tremor. She made herself think about how she was ruining her new gown rather than become paralyzed with fear that this section of cliff would also collapse.

Tory reached the edge and flattened herself on the turf. Below and a hundred yards or so to her left, Jamie was balanced precariously in the fork of a tough shrub that grew from the cliff face. He was safe for now, but the shrub could tear loose at any moment. Jamie might tire and lose his grip on the thin branches. The choppy wind might knock him off.

The child glanced her way. Though bruised and filthy, he smiled through his tears. "Aunt Tory!" His eyes were the same deep blue as hers. He opened his left hand and reached toward her, swaying badly. "I'm scared!"

Tory cringed. "Hang tight to the bush, Jamie! We'll have you safe soon."

He gripped the shrub again, his face woebegone. "Soon!" His voice almost vanished in the wind.

As earth crumbled under Tory's left hand, Edmund exclaimed. "Lady Victoria, come back from there! You can't do anything, and it's not safe."

"Safe enough. Jamie knows I'm here. I won't abandon him." And if he fell— Her heart twisted with agony. It would be an unforgivable betrayal if she was too cowardly to bear witness to his last moments.

After a long pause, he said, "Very well, if you're sure. I'll join the men. When ropes are brought, they'll need someone to go down the cliff and bring the child up. I'm lighter than most, so perhaps I can help."

"Work quickly!" She glanced over her shoulder, fighting tears. "He can't hold on much longer."

"Be careful, Lady Victoria." Edmund headed toward the rescuers while Tory turned back to Jamie. Was the shrub starting to pull out from his weight?

She pushed herself up on her hands for a better view. The soil shifted menacingly. Panic shot through her—until she remembered her despised new ability. If the ground collapsed, she should be able to catch herself and float to safety. Because of her unwanted magic, she was the one person present with nothing to fear.

Ropes had arrived, and Geoffrey was being lashed into a crude harness. She frowned. Of course her brother was frantic to rescue Jamie, but he was tall and broad. Too heavy for the fragile cliff edge. She uttered a desperate prayer as he lowered himself over the brink, his ropes secured by half a dozen men. If Geoffrey were to fall . . .

The onlookers gasped as earth collapsed under her brother's weight. The ropes jerked Geoffrey to a halt and he slammed into the cliff face with bruising force. Though the harness saved him, dirt and pebbles pelted downward, striking Jamie.

The child shrieked and almost lost his grip as his father was pulled to safety through a shower of continually falling debris. *"Papaaa! PAPAAA!"*

Tory could no longer control her tears. Jamie couldn't hold on much longer, and she knew with ghastly certainty that the men would never reach him in time.

She was the only one who could save her nephew.

The knowledge was paralyzing. If she succeeded, she would stand revealed as a mageling in front of everyone important in the county. She would lose everything.

Tory whimpered. She couldn't do this, she *couldn't*. She wasn't even sure if she'd be able to float in the stiff wind. One of the fierce gusts might crash her to the rocks below.

The wind stilled for a moment and she heard desperate sobs from

Jamie. She bit her lip until it bled, knowing she had no choice. She must try to save him.

If she didn't try, no one would know of her cowardice. But Tory would. And she would never, ever forgive herself.

With everyone's attention on the rescuers, she might be able to reach Jamie without being seen. Praying that her mysterious, untrained power wouldn't fail, she turned and fearfully backed into the abyss.

CHAPTER 3

When Tory lowered herself over the cliff, she thought her magic would support her. But to her horror, when she stepped off her footholds she plunged downward with terrifying speed. She gave a strangled shriek and clawed frantically at the cliff face, breaking her nails on the dirt and stone.

Click! She halted in midair. Her hands dug into the cliff, but it was magic that supported her.

She drew a shuddering breath as she looked down at the smashing waves. Her slippers had fallen off and there was nothing but air between her stockinged feet and the sea. Hastily she raised her gaze to Jamie. His eyes were screwed shut and tear tracks marred his round cheeks, but he was holding on.

Glancing up, she saw that the rescue attempts had temporarily halted while the men argued about what to try next. No one was looking at her or Jamie. Perhaps she could save her nephew and get away before anyone noticed her. He was so young and upset that a garbled account of his rescue might not be believed.

Clinging to that hope, she floated to her right. The hundred yards that had appeared short from level ground seemed very long now. Touching the rough, wet cliff face made her feel safer, though she knew safety was an illusion. If her magic failed, she was doomed.

The wind whipped around her, lifting the hem of her gown to indecent levels. Ignoring that, she concentrated on her nephew. *Hang on just a little longer, darling!*

As she neared her nephew, she said softly, "Jamie, I'm here."

He turned his blond head, blinking owlishly. "Aunt Tory," he whimpered. "I knew you'd come." He lunged toward her and tumbled off his branch.

"Jamie!" Heart pounding with fear, she swooped downward and caught him. He was heavier than she expected and for a ghastly instant they were both falling.

She grabbed at her magic and they halted in midair, so low that cold spray from the smashing waves chilled her feet. Trying to sound calm, she said, "Put your arms around my neck and your legs around my waist, Jamie. We'll be safe in a few minutes."

Obediently he latched on like a monkey, his curly head resting on her shoulder. She wrapped her right arm around his solid little body and began floating left and up.

Rising was hard with his extra pounds weighing her down. Grimly, Tory ignored her increasing exhaustion and her aching head. It was worth using all her remaining strength to carry them as far along the cliff as she could manage. The farther they were from where Jamie fell, the less likely they were to be seen.

Wishing she could make herself invisible as well as fly, she used the last of her strength to lift them up and over the cliff edge and on to solid ground. She staggered and almost fell but managed to keep her footing. Dizzy with relief, she set Jamie down and brushed futilely at her muddy gown.

The wind stilled for a moment. In the silence, Tory heard a woman gasp, "Merciful heavens, Lady Victoria *flew*! How could a Mansfield be a mageling?"

Panicking, Tory straightened and saw what looked like every one of her parents' guests. They'd been drawn to the cliff by the drama, and despite the distance she'd traveled, she had come up well within sight of the crowd.

That first shocked cry caused all eyes to turn toward Tory. She froze like a rabbit cornered by a fox as expressions changed from surprise to horror and disapproval. She wanted to disappear, but it was too late.

"Jamie!" Cecilia cut through the crowd, her face radiant with relief. She fell to her knees as she embraced her son, rocking him back and forth.

Jamie grabbed hold of his mother as if he'd never let go. "I'm sorry, Mama," he wept. "I didn't mean to fall."

Bruised and muddy, Geoffrey thundered up after Cecilia. He dropped to his knees and crushed his wife and son in a hug. "God be thanked," he said brokenly. "And thank God for you, Tory!"

With Jamie safe, the crowd's attention locked on Tory, who had just provided shocking evidence that she was tainted by magical ability.

"Disgraceful!" Miss Riddle, the aging heiress to a mining fortune, gave an audible sniff, turned away sharply, and stalked toward the house. She had just given the cut direct, a gesture that proclaimed Tory invisible. Beneath contempt.

Beyond redemption.

Miss Riddle's action was like a breaking dam. A hissing chorus of comments filled the air. "Who would have imagined . . . ?"

"A Mansfield! How dreadful for her family."

"Shocking! Simply shocking. There must be bad blood there."

As Tory watched, agonized, her parents' guests turned away, presenting her with an implacable wall of retreating backs. Friends and neighbors, grown men, dowagers, children—all rejected her. Some faces showed regret, but they still turned away.

With a single act, she had been transformed from "one of us" to "one of *them*."

The Reverend Fisk, Louisa's father, held her gaze for a long moment. Tory spent so much time at the vicarage that the Fisks called her their second daughter.

His lips tightened to a thin line, and Tory knew she'd been judged and condemned. "I never suspected you had bad blood," he said coldly before he pivoted and walked away. Mrs. Fisk did the same, though her expression was sad.

Desperately, Tory looked for Louisa. Surely her best friend wouldn't reject her!

Louisa stood next to Frederick Mason, shock and revulsion distorting her pretty face. "Tory, how *could* you!"

No, not Louisa, too! As her friend took Mr. Mason's arm and fled, Tory cried out, her voice breaking, "Please, Louisa! I'm no different now than I was yesterday! I didn't ask to be like this!"

Louisa didn't look back.

Edmund Harford looked appalled and repulsed, though there was a hint of regret in his eyes. Then he spun on his heel and marched away, leaving only Tory's family.

Lord Roger and Sarah stared at each other, not Tory. His expression was anguished. Weeping, Sarah reached toward him uncertainly. Slowly he took her hand, but as they walked toward the house together, their heads were bowed with misery.

Worst of all, Tory's parents watched with devastation in their eyes. Tory sensed that her mother was also afraid. Frightened for Tory? Or did she fear Tory would reveal that her mother was a mage?

Her father approached with heavy steps. Tall and aristocratic, he had been born to authority, but now he'd aged two decades in as many minutes. "You must go to Lackland Abbey. I hope they can cure you quickly and reduce the damage to our family name," he said brusquely. "Be ready to leave first thing in the morning." Back erect, he took his wife's arm and led the way back to the house.

Only her brother and his wife were left, Jamie secure in his mother's arms. Geoffrey rose and pulled Tory into a hug. She burrowed into him, unable to control her tears. "Geoff, what will I do? Everyone despises me!"

"I don't," he said in a choked voice. "I'll never forget what you've sacrificed to save my son, Tory. You will always be welcome in my home."

"Always," Cecilia echoed as she got to her feet. "If Lord Fairmount is . . . difficult, you may come to us when you leave Lackland." Her shaky smile showed gratitude and full awareness of Tory's plight. "Now I must get Jamie inside and warm him up."

Geoffrey wrapped a powerful arm around his wife and son. "You're a heroine, Tory. I . . . I hope that's some comfort."

Her brother and his small family walked away. Jamie peered over his mother's shoulder. His tearstained face brightened as he waved good-bye before subsiding back into Cecilia's arms.

Tory was alone on the cliff. Shaking, she turned to the sea. The gray-green waves were as familiar as her own heartbeat. Would anyone mourn if she walked off this cliff? She was a mageling, an embarrassment to her family and friends. Everything would be so much simpler if she was gone.

So much simpler . . .

Appalled at her thoughts, she swore an oath that would have shocked her parents. Bedamned to them all! She couldn't help the way she was born. She would not give those who rejected her the satisfaction of destroying herself.

Lady Victoria Mansfield would go to Lackland Abbey and learn to control her magic. She would be home and cured before anyone missed her. She'd be so beautiful and charming that heirs to dukedoms would *beg* for her hand in marriage.

And if the Dishonorable Edmund Harford tried to apologize and make up for treating her so shabbily, she'd . . . she'd *kick* him.

CHAPTER 4

Tory slept like the dead after returning to her room, awaking in early evening. Despair flooded through her as aching muscles and joints reminded her that the rescue and the ghastly aftermath weren't just a horrible dream.

Usually the fete would still be in progress at this hour, but today the gardens were empty except for a few servants cleaning up. The events of the afternoon had cast a pall on the festivities. She opened her door and glanced into the corridor. Was there a guard to prevent her from running away?

No guard. Her father must have known she wouldn't try to escape because she had nowhere to run. She had considered all her family and friends before grimly accepting that even her doting godmother wouldn't take her in. She was an outcast, and she'd starve if she ran away from home.

Tory drifted about her bedroom, fingertips skimming furniture and draperies as if their solid reality could hold her in place. She pulled out drawers, touching small treasures like the first peacock feather she'd ever found and the cameo pin from her godmother and the sparkly nugget of raw gold a friend of her father's had given her.

The Mansfields had lived at Fairmount for centuries. Family legend said that ancestors had owned this land even before the Normans invaded more than seven centuries earlier. The ruins of the ancient Mansfield castle were now a favorite picnic spot. Belonging at Fairmount was as much a part of Tory as her bones.

Yet now, because her mother had brought tainted blood to her marriage, Tory would be exiled from her home. Fury and hatred scorched through her but quickly faded to ashes. It was impossible to really hate her mother.

Countesses usually left their children to servants, but Lady Fairmount would come to the nursery and play games and read stories. She had taught Tory how to run a household and manage servants and pour tea gracefully. Louisa had been envious because her own mother had never had as much time for her.

Tory couldn't bear to think about Louisa.

She realized tears were streaming down her face. She folded into a ball in the middle of the carpet and wrapped her arms around her knees as she rocked back and forth. It wasn't *fair* that she was being punished for doing the right thing!

Eventually she ran out of tears and was left in a state of gray exhaustion. In this house her father ruled, and he had decreed that she was to be sent away. She climbed wearily to her feet. She must pack for school, but her brain was too tired to think about what she should take.

A list. She would make a list.

Her father came to her room while she was deciding what she'd need. Lord Fairmount wore the grim expression of a hanging judge.

"I'll have a servant bring down a trunk, Victoria. Mr. Retter and his wife will escort you to Lackland Abbey. The carriage will be ready directly after breakfast."

"You're sending me with your steward?" she asked bitterly. "You won't even take me into exile yourself?"

"It will reduce the scandal if I go about my usual duties."

She doubted that. Her actions would be a seven days' wonder in the county. People would cluck their tongues and say how sad it was that the Mansfields had a mageling daughter while secretly glad to see the wealthiest family in the area brought low. Her father being at home wouldn't change that. He just didn't want to be with her.

She blinked furiously, determined not to cry. "Does it mean nothing that my wicked magic saved the life of your only grandson? A future Earl of Fairmount?"

"Of course that matters." He scowled. "Losing Jamie would have devastated us all. But that doesn't change the fact that you revealed yourself as a mage in the most public of circumstances. Our whole family has been shamed."

His expression made her feel ill. Though he was usually busy and distant, she'd always thought he was fond of her. But she was only a daughter, and one who had caused a public scandal for the Mansfield family. He would never forgive her for that. "So I am to be thrown out like an old rag," she said, her voice breaking. "The sooner I'm forgotten, the better."

"You will not be forgotten, Victoria," the earl said uncomfortably. "The purpose of Lackland Abbey is to cure young people of their affliction. If you work hard and do well, you can come home. Though you won't make the brilliant match you might have had, very likely you can marry a man of the middling sort and have a decent life."

He thought that marrying "a man of the middling sort" was acceptable for his youngest child? Anger overcoming sadness, she snapped, "Will you allow your guests to see me, or will I be hidden in the attic like a mad aunt?"

His mouth hardened and he left without replying. She closed her eyes, fighting more tears. Her powerful father, one of the great men of England, was too cowardly to speak to his own daughter.

A few minutes later, a footman brought her trunk from the attic. The brassbound box was small to contain a whole life.

She had just packed *Controlling Magic* when her mother arrived wearing a black mourning gown. "Oh, Victoria, I'm so sorry! If there was any way I could save you from Lackland, I would do it."

She caught Tory's hands as if she could physically prevent her daughter from leaving. "My brave, brave girl! What you did took more courage than I've shown in my whole life. I . . . I'll miss you dreadfully."

Tory tugged her hands from her mother's clasp. "Did you even try to persuade Papa to let me stay?"

"Yes." Her mother sighed. "He wouldn't hear of it. On a matter that concerns the family's reputation and honor, he is immovable."

Though Tory knew her mother couldn't overrule the earl, she still felt betrayed. A countess should be able to do *something.* "Today I realized that the weather is always good for the fete, Mama," she said crossly. "Has that just been good luck?"

Her mother glanced away. "What an odd question. Your father would never hire a weather mage for an entertainment."

Which was not an answer. Though her mother wouldn't admit it, Tory was sure the countess had shaped the weather for all these years. *And she'd got away with it!* Tory used magic *once* to save a child's life, and she was exiled. "Weather magic is a very useful power. I wonder how it is done?"

Lady Fairmount's gaze whipped back to her daughter. "You know you mustn't think of such things, Victoria! Magic is alluring—that's why it's dangerous. It seduces people away from proper behavior. At Lackland Abbey, they will teach you how to suppress your power. Concentrate on learning that so you can come home again."

Tory's anger with her mother died away, overwhelmed by her misery. "I want nothing more, Mama."

The countess's expression softened and she gathered Tory into her arms for a hug that said more than the tense words they'd exchanged. "Good night, my darling girl," she whispered. "If you need anything, write to me. I'll send it immediately."

Tory wished the embrace would never end, but finally her mother drew away. Blinking hard, she took hold of the doorknob.

Tory asked, "Is Papa blaming you for my magic? Wondering if you have power since it usually runs in families and no Mansfield has ever been a mage?"

The countess froze. "He has not asked. He does not wish to know." Then she left the room soundlessly.

Tory wondered how many families had questions that weren't asked and truths that weren't spoken. Her mother had lied about her abilities her whole life.

At least Tory wouldn't have to lie. Everyone already knew what was wrong with her. Perhaps, in the long run, she would be luckier than her mother, who had hidden such a great, destructive secret her whole life. Her fear had made her timid.

As she glared at the door, Tory made a private vow. She wouldn't be a liar, and she wouldn't be a coward. Though she had been cursed with this wretched magic, in her own way she would live with honor.

As Tory turned back to her trunk, her maid, Molly, entered and asked, "Do you need help with packing, miss?"

Tory nodded gratefully. "I'm having trouble thinking what I'll need."

"Nothing too fancy. Sensible clothes that you can put on without a maid to help."

Molly opened the upper section of the clothespress and began choosing garments. "Pack your warmest things. Lackland Abbey is right on the English Channel, so there's a cold wind from the North Sea."

"How do you know so much about the school?" Tory asked.

"My cousin was in service to a family whose son was sent there." Molly pulled two pairs of sensible shoes and a pair of half boots from the wardrobe.

Almost afraid to know the answer, Tory asked, "Did . . . did he ever come home?"

Molly nodded. "Aye. Then he went into the army and was killed fighting the Frenchies." She set the shoes in the bottom of the trunk. "Such a *waste*."

Catching the edge in Molly's voice, Tory asked, "What do you think of magic?"

Molly looked up, her expression wary. "Do you want the truth, my lady?"

"Yes," Tory said flatly. "There have been too many lies here."

"People like me think wellborn folk are pure fools to be so set against magic." Molly tucked several pairs of stockings in the trunk. "When my pa was hurt bad in a wagon accident, the local healer saved his life and his leg. That can't be wrong."

"Magic can also be used to harm," said Tory, thinking of all the arguments against using magical power. "It's unnatural. A dishonorable kind of cheating."

"How can magic be unnatural when so many people have it? I wish I was a mage. I'd earn more than I do as a maid." Molly pulled several shifts from the clothespress. "What's unnatural is pretending that magic isn't real when it *is*."

"I guess that makes sense." Tory frowned. "I just don't know what to think. My view of the world has turned upside down today."

"And 'twill change more." Molly regarded her with sympathy.

"Leaving home is hard, miss, but you're strong enough for anything. That was something wonderful, the way you saved the lad. You could have decided that your brother and his wife are young, they would have more, and let the child fall. No one would have been the wiser."

Tory shuddered. "What a horrid way to think!"

Molly nodded, her hands moving swiftly as she folded the shifts and placed them in the trunk. "Yes, but there are some folk selfish enough to put their own comfort over the life of a child." Her upward glance was approving.

What did it say about Tory's life that she was grateful for a housemaid's approval? But maybe a servant could be wiser than a lord.

Together, she and Molly finished packing. When they were done, Molly said, "Good luck to you, my lady." She hesitated. "I have a bit of the Sight, and I think you'll do very well. Better than you can dream of now."

"Thank you," Tory said unevenly. "I need to hear that my life isn't over."

Tory was slipping a book of poetry into her trunk when she had another guest, this time her sister, Sarah. They regarded each other warily.

"Are you and Lord Roger still betrothed?" Tory asked.

Sarah nodded. "I . . . I don't know if I could have come here to say good-bye if he'd broken the betrothal. Roger was shocked to see you flying. Everyone was. But he admires how you saved Jamie. Though his parents will be upset when they learn about you, he is of age and has an independent income, so he can do as he pleases." She blinked back tears. "Thank heaven, he loves me enough to marry me anyhow."

"I'm glad. It's good that he has the courage not to blame you for my failings." Thinking of what Molly had said, Tory continued. "If he had broken the betrothal, would you have wished I'd let Jamie fall? If I hadn't acted, no one would know there's magic in the Mansfield family."

"What a dreadful question!" Sarah looked shocked, then thoughtful. "Losing Roger would be horrible, but losing Jamie would be worse. You did the right thing." She hugged Tory. "Take care, brat. I'm going to miss you."

"I'll miss you, too." Tory ended the hug. "Do you have magic you've concealed?"

Sarah glanced away just as their mother had. "It's said that everyone has a bit of magic, so perhaps I have a touch. But not enough to be a mage, of course."

"Of course," Tory said dryly, thinking her sister protested too much. So the Mansfield women all had some magical talent.

But Tory was the only one who would be punished for it.

CHAPTER 5

No one saw Tory off the next morning. Everything had been said the night before. She climbed into the carriage, feeling like Marie Antoinette on her way to the guillotine.

Her escorts, Mr. and Mrs. Retter, were pale, colorless people. They didn't know quite how to treat her, so they avoided looking at her or talking to her. That made them boring escorts for the journey across England to Kent.

Boredom led to an acute awareness of her surroundings. Tory had always been good at sensing people's emotions, though she'd never thought of that as magic. Now she actively tried to read the people she encountered when they stopped at inns. When they drove into a town on market day, she sensed jolliness before they saw the market square stalls. When they stopped at an inn outside London, she knew immediately that it was a sad place. Later she learned that the innkeeper's old father had died a week before.

She also recognized that her mother was right: Magic was alluring. Tory liked understanding more about her surroundings. Though she desperately wanted to suppress her power, she found herself studying everyone she met, sharpening her magical sensitivity. Rescuing Jamie had opened a door she couldn't seem to close.

Apparently she wasn't a weather mage, since her wishes for rain to slow the journey were futile. The weather was perversely fair, and they arrived at Lackland Abbey on the afternoon of the fourth day. The school grounds were surrounded by a high stone wall that extended a vast distance in each direction.

The dour old gatekeeper opened the massive wrought iron gates and the Fairmount carriage rattled inside. As soon as they passed through the gates, Tory felt as if a suffocating blanket had fallen over her, reducing her magical perceptions to almost nothing. She had become accustomed to a gentle pulse of life in the back of her mind. Now only a feeble trickle of awareness was left. She *hated* the loss of her senses.

As the carriage traveled up the long driveway to a sprawling complex of pale stone buildings, Tory clenched her fists, fighting her anger and distress. The school looked cold and intimidating and old beyond imagining.

But there was one redeeming feature. When Tory climbed from the coach at the entrance to the largest building, she smelled a salt tang on the cool breeze. Molly had been right about the location. Tory felt better knowing the sea was near.

But she hated leaving the luxurious carriage. The velvet-covered seats and Mansfield coat of arms painted on the doors were her last tangible link with home.

Head high, she climbed the steps to the entrance, the Retters behind her. She flinched as she stepped through the heavy arched door. The atmosphere in the building was even more oppressive than outdoors.

A cold-faced porter greeted them. Mr. Retter said, "We are bringing Lady Victoria Mansfield to the school." He reached inside his coat and pulled out a flat packet. "Her documents."

The porter accepted the papers. "Wait here."

The reception area was cold stone with hard wooden benches on two walls. The Retters sat side by side on one bench while Tory paced. She feared freezing if she didn't keep moving.

The porter finally returned. "This way, miss."

The Retters rose to go with her. The porter shook his head. "Your job is done. Leave now."

After a moment of uncertainty, Mr. Retter said, "Very well. I'll see that your trunk is brought in, Lady Victoria."

Expression sympathetic, his wife added, "Best of luck to you, my lady. I'm sure you'll be home again soon."

Then they were gone. Tory had never felt more alone in her life.

"The headmistress is waiting," the porter said brusquely.

She lifted her chin and followed him through another arched door into a dank corridor. Tory sought information with her magical senses, but her awareness was still crushed by the heaviness she'd felt since arriving at this blasted place.

A short walk brought them to another heavy old door. The porter swung it open, revealing a small office. The gray-haired woman behind the desk looked up, her gaze narrowing as she studied Tory. "Summon Miss Wheaton and Miss Campbell," she ordered the servant.

The porter nodded and closed the door behind Tory. Though the walls and floor of the office were more of the pale local stone, a decent carpet warmed her feet. A rather nice painting of a meadow hung on one wall and a vase of late-summer flowers brightened a corner of the massive oak desk.

The headmistress wasn't as pleasant as the office. Her hair was knotted back from her sharp-featured face and her eyes were as cold as the stone. She did not invite her guest to take a seat. "I am Mrs. Grice, headmistress of the girls' school. I see that you are Miss Victoria Mansfield."

Tory stood as tall as she could. "*Lady* Victoria Mansfield."

"We do not use aristocratic titles here. As long as you are a student of Lackland Abbey, you are Miss Mansfield."

"Why?" Tory asked. "My father is an earl. I've been Lady Victoria all my life."

"Practicing magic is the one legal ground by which a peer can disinherit a child," the headmistress replied. "A lord's son can be mad, bad, or criminal, yet legally that son is still his heir. Only magic allows disinheritance. If your father is not satisfied with your progress, he can legally disown you so your title will be stripped from you."

"I . . . I didn't know that," Tory gasped, feeling sick to her stomach.

"The law is not invoked often. Because of natural feeling, most men prefer to give their magic-tainted children a chance to redeem themselves. That is why Lackland Abbey exists." Her voice dropped menacingly. "Your breeding doesn't matter here. Some students boast of their exalted ancestors. Others say nothing because of their shame. I suggest humility. There is no place for pride of birth at Lackland, Miss Mansfield. Not for those who have disgraced their family names."

Tory wanted to explode in fury. Not only had she lost her home, but her very identity was being stripped away.

Instead, she did her best to look meek and biddable. If escaping this horrid school meant humility, she would be the humblest girl in the whole wretched place.

Mrs. Grice handed a pamphlet to Tory. "Here is a brief description of the school's history, purposes, and rules. Read and remember them. Do you have any questions? Most students arrive here remarkably ignorant of what they will find."

Tory glanced down. *The Lackland Abbey Schools* was printed on the front of the pamphlet. "Schools, ma'am?"

"There is a girls' school and a boys' school," the headmistress explained. "The abbey was built for brother and sister religious foundations, and we maintain that separation. Male and female students are very rarely allowed to mingle."

"Why are the schools next to each other when having young men and women together can cause problems? Surely it would be easier if students were separated?"

Mrs. Grice frowned. "Both schools had to be established here because magic doesn't work on the abbey grounds. And don't pretend you haven't tried to use your magic here. Every new student does. That's why you must be cured of your perversion. It's disgusting, *dishonorable,* the way mages can wreak havoc with normal folk!"

No wonder the abbey atmosphere was crushing. Meekly, Tory asked, "Is it known why magic doesn't work here, Mrs. Grice?"

"The ancient monks found a way of blocking magical power so their prayers would not be corrupted." The headmistress looked wistful. "Perhaps their method will be rediscovered someday so magic can be suppressed throughout all of Britain."

"How can magic be suppressed when it's legal?" Tory asked, startled. "Common people use it regularly."

"Which is why they are common," Mrs. Grice said with distaste. "Eliminating magic will make this a better, stronger, more refined nation. Our goal at Lackland is not just to cure young people of good birth, but in time to end magic everywhere."

The headmistress's vehemence was downright scary. While Tory wanted to get rid of her magic, it seemed wrong to take the power away from people like Molly, who found it useful. "How does the abbey cure students, ma'am?"

"You will receive lessons in magical control. When a student's control becomes strong enough, her magic can be permanently suppressed."

"How is that done?"

Mrs. Grice frowned. "Work hard and you will learn when the time is right."

A knock sounded on the door. After Mrs. Grice called admittance, a youngish woman entered. Her appearance was neutral to the point of invisibility. Average size, average face. Brown hair, brown dress, light brown eyes, a darker brown shawl. A wren, not a robin. Tory thought she might be around thirty, though it was hard to judge her age.

"This is Miss Wheaton, teacher of magical control," the headmistress said. "Miss Wheaton, this is our newest student, Victoria Mansfield. Prepare her."

The teacher said in a soft voice, "This won't hurt, Miss Mansfield."

She put a light hand on Tory's head, closed her eyes a moment—and Tory's world changed again. Though her magic had diminished as soon as the carriage entered Lackland Abbey, she realized now that she'd retained some awareness.

Now even that was gone. She felt as if she'd been struck blind and deaf. This stripping away of her remaining power had to be done by magic—yet how could Miss Wheaton do such a thing in the abbey, where magic was supposedly blocked? Miss Wheaton said reassuringly, "Being magically blocked feels very strange, but you'll grow accustomed. Tomorrow your academic and magical abilities will be tested so we will know how best to cure you." She inclined her head. "Good day, Mrs. Grice."

Miss Wheaton left, moving so quietly she probably wouldn't

leave footprints in mud. The headmistress said sternly, "Don't waste time thinking about your former life, Miss Mansfield. Your future depends on how hard you are willing to work at being cured of your vile abilities."

Another knock sounded at the door. "Come in," Mrs. Grice called again.

This time a young girl entered the office. With her slight build and flaxen hair spilling about her shoulders, she looked like a child, but her huge, pale green eyes were not young.

"Miss Campbell will show you around the school, then take you to your room." The headmistress pursed her lips. "There is only one empty bed available, so you must share Miss Stanton's room. Work hard, Miss Mansfield, and Lackland Abbey will serve you well." She looked down at her papers.

Silently, Tory followed her guide from the room. Her prison sentence had begun.

CHAPTER 6

In the passage outside the headmistress's office, Tory's guide turned right, away from the front entrance. The other girl was shorter than Tory, who was not tall. As they fell into step together, Tory asked, "Do you work here, Miss Campbell?"

"No, I'm a student also," the other girl replied. "We usually use Christian names here. I'm Elspeth."

"My name is Victoria, but I'm called Tory." After half a dozen steps, she asked hesitantly, "What did you do to get sent here?"

"We don't talk about such things." Elspeth gestured toward the pamphlet Tory carried. "That tells you the official rules, but new students are always given a tour by an older student who can explain the unofficial rules." Her fleeting smile was visible more in her eyes than her face. "I'm often called on because I'm a useful bad example."

"Why is that?"

"The average stay at Lackland is about three years. I've been here for five."

Five years? That was forever! "What did Miss Wheaton do to me? It was *awful*."

"The school governors claim magic doesn't work at Lackland, but that's not quite true," the other girl said. "People with very strong power usually retain some magic, so Miss Wheaton blocks that. You must have a great deal of ability to feel it so much."

Tory bit her lip, not wanting to believe she had strong power. "Since I now have no magic, am I cured? Can I go home?"

Elspeth shook her head. "You're not cured. If you left the abbey grounds, most of your power would return immediately, and Miss Wheaton's suppression spell would fade very soon after that."

Puzzled, Tory said, "She must be very powerful to be able to suppress students when the abbey grounds block most magic."

"She has a way of resisting the dampening effect Lackland has on everyone else," Elspeth explained. "She needs that to evaluate students and teach magical control."

"Is there a male teacher like her on the boys' side?"

Elspeth nodded as she swung open the oak door at the end of the passage. "Yes, Mr. Stephens. He and Miss Wheaton were both Lackland students. They chose to stay and help cure others. Very noble of them." There was unmistakable sarcasm in her voice.

They stepped outside into a cloister garden. Roofed walkways ran around all four sides of the courtyard so students could stroll protected on rainy days. "This is the heart of the girls' school," Elspeth said. "The boys' school is a mirror image."

Tory studied the ancient, weathered stone walls. Bright beds of blooming flowers and a softly singing fountain in the center of the courtyard made a lovely, serene garden.

Yet every student in this school was here against her will. All were trapped and frantically trying to find a way out. The knowledge increased her feeling of suffocation. "How do you stand it here?" she burst out. "I arrived less than an hour ago, and already I am desperate to leave."

Elspeth sighed. "One can learn to endure almost anything. Even Lackland." She pointed to her left. "Classrooms are on that side and our living quarters are on the right. Teachers have separate rooms in another building. The section opposite has student public rooms like the dining hall and library and kitchens."

"What subjects are taught besides magical control?" Tory asked as they stepped into the garden.

"There are different academic courses, depending on how well educated a girl is when she arrives here." Elspeth's eyes glinted. "You'll also be evaluated for ladylike 'accomplishments,' like music and drawing and embroidery."

"Anything that makes a girl more marriageable is useful," Tory agreed. "Especially since having magic makes us less desirable."

"Marriage is not the only possible path for a woman," Elspeth said calmly.

Tory stared, so shocked she didn't know how to respond. Marriage was the goal of all normal women, though it wasn't always achieved.

Of course, Elspeth wasn't normal. Most people would say Tory wasn't normal, either. "Why have you been here so long?"

"You want to know so you can avoid my failings?" Elspeth asked with another fleeting smile.

"Exactly," Tory said, not smiling.

"Mrs. Grice would say I'm uncooperative." Elspeth's pale green eyes narrowed like a cat's. "She is right. But they can't keep me here when I reach twenty-one. Lackland isn't a prison. Not quite."

Giggles echoed from above, followed by projectiles hurtling downward. Tory jumped backward. "Look out!"

Swiftly, Elspeth raised one hand. The objects were deflected and crashed into the lawn a yard away. They proved to be half a dozen eggs, now smashed to messy bits.

Tory had never seen magic in action, and she found it unnerving. No wonder everyone at the Fairmount fete had been so perturbed by what she'd done. "Why is someone throwing eggs at us?"

"Don't worry, the eggs weren't aimed at you," the other girl said, unperturbed. "I'm not popular in some quarters."

"So you protected us with magic." Tory wondered if she would have been able to do the same. She would need to . . .

No! She mustn't think about such things. "You must be a very powerful mage to use magic here in the abbey."

"I am." Elspeth trailed her fingers in the water as she walked by the fountain. "My power is reduced here, but it's strong enough to deal with flying eggs."

"Might someone do something worse to you?"

"They wouldn't dare." Elspeth resumed her walk across the garden.

Tory decided she didn't want to make an enemy of Elspeth. "Why are you disliked by some of the students?"

"Because I like magic. Perhaps they fear my liking will rub off and they'll start liking their magic, too." Elspeth led them into an open passageway that cut through the building opposite. "That tower on the other side of the school is our chapel. Every morning we must attend services so we can pray for the cure of our magical afflictions."

A daily service in a cold, drafty chapel was not appealing. "Do prayers help?"

"Not that I know of," Elspeth replied. "Lackland students fall into three categories. The majority want nothing more than to be cured as fast as possible so they can go home, so they obey the rules and don't cause trouble. A few are so furious at being sent here that they lash out in all directions."

"And throw eggs. What is the third group?"

"People like me who embrace our powers despite all the pressure to give it up." Elspeth gestured toward the right side of the passage. "Since this is an abbey, the dining room in there is called a refectory. The food isn't usually dreadful."

"Faint praise." Tory thought wistfully of the skilled chef back at Fairmount Hall. They stepped into the gardens behind the school. "How pretty," she said as they started along a herringboned brick path that led between formal flower beds.

"Orchards and vegetable gardens are on the right, beyond the ornamental gardens." Elspeth pointed. "To the left is the boys' school. On the other side of the stone wall with iron spikes on top."

The wall was perhaps a dozen feet high and the spikes had wicked points. Still, if Tory's magic worked here, she could float right over the top. . . .

She immediately stamped on the thought. "How successful are the schools at keeping males and females separate?"

"Not as successful as they like to think." Elspeth turned onto a path that led along the spiked wall. This close, Tory could see that the divider was actually a heavy stone lattice. The boys' school was clearly visible through the square, hand-sized holes.

Elspeth halted and stretched a bit to peer through an opening. "Naturally students on both sides talk whenever they get the chance."

Tory looked through an opening at her eye level and saw that a playing field was on the other side and a game of football was in progress. The players ranged from boys of eleven or twelve to full-grown young men. Half wore red ribbons tied on one arm, the other half wore blue. "If the official policy is to keep males and females apart, why don't they brick up these holes?"

The other girl laughed. "One of the charming oddities of Lackland is that this wall has some ancient magic that makes bricks fall out of the holes if anyone tries to close them. The magic interferes with all forms of blocking as well as making it almost impossible to tear the wall down."

"So boys and girls meet and flirt." Tory pursed her lips and estimated the thickness of the stone. "The wall is too thick to allow kissing, but fingers can touch. Notes can be passed."

"The wall is very romantic." Elspeth's voice was ironic. "On the other side are attractive members of the opposite sex who share the curse of unwanted magic. So near, yet impossible to do more than a fleeting touch of the fingers! Courtships aren't uncommon, with students marrying once they're released from Lackland."

Tory glanced up, thinking the spikes weren't that great a barrier. "The viewing holes would make it easy to climb over the wall. They're rather like a ladder."

"Ah, but the wall magic includes an invisible veil of power that causes excruciating pain if someone tries to climb over," Elspeth said. "Or so I'm told."

"That sounds much more discouraging than spikes." Tory's gaze returned to her viewing hole. Her attention was caught by a tall young man with dark hair and a quick, athletic figure. She felt a strange flicker inside, rather like the flutter she felt when trying to float. "When students leave, do they go back to their old lives?"

"No one ever leaves the same as when they came." Elspeth's soft words sounded like an epitaph.

"Change is probably inevitable," Tory said with reluctance. "But what happens to most students after they're cured and leave Lackland?"

"Most find a place lower in a social order than the one they were born to. Boys go into some profession like the army or navy, or perhaps they study law or become vicars. Girls look for the best husband who will have them. It isn't uncommon to marry a well-off merchant who wants to be connected to an aristocratic family. If they can't find husbands and their families cast them off, usually they become governesses."

Though Tory liked learning, she had no desire to spend her life as a governess. "What about those who embrace their power, as you do?"

"We become mages and are disinherited by our families," Elspeth said dryly. "Some move to the colonies, where magic is more acceptable."

"What do you hope to do?"

"Go somewhere far from here," Elspeth said with even more dryness.

Thinking it was time to change the subject, Tory watched as the dark-haired young man raced down the field, expertly controlling the ball as he headed toward the goal. "Who is the tall fellow with the ball?"

"That's Allarde." Amusement sounded in Elspeth's voice. "You have a good eye. He's the Marquis of Allarde and a second cousin of mine. As the only son of the Duke of Westover, he's the most eligible male at Lackland."

"I thought students don't use titles."

"Not usually, but there are exceptions." Elspeth turned and continued on to a footpath that led away into a pasture scattered with sheep and ancient, half-ruined outbuildings.

Tory was happy to move away from the stone heaviness of the abbey. Though walls enclosed the grounds on both sides, this green openness was a pleasant change from the school. She felt even better when she heard the cries of gulls and realized they were near the sea.

A five-minute walk brought them to a cliff high above the English Channel. The port of Dover was only a few miles south, and Lackland shared the famous white chalk cliffs that Dover was known for. Tory inhaled the tangy air. "This is like my home. I grew up with the cliffs and the sea."

"Beautiful, isn't it?" Elspeth's flaxen hair whipped behind her in the stiff breeze. "We're right on the Straits of Dover, the narrowest part of the channel." She pointed. "See that dark line? It's the French coast. Strange to think that Napoleon's armies are so near. It's the sea that keeps Britain safe."

Tory shivered, and not only because of the brisk wind. France looked so *close*. She found it uncomfortably easy to imagine regiments of French troops lined up on the other side, armed and eager to cross the channel. "Knowing how close we are to France makes the war seem much more real than it did at home."

"Sometimes I have nightmares that the French have invaded and are burning and killing everything in their path. They will land along this coast. Perhaps on the beach right below this cliff." Elspeth's face tightened and she turned away from the channel.

Tory lingered a little longer. She had an uncanny feeling that this place and the enemy across the water would be very important in her life, though she didn't know how.

She turned and walked quickly to catch up with Elspeth. "How are we cured of magic? Mrs. Grice said I'd find out when the time came."

"Once a student becomes really good at control, Miss Wheaton will cast a locking spell that seals the magical power so tightly it can never be used again." Elspeth laughed a little. "Ironic, it? Magic is used to cure magic."

"Maybe it's inevitable." Tory frowned. "So the quicker I learn to control my magic, the sooner I can go home."

"Yes." Elspeth gave a slanting, enigmatic glance. "If that's still what you want."

"Of course that's what I want!"

"Don't be so sure," Elspeth said softly. "Desires change."

Tory didn't want to believe that. But—she did.

Blast it, she did.

CHAPTER 7

Back at the school, Elspeth led Tory into the residence hall and up the stairs. "This is a sitting room for general use." She opened the door to reveal a collection of chairs and sofas before continuing to the end of the corridor.

She halted at the last door. "Your room has a fine view of the sea. Classes are ending now, so Cynthia Stanton should be back soon."

"Thank you for the tour and the information," Tory said. "I'll see you at dinner."

Elspeth smiled. "You won't want to be seen talking to me. It would be bad for your reputation. Good day to you, Tory." She turned and walked away. With her flaxen hair falling to her waist, she looked like a child from the back. She'd been an unnerving guide, but Tory had liked her straight answers.

Wondering what Miss Cynthia Stanton was like, Tory opened

the door and regarded her new quarters gloomily. Her trunk was waiting, so this must be the right place, but the room was a far cry from her lovely lady's chamber at home. This was more like the quarters of an upper servant. A housekeeper, perhaps.

She advanced into the room. The size was reasonable, and Elspeth had been right about the fine view of the sea. But while the pale blue walls·were soothing, the furniture was shabby and hadn't been elegant to begin with.

The two halves of the room had been furnished as mirror images. Each side had a bed, a small desk, a clothespress, a washstand, and a chair. The bed on the right side must be Cynthia Stanton's since a carpet lay beside it and extra pillows had been added.

The left half should have been Tory's, but her roommate had colonized all the space. Expensive gowns were tossed on the bare mattress, books and papers and bottles were carelessly stacked on the desk, and the clothespress bulged with clothing. Cynthia Stanton must have brought everything she owned—and she owned a lot.

Tory was wondering whether she should wait for her new roommate or start clearing space when the door opened and a tall blond girl swept in. She was quite beautiful, with good features and golden hair twisted into an elegant knot. Her green silk brocade gown was more suited to a London lady than a country schoolgirl.

Tory opened her mouth to introduce herself, but she was cut off when the other girl snapped, "Who are *you?*"

"Victoria Mansfield," she replied, startled. "Tory. I'm your new roommate. You must be Cynthia Stanton."

The blond scowled. "This is *my* room!"

"Mrs. Grice said no other space was available." Tory gave a placating smile. "We're stuck with each other."

Cynthia glanced at Tory's trunk. "At least you don't have many things. You can use your trunk for storage."

Her new roommate expected to keep using Tory's clothespress? Unacceptable. Cynthia Stanton might be older, taller, and better dressed, but that didn't give her a right to occupy the whole room.

Tory wasn't an earl's daughter for nothing. "I will use my clothespress," she said with calm assurance. "I'll help you move your things." She opened her clothespress and pulled out a stack of folded stockings. "Where shall I put these?"

"Back where they belong!" Cynthia glared at her.

Tory faced the other girl, knowing she must stand her ground or Cynthia Stanton would make her life miserable. "If you choose not to move your possessions . . ." She pulled out a folded morning gown made of rose-colored cotton and trimmed with gaily embroidered ribbons. "I'll have to cut this down quite a bit to fit me," she said, holding the garment in front of her. "But the color will suit me well."

Cynthia snatched the gown from Tory. "How dare you! My father is a duke!"

"How nice for you. Mine is an earl. Not so high a rank, of course, but a very old title." Tory watched warily, wondering if the taller girl would resort to physical violence. Probably not. And if she did—well, though Tory was smaller, she had been a tomboy who had climbed trees and wrestled with neighborhood boys when she was small.

But she didn't want to fight. *Control is a matter of will.* The phrase from her book of magic popped into her mind.

Though the topic had been controlling magical power, the words could be applied anywhere. How should she deal with the haughty Cynthia? Tory didn't want to challenge her, but she must make it clear she wouldn't be bullied.

She caught Cynthia's gaze and focused her considerable will. "Of course you don't like having someone move in when you've had the room all to yourself, but we must make the best of the situation. I won't be a difficult roommate, but I do need my share of space and furniture."

They stared at each other like wary cats. Cynthia broke first. "These rooms aren't large enough for two people," she said sulkily.

Tory managed not to point out that there wouldn't be a problem if Cynthia didn't have so many things. "This is not what either of us are used to," she agreed as she removed a stack of the other girl's shifts and placed them neatly by the wall on Cynthia's side of the room. "Have you asked if they could bring in another clothespress? Or perhaps the estate carpenter could build shelves for you in that empty corner."

Cynthia frowned at the corner. "I suppose that would work."

The door opened and a maid entered with a pile of bedding. She stopped nervously. "I'm sorry, my ladies. I didn't know anyone was here. I was sent to make up the bed for Miss Mansfield."

"Come in." Tory scooped an armful of Cynthia's garments off her bed and deposited them over the back of the other girl's wooden chair. "Do you know if there is a spare clothespress anywhere? Miss Stanton needs one."

"I believe there's one in the basement," the maid said. "'Tis worn but usable. Shall I ask if it can be brought up, Miss Stanton?"

"Have them bring it *immediately*, Peggy," Cynthia said grandly. "I do not wish to be kept waiting."

The maid nodded, then concentrated on making the bed as quickly as possible so she could escape. Tory suspected that Cynthia was the sort of female who threw hairbrushes and perfume bottles at servants like Peggy.

When the maid was gone, Tory remarked, "I'm glad we have servants. I wasn't sure what I'd find here."

"Of course we have servants! Our families certainly pay enough for us to attend Lackland. We're entitled to basic comforts." Cynthia sounded scandalized at the thought that students might be expected to look after themselves.

"Our families pay for us?" Tory asked with surprise. "I thought Lackland was run by the government, like a prison."

"It's the most expensive school in Britain," Cynthia said with perverse pride. "One must come from a wealthy family to afford it. Lackland isn't luxurious, but Allarde tells me it's better than Eton, which he attended before he was sent here."

Tory's interest quickened. Had Cynthia been flirting with Allarde through the wall? "I saw Lord Allarde playing ball. Elspeth said he's heir to a dukedom?"

Cynthia nodded. "It's said his father doesn't want to disinherit him, but even if Allarde inherits the dukedom, now that it's known he's a mageling he'll have trouble finding a wife of equal rank." She glanced in her mirror with a smile of satisfaction. "Likely he'll find a wife who has also been at Lackland."

It didn't take magic to guess who Cynthia saw as a suitable wife for Allarde. Well, she'd have to catch him first. Surely Allarde's family would prefer he marry a girl from a nonmagical family, even if her rank was lower.

Tory busied herself with unpacking. A battered old clothespress arrived with surprising speed. She wasn't sure if it was Cynthia's rank or her bad temper that prompted such quick service.

Her new roommate left the piles of displaced clothing where Tory had set them. The maid, Peggy, would have the job of putting everything away later.

Tory was just finishing her own unpacking when a bell rang through the corridors. "Dinner." Cynthia swept from the room without waiting for Tory.

No matter. Tory did not think they were destined to become confidantes. With a pang, she thought of Louisa and the closeness they had shared, now gone forever.

She glanced in the small mirror on the clothespress door to check that she looked respectable. After smoothing down her hair, she stepped out into the corridor and saw other girls emerging from their rooms. A plump, cheerful brunette said with a smile, "You're new. I'm Nell Bracken."

Tory returned the smile, grateful for uncomplicated good nature. "I'm Tory Mansfield. I just arrived this afternoon."

"Come sit with me and my friends, Tory." Nell lowered her voice confidentially. "We're the most normal lot here."

Tory smiled wryly. "Normal would be very good."

Nell kept her voice low. "My sympathies that you're stuck with the duke's darling daughter."

Tory managed to suppress a laugh, barely. They clattered down the steps to the ground floor, then followed a passage that led to the refectory. Half a dozen long tables were laid out for the meal. There were settings for forty or fifty students.

Nell led her to a table at the far end of the hall, where a dozen other girls were already seated. "Meet our newest student, Tory Mansfield," she said, before rattling off introductions to her friends.

Tory smiled and tried to remember all the names. All were within a year or two of her age, and they seemed pleasant. No one scowled or threw eggs.

Tory sat down quietly, thinking it wise to hold her tongue until she understood Lackland better. Clearly Nell and her friends were part of the majority who wanted only to behave and go home as soon as possible.

Cynthia had joined a group of high fliers at another table. She and her friends seemed dedicated to making life difficult for the serving maids. They definitely looked like egg throwers.

Elspeth sat with another, smaller group. They were relaxed and happy with one another, and ignored by everyone else. They must be the students who embraced magery.

As Elspeth had said, the food wasn't dreadful, but the oxtail soup, boiled beef, and potatoes were a far cry from Fairmount Hall.

When the main meal was finished and they were waiting for their pudding, she asked, "What are the teachers and classes like?"

A girl called Marjorie made a face. "Miss Wheaton is the only one who really matters since she has the power to let us go home."

"I met her briefly this afternoon. She was . . ." Tory hesitated, unsure how to describe her. "Very quiet."

"She is, but at least she isn't mean," Nell said. "Tomorrow you'll be tested in French and figuring and other subjects so they'll know what you need to be taught."

"Why do they teach these things?" Tory asked, curious. "To keep us busy so we won't get into trouble?"

Another girl, whose name Tory couldn't remember, said, "The real reason is so we can get work as governesses if we can't find husbands."

"Governesses, or housekeepers," Marjorie said gloomily.

Tory shuddered at the thought. "How often does that happen?"

The girls exchanged glances. "Too often," Nell said.

"What should I know about the teachers?"

"Miss Macklin is dreadful," Nell said. "Speak as little as possible."

Other frank comments followed. Tory made mental notes. "What else should I know? Elspeth Campbell showed me around today. She said there are unofficial rules."

"Avoiding Elspeth is one of them," Marjorie said earnestly. "She's nice enough, but you don't want to be seen with that lot. They *like* having magic."

Tory nodded to the angry group. "What about those girls?"

"Keep your distance," Nell said. "If you can. They're mean as snakes." Her gaze moved to Cynthia. "Like us, they want to be cured as soon as possible so they can go home, but they're fearful snobs. As if they were the only ones with lords for fathers!"

The serving girl came to serve a crock of bread pudding, so conversation ceased. Tory dug into the sweet. The pudding was quite good, with apples and cream.

She had survived her first day at Lackland Abbey.

Tomorrow would be worse.

CHAPTER 8

The wake-up bell clanged so loudly that Tory jerked awake, wondering if she had fallen asleep in a church tower. Then she remembered she was at Lackland. Yawning groggily, she sat up in her bed. The other girls had told about the bells the night before. Students had half an hour to rise, wash, dress, and walk to the chapel for the morning service. Then to the refectory for breakfast.

Tory hadn't slept well in the strange room, and Lady Cynthia had snapped at her for tossing and turning. At home, the day started when one maid carried in hot water for washing while another brought her a tray with steaming hot chocolate, fresh-baked bread, fruit preserves, and sweet butter.

She blinked back incipient tears. Why hadn't she appreciated those comforts when she had them?

Reminding herself that at least there was a maid—and Peggy

had brought up pitchers of water the night before—Tory swung from the bed. The floor was *cold*. But she would not complain. She would be a model of good behavior, so cooperative and nonmagical that they would send her home within a fortnight. But in case that didn't happen, she'd write her mother and ask for a small bedside carpet, like Cynthia's.

After washing up in the cold water, Tory went to her clothespress and studied the contents while she shivered in her shift. First her stays, a light comfortable set that laced up the front.

She considered what gown she should wear, given that she wanted to look demure and nonmagical. Not the dark blue morning dress; it made her eyes look too brilliant. Nor her rose muslin, which made her complexion look too fine. The brown linen would be best. Though the dress was well cut, brown wasn't her best color and the effect was subdued.

She pulled the gown on, glad she'd followed Molly's advice and brought clothing she could don without help. She'd rather ride naked through Coventry like Lady Godiva than ask Cynthia for help.

Well, maybe not that, but the less she had to do with the duke's darling daughter, the better. She released her hair from the braid she wore to bed and began to brush it out.

Cynthia was only now sliding from her bed, her movements languid. As she drew on a warm wrap that had been draped over a chair, she said, "What is it like to go through life looking like a plain brown wren?"

Tory froze, shocked by the other girl's meanness. Cynthia had a gift for finding a weak spot. Tory had always been aware that her sister, Sarah, was the family beauty, though Sarah had never flaunted that. She'd always been quick to say that Tory was just as pretty in a different style, which was kind if not true.

But Cynthia was not kind, and she'd placed her dart well. Knowing it would be fatal to show the words hurt, Tory said coolly, "Wrens are quite pretty and charming. What's it like to go through life as a sharp-tongued shrew?"

Cynthia gasped with fury. "How *dare* you!"

Tory coiled her hair in a knot on her nape and stabbed pins in with more force than necessary. "I dare because I will not allow you to insult me with impunity." She turned and stared at her roommate. "Treat me rudely, and I shall return that. Treat me with civility, and I will return that, too."

Cynthia looked like a teakettle on the verge of boiling over, but she was spared having to answer when another girl entered the room. Tory recognized her as one of Cynthia's dinner companions. She looked like a rather pretty rabbit, with light brown hair and blue eyes that blinked too fast. Like Cynthia, she wore clothing that was too elaborate for a school day.

The newcomer studied Tory. "This is the girl they forced on you?"

"It is," Cynthia said brusquely. "She's just leaving now. You're late, Lucy. You'll have to hurry to dress my hair before chapel."

Guessing that Cynthia had bullied the girl into acting as her personal maid, Tory said with her most charming smile, "How lovely to meet you, Lucy. I'm Victoria Mansfield. Please call me Tory. I'm sure we'll be seeing more of each other."

Lucy blinked. Cynthia's description of her new roommate had surely painted Tory as dreadful. "It's a pleasure to meet you, Miss Mansfield," the other girl said with a shy smile. "Tory."

Pleased to see Cynthia fuming, Tory collected her plainest shawl and left the room. As she neared the stairs, two girls emerged from the last room on the corridor. Penelope and Helen had been part of the group she'd dined with the night before, and they greeted her pleasantly.

After greeting them in return, Tory asked, "Can I go to the chapel with you? Elspeth Campbell pointed out the tower yesterday, but I haven't been there."

"You're in for a treat," Helen said dourly. "It's cold as a crypt even in high summer. Come January, we'll be huddled together like sheep for warmth."

"I don't suppose we get heated bricks for our feet like we do in my family's church at home," Tory said as she fell into step with the other girls.

Penelope sighed. "Conditions at Lackland are rather better than a workhouse, but this is not what any of us are used to."

At the bottom of the stairs, they turned left through a door that led behind the building. Fog from the sea lay over the grounds. The chapel was barely visible, floating uncannily in the mist. "I feel like I've wandered into a Gothic novel," Tory murmured.

"But no handsome count named Orlando will rescue us," Helen said with a smile.

Chuckling, the girls joined the stream of students entering the chapel. Yet despite the biting cold inside, Tory found the chapel more appealing than the main abbey. Nuns had prayed and sung here for centuries. Perhaps the walls remembered their devotion.

Tory sat at the end of a wooden bench next to her companions. As the chapel filled, she saw that the girls separated into groups as they had at dinner.

Elspeth was one of the last to enter. Her gaze met Tory's and she raised an ironic eyebrow as if saying, *Now you understand why it's best not to be seen with me.* She took a seat in the last row, her face composed.

Tory felt a twinge of guilt. She would like to become better acquainted with Elspeth, but since she wanted desperately to be cured and leave Lackland as soon as possible, she should be with girls who shared her goals.

A sour-faced cleric entered the chapel and scowled at the students. The group quieted obediently. "His name is Mr. Hackett," Penelope whispered.

His gaze swept the congregation and settled on Tory. "A new student," he said harshly. "Give thanks, girl, that you are able to attend this fine school and have the evil purged from your filthy soul!"

Tory blanched at his venom. Luckily, his attention moved away as he began intoning a prayer. That was followed by the vicar's condemnation of magic and mages, descriptions of how the girls would suffer in hell if they didn't renounce their evil natures, and orders to pray for deliverance.

Tory felt whipped by Hackett's words. If she dared, she would have walked out. She was what God had made her, and while her magic was unacceptable, she wasn't *evil*. Letting Jamie die when she could have saved him—that would have been evil.

A few girls were nodding agreement with the curate, but most wore blank expressions. They must be used to Hackett's virulence. Realizing that she must learn to ignore the man's venom, Tory gazed straight ahead and tried to think of better things.

The image of a swift, powerful athlete came to mind. Allarde. Dreaming of the Marquis of Allarde would make the time fly.

When the service ended, a hungry herd of girls poured out into the foggy morning and headed to the refectory. Tory fell in alongside Elspeth Campbell. Speaking softly so as not to draw attention, she asked, "Is Mr. Hackett always that bad?"

"Often worse," Elspeth replied. "Especially on Sundays, when he has more time to chastise us."

"If he despises magic and those who have it, why does he work here?"

"I think he enjoys screaming vile threats at a roomful of attractive young ladies."

Tory thought of the cleric's feverish intensity as he lashed out with his words. "I suspect you're right. How do you bear it every day?"

"I run through magical control exercises in my mind." Elspeth grinned. "It's excellent for my discipline because for half an hour, there's nothing better to do."

Telling herself that was a better use of time than daydreaming about a young man she'd barely glimpsed, Tory said, "I'll do that tomorrow. Anything is better than listening to Mr. Hackett."

Outside the door to the refectory, Elspeth said quietly, "Good luck with your evaluations." Then she crossed the room to join her friends.

Tory scanned the long room. The tables had steaming teapots, tableware, and small jars of preserves and butter. At the far end a long table was set crosswise to the others. Two kitchen maids presided over the food while students lined up to be served.

As Tory started toward the serving table, a tall girl with a haughty nose approached. Tory had noticed her the night before as part of Cynthia's group.

"I'm Margaret Howard, the head girl," the girl said curtly. "After breakfast, go to Miss Macklin's office in the classroom building."

Before Tory could ask for better directions, Margaret was gone. Head boys and head girls were traditionally older students chosen to have authority over the their fellows. Tory's brother, Geoffrey, had said the head boys at his school, Eton, were usually dreadful prigs. Margaret Howard seemed that sort.

Remembering that the night before the other girls had labeled Miss Macklin particularly difficult, Tory joined the line for breakfast. She was the last girl, and by the time her turn came, the hot porridge had run out. Only bread rolls were left, so she took one and headed to Nell Bracken's table.

Nell poured a cup of tea and slid it toward Tory. "Good morning. How did you sleep?"

"Well enough." Tory stirred sugar and milk into her tea before taking a deep gulp. Grateful for its warmth, she said, "I've been ordered to report to Miss Macklin's office after breakfast. Where is it?"

"When you enter the school building through the main entrance, it's the first room on the right," Helen said. "Good luck with the evaluation."

Tory frowned. "You're the second person to wish me luck. Why do I need it?"

"Miss Macklin believes that students come here too full of pride because of our birth," Nell replied. "And that it is her duty to knock the pride out of us."

Miss Macklin hadn't succeeded with Cynthia Stanton, but Cynthia was probably a hopeless case. Tory said, "I shall be the most humble student she has ever evaluated."

"That might help," Penelope said, but she didn't look optimistic.

Since Miss Macklin couldn't be avoided, Tory reached for the pot of gooseberry preserves. Facing a difficult teacher would be easier on a full stomach.

CHAPTER 9

"Come in," Miss Macklin barked in response to Tory's knock.

Tory's heart sank when she saw the teacher, who was thin, prune-faced, and practiced in disapproval. Looking as meek and nonmagical as she knew how, Tory said, "I'm Victoria Mansfield, Miss Macklin. I was told that you wish to see me."

Miss Macklin pursed her lips as she studied Tory. "Most girls who come here have the so-called ladylike accomplishments like music and watercolors and embroidery, but are appallingly ignorant of academic subjects. Have you studied the globes? Literature? Mathematics?"

"Yes, Miss Macklin," Tory said, clamping down on her distaste for the woman. "My father believed girls should be educated, so we had a very accomplished governess."

Miss Macklin did not seem to find that gratifying. She kept Tory standing as she rattled off questions about geography, Shakespeare, and several poets, then tested Tory on her sums. Tory found the questions easy.

Looking even angrier, Miss Macklin switched to French and asked if Tory could speak the language. Like most children of aristocrats, Tory had learned French early, and her tutor had been born in Paris. "*Oui,* Mademoiselle Macklin."

After several minutes of conversation, Miss Macklin said grudgingly, "Your French is passable. Do you speak Italian?" After Tory shook her head, the teacher said, "Hold out your hands palm up."

Obediently, Tory held out her hands. The teacher raised a brass ruler and smashed it viciously down on Tory's palms.

"Why did you do that?" Tory gasped, blinking back tears.

"You are arrogant, Miss Mansfield," the teacher said triumphantly. "Arrogant and full of pride. Girls like you think your birth will protect you from unpleasantness. In the world outside that may be true, but not at Lackland Abbey. Your family sent you here because you are tainted by magic, and it is the school's duty to do whatever we deem necessary to make you fit for decent society."

Tory stared at her hands, where welts were forming. "But I didn't do—"

Her protest was cut off when Miss Macklin lashed out with the ruler again, this time across Tory's fingers. "That is enough, Miss Mansfield!" the teacher snarled. "Do not ever talk back to me!"

Hands in agony, Tory stumbled back from the desk and banged against the door. She wanted to strike back any way she could, but defiance was exactly what Miss Macklin wanted. The teacher craved an excuse to cause more pain.

Forcing herself not to lash out, Tory stammered, "I . . . I will remember not to talk back, Miss Macklin. Do you wish to test me on any other subjects?"

The teacher looked disappointed by the meek answer. She lifted her quill pen and wrote several lines on a piece of paper. Handing it to Tory, she said, "These are your classes. You'd best work hard. For a girl like you who is both plain and cursed with magic, being governess to a family of the middling sort is the most you can hope for."

Even life as a governess would be better than staying in this horrible school. Fighting to keep from breaking down, Tory said, "Good day, Miss Macklin."

She bolted out into the corridor, her hands hurting so much she could barely grasp the doorknob. As she turn to flee, she crashed into another person. Before she could take off again, a quiet voice said, "Come into my office, Miss Mansfield."

Tory blinked back her tears and saw that it was Miss Wheaton, the mage teacher who'd examined her the day before. Though she was again drably dressed, her eyes were compassionate as she held open the door on the opposite side of the corridor.

Warily, Tory stepped into Miss Wheaton's office. The room was small but welcoming. Pretty watercolors of flowers brightened the walls, the floor was softened by a worn but cheerful rug, and the small bookcase was full to overflowing.

Miss Wheaton frowned at the welts caused by the ruler. "Your hands must hurt."

"All I did was answer Miss Macklin's questions." Tory tried to keep her voice from shaking. "I was trying to show her that I was cooperative and wouldn't cause any trouble. But she hit me with her ruler. T . . . twice."

"Lackland students are used to wealth and privilege, and sometimes they need to be reminded of their changed situation," Miss Wheaton said in a neutral voice. "Some teachers feel that point must be made very emphatically."

"So they want to break us as horses are broken to the saddle," Tory said bitterly.

"Not everyone agrees with that approach." Miss Wheaton took

gentle hold of Tory's hands. "Let me see if I can do something about the pain."

Tory winced as the teacher carefully straightened her swelling fingers but managed to avoid whimpering. Miss Wheaton moved her hand through the air above Tory's. "Fortunately no bones are broken."

"Does that beastly woman break bones?" Tory gasped, forgetting that she shouldn't criticize one teacher to another.

"Sometimes, usually when a girl does particularly well on her academic examination. Perhaps she believes that a good education makes one prideful." Miss Wheaton cradled Tory's right hand between her palms. "Let's see what I can do."

Warmth began flowing into Tory's palm and fingers. After a minute or two, Tory exclaimed, "The pain is going away! You must be a healer."

Miss Wheaton nodded and transferred her attentions to Tory's left hand. "I could do more away from Lackland, but I have some power even here."

"Are students beaten regularly?" Tory asked warily. Though she'd been spanked sometimes as a little girl, her parents thought it unseemly to spank an older child.

"The boys are, but not usually the girls," Miss Wheaton replied. "I can't say I approve, but all boys' schools allow caning."

"My brother said that at Eton, students were told caning builds character. I suppose girls are caned less because we aren't thought to have much character."

"Which is the sort of thing males say when they don't know any women." Miss Wheaton chuckled, looking younger and much prettier. "The fog has lifted, so I'll take you to the village for your magical evaluation."

"Away from Lackland?" The prospect cheered Tory. She brushed at her face, hoping there were no tear tracks. "That would be lovely."

Seeing Tory's gesture, Miss Wheaton said, "I'll lend you a shawl and bonnet so you don't have to go back to your room."

Miss Wheaton was so *nice*! This was like talking to Tory's sister, Sarah. Yet despite her kindness, Miss Wheaton held ultimate power over the girls of Lackland.

As the teacher retrieved shawls and bonnets from a clothes peg, Tory studied her class schedule. All her academic classes were marked as advanced, except for Italian language and literature with Miss Macklin. Though Tory had always wanted to learn Italian, she did not look forward to having such a beastly teacher. She'd sit in the back of the class.

There was also a note that her "accomplishments" would be evaluated. Nell had mentioned this at dinner. A governess must teach drawing, music, and needlework, but virtually all girls sent to Lackland had such skills, and Tory was no exception.

Academic subjects were another matter. Some girls arrived at Lackland ignorant of anything beyond reading, writing, and basic arithmetic. Though Tory was still angry with her father, at least he believed in educating his daughters as well as his son. Tory and Sarah had learned Latin as well as watercolors and how to play the pianoforte.

Miss Wheaton handed a straw bonnet and a blue knit shawl to Tory and they set off. The day was pleasant, with more sun than clouds. A good day for walking.

A footpath led across the grounds to the main gate. When they reached that, Miss Wheaton said, "It's time to remove the block I put on you yesterday." She closed her eyes and briefly touched the heel of her palm to Tory's forehead.

Then they walked through the gate. Tory gasped at the flood of sensations. In the day since her arrival, she'd started to adapt to the abbey's suffocating atmosphere. Now she felt as if she were waking after heavy sleep. She turned in a circle, reveling in the vitality of the normal world. "Everything feels so *alive*."

"You're now restored to your full self." Miss Wheaton led the way across the road to a public footpath that ran between two barley fields. "Having been deprived of your magical senses for a time, you should be extra aware now."

Tory winced. "So I'll feel even worse when I return to the school?"

"The more aware you are of your abilities, the more you'll miss them when they're blocked," the teacher said. "But today is a day for learning and understanding. You can ask me anything you want about magic, and if I know the answer, I'll be happy to explain it."

What Tory really wanted to ask was *Why me?* but that wasn't a question Miss Wheaton could answer. "Do students who have their magic locked down ever regret having that done?"

"No one has ever asked me that." The teacher's brows furrowed. "Not that I know of, but of course I don't see students after they leave Lackland. In the nature of things, there must be a few who later regret denying that part of their nature."

Tory didn't find that comforting. "I will miss this intense awareness of nature. I've always had it, but it's stronger now that my magic has awakened."

"Can you describe how you feel?"

Tory searched for the right words. "Everything around me pulses with life, even the grass. Or . . . it's like a subtle hum that adds richness to being alive."

"Well said. Can you tell the difference between grass and a tree?"

Tory tried for a dozen steps. She sensed a slow living current of . . . of *greenness,* but nothing more specific. "No. Should I?"

Miss Wheaton grinned. "No, it's just a test of sensitivity. If you could distinguish between tree, grass, and shrub so soon after awakening to your magical ability, you'd probably have strong healing ability. But in itself, identifying plants isn't particularly useful. The difference between plants and animals can be handy, though. What can you tell me about that bramble bush ahead?"

Tory turned her attention to the brambles, consciously looking for different energy patterns. Frowning with concentration, she said, "The bramble is quietly alive, but there are sparks of a brighter energy within it. Rabbits?"

"Blackbirds, but you do well to sense the difference."

Tory felt pleased, until she remembered that she didn't want Miss Wheaton to think Tory had strong magical power. A sudden suspicion struck her. "Do you use magic to persuade girls to talk to you freely?"

Miss Wheaton made a face. "Yes, though students seldom realize that."

"It isn't enough to control our bodies!" Tory blurted out, feeling betrayed. "You want our minds as well. If we say the wrong thing, do we have to stay here longer?"

"No!" Miss Wheaton said sharply. "I dislike using magic in this way, but I need to know a student's true thoughts about her magical gifts so I can help her choose the path that is best for her. Nothing you say will be used against you."

"You say 'gifts,' but for most of us, magic is a curse," Tory retorted. "That's why we're in this prison!"

The teacher was silent for the space of dozen steps. "The difference between a gift and a curse can be how one feels about it. Most magelings feel that magical power enriches their lives, so for them, magic is a gift. Many would envy your ability."

Tory thought of her maid, Molly, who'd wished she had magic. "That may be true for the lower orders, but for those of us who are wellborn, magic is a disaster."

"The damage comes from society, not magic itself," Miss Wheaton pointed out. "Though the price of magic is high for aristocrats, embracing one's talents can be deeply rewarding. That is why I choose to teach at Lackland—so I can help girls decide what they truly want."

"Are you trying to persuade me to embrace magic?" Tory asked incredulously. "You're supposed to cure me!"

"Refusing magic is as costly as embracing it." There was deep sadness in Miss Wheaton's voice. "My job is not to persuade, but to inform my students so they fully understand the consequences before they choose which path to take."

Tory's anger faded. "Were the consequences dire for you?"

"Magic brings me great joy and rewards," the teacher replied. "But I wish I hadn't had to choose between my abilities and my family."

"I don't want to have to make that choice," Tory said flatly. "I want my family and normal life. How is magic locked down? Or is that a secret?"

Miss Wheaton's expression suggested that Tory didn't yet know what she wanted, but she merely said, "All students study magical control. Think of those controls as chains. When the chains are strong enough, a mage can use them to tie up magical ability like the bonds that secure a bull."

That made sense, but Tory frowned. "So after I'm cured, I'll always feel as dull and heavy as I do at Lackland."

"You will adapt and feel the same as most people feel their whole lives," the teacher reassured her. "That's not a tragedy. But remember that having one's power locked down isn't a true cure since magical talent can still be passed to one's children."

"Which is a disadvantage in the marriage mart." Though Tory had learned at Lackland that she didn't like losing her magical perceptions, it would be wonderful to return home even if she could no longer expect to find a husband of high rank. A husband she could love. meant more than a title. "How long does it take to develop enough control to have one's power locked down?"

"I don't believe anyone has been cured in less than a year." They reached a fence, and Miss Wheaton used the ladderlike steps of a stile to climb over. "Unusually powerful students generally need more time to develop sufficient control."

"I don't have much power! Hardly any at all." Tory climbed over the stile, wryly aware that she was echoing what her mother and sister had said. "It's the merest chance I was publicly seen doing something magical."

"Your father's letter said you could fly. That is major power."

"Not *fly*," Tory said uncomfortably. "I just . . . float a bit."

Miss Wheaton smiled. "Show me." Seeing Tory's hesitation, she added, "There's no need to conceal your abilities from me. You are what you are. I hope you believe that I want to help you."

"I do." Tory's voice was edged. "But are you using magic to make me trust you?"

"No." Miss Wheaton held Tory's gaze. "Magic can't induce real trust, nor would I do such a contemptible thing if I could."

The teacher's words were convincing, but even if she was lying, what could Tory do about it? She was trapped at Lackland until Miss Wheaton allowed her to leave. Cooperation was the only choice.

She closed her eyes. Cleared her churning mind. Thought about fluttering in her midriff, the click . . .

"Good heavens!" Miss Wheaton gasped.

Tory's eyes shot open as she swooped upward. She gave a squeak of surprise at her swift ascent and grabbed wildly at a tree branch. She didn't want to find out how high she could go, but she felt exhilarated as she clung to the bobbing branch.

"I've never had a student who could do that before." Miss Wheaton sounded envious. "Are you all right up there?"

"I'm still not used to this!" Tory peered between the branches and saw two young owls staring from a hole in the trunk. Mentally she told the owls she meant no harm, hoping they understood. They blinked at her but didn't vanish into the hole.

She turned her attention to the countryside. Lackland Abbey lay behind, its massive walls forbidding. Ahead she saw the spire of the parish church in Lackland village. The sea was a silvery shimmer to her left while fields and hills unrolled in other directions. She felt gloriously free. Though if she took up flying regularly, she would need to wear something more modest than skirts and petticoats!

But, of course, she wouldn't fly again. This was only for Miss Wheaton's evaluation. Excitement gone, she chose a spot on the ground and concentrated on gliding down safely. She stumbled as she landed, but she was improving with practice.

Miss Wheaton caught Tory's arm to steady her. "Your control is surprisingly good for a new mage. Did you take lessons?"

Tory shook her head. "There was a book in my father's library, *Controlling Magic* by An Anonymous Lady. It talked about pulling one's energy to one's center in order to find balance. Are you familiar with that book?"

The teacher laughed. "I wrote it. The exercises are very similar to what you will study in my classes, though I've learned some new techniques since I wrote the book."

Tory blinked. Miss Wheaton had unexpected depths. She studied her teacher, using all her senses. "You have many secrets."

"Doesn't everyone?" Miss Wheaton changed the subject. "How did you discover you could fly?"

"I woke up from a dream floating over my bed," Tory said. "I thought I'd be able to conceal my ability and carry on as usual, but . . . that wasn't possible."

"Your father's letter described how you saved your nephew." Miss

Wheaton resumed walking along the path. "You showed great courage, Miss Mansfield."

Tory shrugged as she fell into step with her companion. "Not really. I was terrified, but I couldn't just stand there and watch Jamie die."

"That is the definition of true courage," the teacher said quietly. "Being frightened, yet still doing what is right."

Being brave hadn't prevented her father from sending her away. Tory hoped she'd get her reward for saving Jamie in heaven, since it hadn't happened on earth.

CHAPTER 10

Lackland was a pretty fishing village built around the mouth of the Lack, a small river that cut through the chalk cliffs to empty into the English Channel. A few houses were scattered along the cliffs above, but most of the village was stepped down the hillside that led to sea level.

The narrow streets lined with narrow houses reminded Tory of the village near Fairmount Hall, though the cliffs were much whiter here. As they passed the parish church, she remarked, "I see the church is Saint Peter's by the Sea. I suppose that's because Saint Peter was the patron saint of fishermen?"

"Yes, and it's a pretty place. Would you like to go inside?" When Tory nodded, Miss Wheaton led the way in.

Tory sighed with relaxation. The church was indeed lovely, and they had it to themselves. Unlike the school's chapel, there was no unpleasant vicar to ruin the peace. As they drifted about the church, admiring the stained glass and the bouquets of flowers and leaves, Tory asked, "What kind of magic is the most common?"

Miss Wheaton considered. "Most magelings have at least a little healing ability, but intuition is even more common. That's the ability to know something without rational knowledge. Many people who don't consider themselves magical have intuition, though they don't always use it."

Tory frowned. "How does one tell intuition from simple emotions? Wouldn't wanting something a lot get in the way of a mystical feeling?"

"Like anything else, it takes practice," the teacher replied. "The next time you need to decide something, clear your mind and see which choice feels right. The more you do it, the more accurate you become."

Still skeptical, Tory asked, "Is your intuition always accurate?"

"Sometimes my emotions get in the way," Miss Wheaton admitted. "But if I take the time to really clear away thoughts and feelings, what is left is usually true."

"I'll try that." Tory closed her eyes. "Let's see . . . I'm hungry, and now that I clear my mind—I have a powerful intuition that somewhere near the harbor, there is a tea shop that will cure the problem."

The teacher laughed. "What excellent intuition! I do believe there is just such a tea shop. Shall we go find it?"

Smiling, they continued down the hill, Miss Wheaton describing different kinds of magical ability. The tea shop was very pleasant, with excellent sausage rolls and iced cakes. Tory was pleased when they were seated by a window with a view of the small harbor. She was happier than at any time since she woke up floating over her bed.

As they left the tearoom, she asked, "Have I been sufficiently tested?"

Miss Wheaton nodded. "You have a good deal of power, and have a decent start on controlling it. I'll put you in my intermediate class."

At least Tory didn't have to start with the beginners, but she'd still be imprisoned at Lackland Abbey for at least a year, probably more. She looked wistfully at the harbor. Several piers jutted out into the water, small boats moored alongside. The larger boats would be fishing in the channel now. "Do you bring students here often?"

"Regularly, but not as often as they'd like." As they turned to retrace their steps, Miss Wheaton halted, surprise on her face. "That gentleman at the corner is one of the teachers from the boys' school, Mr. Stephens."

Tory's eyes narrowed. The male teacher had a compact build and a quick, forceful way of moving. "He's a mage, isn't he? Does he teach control classes like you?"

"You have a definite talent for reading people, Miss Mansfield." Miss Wheaton hesitated. "I need to speak with him. Would you mind going off on your own to visit the waterfront? I'll collect you when I've finished my discussion with Mr. Stephens."

To wander freely, even if only for a few minutes! "I'd like that." Since Miss Wheaton still looked doubtful, Tory added, "I don't see how anyone could get into trouble in a village this small."

"No doubt you're right. Very well, I'll see you in a few minutes." Miss Wheaton headed down the street toward Mr. Stephens. Tory saw the male teacher's energy flare when he saw Miss Wheaton approaching.

Curious, she watched as they met. They didn't touch or do anything improper, but as Miss Wheaton looked up at Mr. Stephens, they *glowed* at each other. So Miss Wheaton had a beau. And they had Lackland's high stone wall between them and probably few opportunities to meet.

Finding the thought perversely satisfying, Tory walked down the hill to the waterfront with long, swinging steps. She enjoyed the illusion of freedom. There was nothing to stop her running away from Lackland, except common sense.

She walked out on the longest pier, breathing in the mingled seaside scents of seaweed and salt air. The breeze fluttered her skirts and bonnet, so she pulled off the bonnet so she could feel the wind in her hair.

A gull glided down to perch on the nearest piling, its expression hopeful. Since Tory had saved a ginger biscuit from the tearoom, she broke off a corner and tossed it toward the piling.

The gull swooped down and snatched the tidbit from the air and returned to its piling. Other gulls appeared. Tory shook her head. "Sorry, the rest is for me."

An amused voice behind her said, "Do the gulls talk back?"

Startled, she swung around to see a young man about her age. He had lovely thick blond hair and a mischievous smile.

"I don't speak gull," she replied, "but I imagine they're saying 'More, more!'"

"That's a safe guess." He looked her up and down with unabashed curiosity. "Since you're one of the poor fools from the abbey, maybe you really can speak to birds."

Tory bristled. "No gentleman would call a lady he's just met a fool."

"You're likely a lady, but I'm no gentleman," he said cheerfully.

"That's obvious," she said tartly. "Anyone trapped in Lackland Abbey deserves sympathy, but why do you call us fools?"

"Because you have the grandest talents anyone can ask for, and you're trying to destroy them."

She narrowed her eyes and studied him on all levels. His clothes and accent were decent, if not out of the top drawer, but his broad shoulders were splendid. She guessed that he might be the son of a

prosperous local merchant or professional man. More than that . . .
"You have magic yourself," she said flatly.

"Aye, and proud to be a mage. I'm Jack Rainford, and the best
weather worker in Britain." Seeing Tory's brows arch, he grinned.
"Well, the best in Kent, anyhow. There have always been weather
mages in my family and my mother says I cut my baby teeth on
clouds. This nice sunny day you're enjoying? You can thank me for it."

She laughed. "And here I thought God made the weather."

"He makes it, but I can alter it." Jack gestured to the south. "See
that dark line of rain clouds moving out into the channel? They
would have been raining here, but we've had enough rain, so I
pushed the clouds south, where it's been dryer."

Remembering that her mother had some weather ability, Tory
asked, "How is weather controlled?"

"It's hard to explain." His brow furrowed. "You have to have the
weather talent, of course. Then it's a matter of reaching out and feeling the air. I can sense winds and storms far away. Over the Atlantic,
on the Continent. I can't conjure a storm out of still air, but I can
herd storms a long way and build them up as they come closer. It's
easier to push clouds away if I want some sunshine."

"Can you show me?"

"It's a waste of power," he said, "but since you have such pretty
blue eyes . . ."

Tory wanted to think that Sarah was right about her bewitching
eyes, but more likely Jack Rainford was an incorrigible flirt. It was
interesting to talk to someone who was a mage and proud of it,
though.

Jack focused his gaze on the rain clouds he'd pointed out. Tory
felt a kind of . . . tension in the air. She guessed that it was the feel
of strong magic being exercised.

After several minutes of silence, he muttered, "This storm is a
stubborn one. It's giving me a headache."

"Or perhaps you aren't really a weather mage," she said, disappointed.

"I am so!" He scowled at the storm—and a chunk of dark clouds split away from the main storm and headed in their direction, moving unnaturally fast.

She caught her breath. "You really did that?"

"If you don't believe me, I'll let it rain right on your head!"

Tory could see raindrops pelting down from the approaching clouds. "That's not necessary," she said hastily. "I'm convinced, and I don't want to get wet."

"I'll release the clouds since I don't want to get wet, either." He gazed intently at the cloud. It stopped moving toward them in that unnatural way and began drifting east across the channel on a track parallel to the main storm. "Let it rain on the Frenchies," Jack said in a hard voice. "Keep their powder wet so they can't invade."

Elspeth had also talked of possible invasion, and her words had stuck in Tory's mind. "Do you think they'll try to?"

"If they can, they will," he said brusquely. "The French and the English have been at each other's throats forever. You know any history? The last successful invasion of England was William the Conqueror, and he was Norman French."

"1066." The date was engraved in the mind of every English schoolchild. "But the channel has kept us safe ever since."

"I wouldn't count on that always being true." Jack frowned at the French shore.

Tory looked across the water and imagined massing armies intent on conquest. "We must put our faith in the Royal Navy."

"That and magic." Jack was no longer smiling. "Mages can help keep England safe. That's why it's so stupid that people like you throw it away."

"It's not my choice to be at Lackland!"

"But you'll go along with it like a good little sheep," he said, not bothering to keep contempt from his voice. "A pity. All that power, wasted!"

"Even if I kept my magic, girls can't be soldiers or sailors." Angry, she donned her bonnet again. "Not to mention that being a mage would cost me much of my family."

"You'd be useless in the infantry, but your magic could still be of value. Female mages can be as powerful as men." He turned his full attention to Tory. "When the French come, you could fight to protect your country just like me. But you won't. You'll be shivering in your fancy school and hoping the Frenchies won't hurt you."

"If I weren't a lady, I'd push you off the pier," she said through gritted teeth.

"I should like to see you try!" Good humor restored, he said, "I shouldn't tease you. All you poor, talented aristocrats are raised to hate yourselves. Only a few have the courage and wit to break out and learn how to be real mages."

Tory had a sudden mental image of Elspeth on the headlands facing France, her arms raised into the wind as she used her power to stave off invasion. "Some of Lackland's students will be standing beside you if invasion comes. But most of us just want to go home. Is that so wrong?"

"You can't go home again, not really, and you know it. Poor fools, like I said before." He regarded her thoughtfully. "But you're right, not all the students at Lackland are sheep. You'd be surprised what goes on out there at the abbey."

"I only just arrived, so everything about the place surprises me," she said wryly.

He glanced at the white cliffs that rose above the village. "These chalk cliffs are fairly soft. Did you know they're digging tunnels in the chalk under Dover Castle as quarters for soldiers to defend against invasion?" His gaze flicked toward her. "They say there are secret tunnels under Lackland Abbey, too. Old ones that go back to when it really was an abbey."

"I haven't heard anyone mention them," she said, intrigued.

"Those who know wouldn't want to talk about them, would they? The tunnels being secret and all," he said with elaborate patience.

Pushing the irritating chap off the pier really would be satisfying, but he was too large. Unless she caught him off balance . . .

Suppressing the impulse, she asked, "Do some students use the tunnels to get away from the abbey at night?"

"Maybe. Or maybe they go courting, since tunnels must run under both sides of the abbey. I wouldn't know, me not being a gentleman or a Lackland student." He chuckled. "And since I'm no gentleman, I'm going to ask your name even though we haven't been properly introduced."

A young lady wouldn't give her name to a stranger—but as a student at Lackland, she was no longer a young lady. "I'm Victoria Mansfield."

"Lady Victoria, I'm sure. Or maybe the Honorable Victoria Mansfield?"

She made a face. "I used to be Lady Victoria, but not at Lackland."

"Miss Vicky. It suits you."

"That's Miss Mansfield to you, Mr. Rainford," she said frostily. "No one ever calls me Vicky!"

"Then I'll call you Tory. Victoria is just too stiff." His smile was engaging. "You can call me Jack."

Did he use intuition to guess she was Tory, or was it just a lucky guess since Tory was another nickname for Victoria? Before she could decide, a movement from land caught her eye. She turned to see Miss Wheaton stepping onto the pier. "Saved by the teacher," Jack said cheerfully. "I was just thinking it's a good thing I can swim."

She stared at him. "Can you read minds?"

"No." He gave that infuriating grin again. "But you looked like you were ready to forget being a lady."

Deciding she'd better get away from him before she lost all claims to good behavior, she pivoted and stalked toward Miss Wheaton. When they met, the teacher said dryly, "I see you've met Mr. Rainford. He likes trying to corrupt my students."

"They need corrupting, Miss Wheaton," Jack said earnestly.

"I'll have none of your nonsense," the teacher said, but there was amusement in her eyes. "You've been showing off for Miss Mansfield, and it's given you a headache." She pressed her palm to his forehead.

Subtle lines of strain in his face eased. "Thank you for fixing my headache. A pleasure meeting you, Lady Vicky." He walked away with a grin.

Tory said through gritted teeth, "Has anyone ever pushed him into the water?"

"Not that I know of, but not everyone is lucky enough to meet him on a pier where it would be possible." Miss Wheaton's voice was indulgent. "Mr. Rainford is quite a gifted young mage, so he's always interested in meeting new Lackland students."

"To corrupt us?"

"It's not a bad thing to meet mages who are comfortable with their abilities." Miss Wheaton led the way back to shore. By the time they reached land, Jack Rainford had disappeared down a cross street.

Tory said, "He talked of French invasion and how England needs its mages for defense. Are the French really going to invade?"

"I don't know." Miss Wheaton looked troubled. "It's certainly possible."

"Are there no mages who can tell us what will happen?"

"Seeing the future is called foretelling. Knowing in advance.

Though some mages have ability in that area, the future isn't fixed. Since it can change, even the best foretellers only see possibilities."

"The future changes?"

"Think of following a map through the countryside," Miss Wheaton explained. "When you come to a fork in the path, you must decide whether to go right or left. If you go left, the path will take you to a different place than if you choose the right fork. Each path leads you to more forks, more choices, and different futures."

"I see. It's free will in action," Tory said thoughtfully.

The teacher nodded. "Sometimes a particular event will be so close or so inevitable that it can't be avoided, but usually we can't be sure of the future, and that's just as well. How dismal it would be to believe our futures are carved in stone!"

Dismal indeed. Tory needed to believe in change. Miss Wheaton was right. It was better not to know what lay ahead.

As they headed back to the abbey, her thoughts turned to Jack Rainford's claim that female mages could fight for England. Tory's ancestors had been warriors—that's why her family had wealth and status now. The blood of those warriors ran in her veins.

Tory loved England as much as any man. The thought of invasion, of rape and burning and slaughter, horrified her. Could she learn how to help defend her country without losing her family?

She intended to find out.

CHAPTER 11

. . . bong, bong, bong. Tory counted as the chapel clock struck the hour. Midnight, and Cynthia Stanton slept with slow, regular breaths that weren't quite snores.

Cautiously, Tory slipped from her bed, fully dressed except for her shoes. After arranging the blankets in a long roll under the coverlet, she wrapped a shawl around her shoulders, picked up her shoes, and tiptoed from the room.

In the week since her evaluation, life had settled into a regular routine of chapel, meals, classes, and studying. She was now an accepted member of Nell Bracken's group, and her relationship with Lady Cynthia was easier, largely because Cynthia refused to speak to her. Tory had found that giving her roommate a cheerful smile infuriated the other girl, and it was wickedly satisfying.

Though most of her attention was given to school and her new friends, she couldn't stop thinking of what Jack Rainford had said. Tunnels beneath the abbey. Surprising things might be happening down there.

Tory's casual questions about possible medieval tunnels had received only blank stares from the other girls. Maybe interesting things happened only on the boys' side, with no access for the girls. But that didn't mean Tory couldn't look.

Elspeth Campbell was the most likely to know about abbey mysteries, but the other girl was maddeningly elusive. Tory saw her between classes or across the refectory, but Elspeth always slipped away before Tory could intercept her.

So Tory had started quietly exploring on her own. She guessed that the entrance to any tunnels would be from the cellar of an abbey building. Most of those cellars were locked away from students, so Tory couldn't investigate them.

She'd explored those cellars that she could enter. Under the refectory were sacks and bins of food, including far too many turnips stored for winter, but nothing that looked like an entrance to a tunnel.

There was also a dank, unpleasant cellar below the classroom building. She found trash and spiderwebs, but there were no signs of regular traffic except by small creatures she preferred not to think about.

Her searching was easier because Miss Wheaton hadn't reinstated Tory's suppression spell when they returned to the abbey after the evaluation. Tory wasn't sure if that was by accident or design, but she was grateful not to feel as smothered as she had her first day at the school.

She practiced her intuition whenever she had the chance. Though it hadn't led her to any hidden tunnels yet, she did have clearer feelings about what was likely or not. Now her intuition was suggesting that a tunnel entrance might be concealed in one of the crumbling old abbey outbuildings.

There was no one stirring as she made her way along the dark corridor and down the stairs. The day had been gray and rainy. Though the skies had cleared and a waxing moon illuminated the abbey grounds, the grass was wet and the air bitingly cold. Tory pulled her shawl tighter around her shoulders. Winter wasn't far away.

She made her way to the edge of the gardens that led toward the sea. The pastureland contained scattered outbuildings and crumbled ruins that might have been chicken coops or granaries in the old days.

She let her mind drift. Which one . . . ?

There. That rocky ruin just beyond the kitchen garden. Her shoes were saturated by the time she reached it. The original building had been no larger than a bedroom, and loose stones had fallen into piles at the base of the irregular walls. The site didn't seem very promising, but her intuition said to look closer.

She squinted at the ruins, glad for the moonlight. *Hmm.* Grass was flattened into an almost invisible path that led to the highest surviving wall. She shoved at the stones with her foot. Nothing. Then she pushed at the wall. This ruin was more solid than it looked. She pulled and pulled every way she could think of without getting a response. Yet that faint trail in the grass remained.

She closed her eyes and calmed her mind. How . . . ?

Tory bent over and twisted the nearest stone toward herself. The whole rocky pile moved smoothly to one side, revealing a hole with steps leading downward. Good heavens, there really was a hidden tunnel!

Now that she'd found a secret passage, she realized she hadn't thought about what might happen next. Without a torch or lantern, she couldn't go far in the darkness. But the moonlight made the first few steps visible.

Cautiously, she stepped inside. Another step. The pale chalky walls reflected every bit of available light, so it wasn't as dark as she'd expected.

When her head was below ground level, the hatch over the tunnel rolled shut above her. Her heart jumped again. She stretched up and pressed her palms against the hatch. To her relief, it moved easily. She wasn't trapped in a chalky tomb.

More surprising, the tunnel wasn't dark. As her eyes adjusted, she saw that several steps lower there was a landing several feet square. On the left side, several dimly glowing spheres about the size of an apple rested against the wall.

She knelt to examine the pile of glowing lights. They weren't candles or lanterns but pure light. Warily, she touched the sphere on the top of the pile, using her left hand in case it was dangerous. The light tingled, but she didn't get burned and her fingers didn't fall off. The light continued to glow gently.

So. A magical light. A girl who could float in midair shouldn't find this surprising, though she wondered how such powerful magic could work within the Lackland precincts. But she wasn't exactly *in* Lackland; she was below it. That seemed to make a difference.

Was it possible to hold one of the lights? She slid her hand under the one closest to her. It settled neatly in the middle of her palm, tingling slightly. She now had enough light to continue down the stairs.

She counted the steps as she descended. After thirty-two, she reached the bottom. A tunnel stretched ahead. The passageway was roughly rectangular, with tool marks showing on walls, ceiling, and floor. Though she had headroom to spare, a tall man might risk banging his head.

The center of the shaft was shiny and hollowed out from centuries of wear. Tory could feel ancient energy in the cool, damp air. An image flickered through her mind of nuns gliding along this passageway on light, silent feet. She started down the tunnel cautiously, wishing she had more light.

The ball brightened.

Had the light responded to her thought? How bright could it get?

The ball blazed so fiercely it hurt her eyes, and the tingle increased so dramatically that she dropped the ball. That was too much light! She wanted it dim again.

By the time the ball drifted to the floor of the tunnel, it had dimmed to its original intensity. So, magic did work here below the abbey. What about her floating ability?

An instant later, her head cracked the ceiling. Muttering an oath, she floated down, making sure to do it slowly.

She was positively buzzing with energy. She scooped up the ball and wished it just a little bit brighter. The light obeyed her very nicely, so she proceeded down the passage.

Tory almost jumped from her skin when she saw a flicker of movement ahead of her. She exhaled with relief when she realized that it was a sleek gray tabby cat. She hoped it was keeping the tunnel vermin-free.

The tunnel swung to the right and intersected another tunnel that looked exactly the same. She halted. It would be very easy to get lost in these featureless passageways.

Or were the walls featureless? As she scanned the walls and corners, she spotted a faint blue glow near the ceiling on her right. She reached up to touch the glow. The color brightened for a few moments before fading again. When she moved forward a few steps and turned, she saw a matching blue spot visible to someone coming the other way.

Curious, she checked the cross tunnel and found golden glows in the same relative locations. She touched them to brief life. Guessing that the colors marked the way, she continued down the blue-coded passage.

The next cross passage was marked with pale green. Would people without magic be able to see the patches of color? She suspected not.

They would get lost, which was probably why the tunnels had been excavated in such a confusing way. Tory had always had a good sense of direction, and she thought she was under the boys' school. But she could easily be wrong. How far did these blasted tunnels go?

She heard a faint noise ahead. As she continued along, it became a murmur of voices. The soft, whispery sounds made the hair on her neck prickle.

She bit her lip, suddenly nervous. Though she'd assumed anyone down here would be from the school, what if smugglers had found the tunnels? They often used sea caves to hide brandy and silk and other goods brought illegally from France. They would love nice tunnels like these, and they didn't treat strangers kindly.

She closed her eyes and used magical perception to explore those murmuring sounds. A great roar of magic rolled over her. Magelings ahead, not smugglers.

Taking off her shoes, she moved ahead soundlessly. After a last turn, the passage ended abruptly in a large room with higher ceilings. About two dozen young people sat in two irregular circles, with more boys than girls.

"Look!" a male voice said.

As Tory caught her breath, several people rose and came toward her. The nearest was a flaxen-haired girl.

"I wondered how long it would take for you to find us," Elspeth said with a slow smile.

CHAPTER 12

"What is this place?" Tory asked, relieved to see a familiar face. "Did you expect me to come here?"

"We certainly did." A grinning Jack Rainford loomed behind Elspeth. "I knew as soon as we met that you weren't one of the sheep, Vicky."

"It's Tory," she retorted. "What are you doing here?"

"Back to your class, Jack. There will be time to talk later." The speaker was Mr. Stephens, the magic-control teacher from the boys' school. With him was Miss Wheaton. *Teachers* were part of these mysterious goings-on!

Miss Wheaton made a shooing motion with her hand at Jack and Mr. Stephens. "Both of you go. Elspeth and I will explain the Labyrinth to Miss Mansfield."

Smiling, both males returned to their groups while Tory studied her surroundings. "This place is called the Labyrinth? It's well named."

The hall was furnished like a spacious but shabby drawing room, with clusters of furniture and a lecturer's dais facing a group of chairs. Magical lamps made the center of the room as bright as day. Even the most dazzling of candlelit ballrooms was dark compared to this glorified cave.

Miss Wheaton led Tory and Elspeth to a distant group of worn wing chairs. The teacher took a seat, gesturing for the girls to do the same. "Students who seem seriously interested in magic are provided with enough clues to come looking for the Labyrinth. It didn't take you long at all."

"Jack Rainford told me that mysterious things might be happening under the abbey." Since this corner of the room was dark, Tory mentally told the ball of light she still held to brighten until she could see the faces of her companions.

Miss Wheaton asked, "Do your abilities seem stronger down here?"

Tory rubbed the sore spot on her head where she'd hit the ceiling. "They certainly are!" Wanting to free her other hand, she directed the light to hover above them. The globe floated up and stayed. "These lights are wonderful!"

"Mage lamps," Elspeth said. "Not everyone can create them, so light globes are left at each of the entrances to the Labyrinth. You're doing well with that lamp."

"The tunnels are coded with color, aren't they?" When Elspeth nodded, Tory asked, "How can magic work here when it doesn't aboveground?"

"The official belief is that Lackland Abbey was built to suppress magic," Miss Wheaton replied. "In fact, the exact opposite was true.

Magic doesn't work well on the surface because Lackland's creators wished to concentrate the power belowground, where they trained novices. It's said that Merlin himself built these tunnels."

"Merlin?" Tory asked incredulously. "He's just a legend."

"Very likely," the teacher agreed, "but one that fits us. Merlin and King Arthur and the Knights of the Round Table were dedicated to defending Britain."

"Because we aren't here just to study magic." Elspeth's pale green eyes were grave. "We are preparing to defend Britain against Napoleon if there is an invasion."

Tory's jaw dropped. "Is invasion really coming, Miss Wheaton? You told me no one can predict the future reliably."

"True, but every British foreteller agrees that the odds of Napoleon invading are very high." The teacher's expression was bleak. "I have nightmares about what might happen. Britain and France have been blood enemies for centuries, and now we are Napoleon's fiercest foes. If the French come . . ." She shook her head.

"Napoleon might not invade, but if he tries—well, some of Britain's best mages will be standing against his armies." Elspeth's eyes narrowed like a cat's. "The army and militia are Britain's regular troops, so we call ourselves the Irregulars. Merlin's Irregulars."

Tory considered what kind of magic could prevent an invasion. "Would you use weather magic? That might stop invaders like the hurricane that smashed the Spanish Armada in 1588."

"British mages conjured that hurricane," Miss Wheaton said with a smile. "The channel has always been our greatest defense. God willing, it will be again."

"Is that why Jack Rainford is here?"

"Yes, he's our strongest weather mage. Several other talented local mages are also Irregulars." Elspeth's gesture encompassed the room. "Most of us are from Lackland Abbey, but no matter what our rank in society, we share the same determination to develop our magic and use it to defend our homeland. We call each other by our given names to remind ourselves that we're equals in our study of magic."

The cause was vital, yet being a patriot and embracing magic would mean complete estrangement from normal society. Tory bit her lip. Though she wanted to be a warrior for England, she also wanted to go home. "Does every student who finds her way down here join the Irregulars?"

Miss Wheaton shook her head. "Though students may be drawn to magic, choosing to become an Irregular is a path into the unknown."

"What happens to those who decline? Surely they tell others what they found here."

"Mr. Stephens or I bespell them so that they wake up the next morning thinking they were dreaming," Miss Wheaton said. "The dream fades, and they have no inclination to talk about it."

Tory asked, "Are only weather mages useful?"

"Everyone with magic can help, no matter what their special gifts," Miss Wheaton said. "Besides general training, we also teach the Irregulars how to share magic with each other. If a dozen mages are lending power to Jack, he can pull weather from greater distances and build stronger storms than he can on his own."

"It's the same with healing," Elspeth said. "When several of us work together, we can do more than even the best individual healer."

Tempted by the idea of learning more magic, Tory said hesitantly, "My abilities aren't very useful, but I could probably help others. Do you meet here every night?"

"Only three nights a week. We mustn't deprive you of too much sleep!" Miss Wheaton replied in a very schoolmistressy voice.

"Are the governors of the school bespelled so they won't find out about the tunnels?" Tory asked.

Elspeth smiled wryly. "The governors of the school do know

about the Labyrinth, though probably not exactly what we do. Every now and then they raid the tunnels to try to catch us. They aren't very successful. It's too easy to get lost down here if you can't see the magical color codes."

"Why don't they just block the entrances?"

"They try, but the blocks never last," Miss Wheaton said. "Labyrinth magic is so powerful that entrances always reopen. The authorities are frustrated, but they've been unable to stop our work. They've decided to ignore us as long as we don't cause any trouble aboveground."

"Do they know you and Mr. Stephens teach magic down here?"

Miss Wheaton shook her head. "They can ignore the students, whose families are paying high fees, but we teachers would be dismissed immediately."

"The Labyrinth is due for a raid," Elspeth said thoughtfully. "There hasn't been one in at least a year."

"I should like to think the governors have given up, but I expect we won't be that lucky," the teacher said with a sigh.

Tory had imagined herself as a patriotic warrior for her country, as courageous as any man. Bur now that she had the chance, she didn't know if she was up to the challenge. "Must I decide now?"

"Not quite yet, but before you leave tonight. Think about it. Talk to Elspeth. If you decide to stay, I'd like to talk to you again." Miss Wheaton touched Tory's shoulder lightly before returning to the classes at the far end of the room.

Elspeth asked, "Do you have any other questions?"

"I don't know what to ask." Tory shook her head. "It's a noble cause, but I don't know if I'm brave and noble enough."

"From what I've heard, no one knows how brave she is until face-to-face with danger." Elspeth toyed with a strand of her pale hair. "I hope I'll be equal to whatever comes, but I simply don't know. When

I was little, I was always terrified when other children attacked me because of my magic."

Tory winced. "You came into your power young?"

"Too young. I managed to conceal what I was from my parents for some time, but other children sensed I was different even before my magic began to manifest." Her eyes were shadowed by bad memories.

"Yet now you face down students who despise you for accepting your magic."

Elspeth's smile was knife-edged. "Learning how to use my power has given me confidence. I may still be afraid in the future—but perhaps not so much."

"So if I refuse to join the Irregulars tonight, I'll be sent home and made to forget about the Labyrinth," Tory said. "What if I decide to learn more about magic, then change my mind later? Will I be punished?"

"No, you'll just be placed under the forgetting spell."

"So I can say yes now, and back out later?" When Elspeth nodded, Tory asked, "Would that be considered dishonorable?"

"No, but it's uncommon. Most Lackland students find they enjoy learning how to master their magic." Elspeth shook her head. "Using one's power is exhausting, sometimes frightening, but also intoxicating. Haven't you experienced that?"

Tory remembered the fear and exhilaration of flying. "I have. It seems wrong to enjoy something so much."

"How is it wrong if we do no harm? The church doesn't condemn magic. Only the aristocracy thinks that it's a disgrace to our elevated breeding."

"I've been thinking about that ever since my magic appeared," Tory agreed. "But the people who despise magic are our friends and families."

Elspeth looked wistful. "I've often thought that I would have been better off born a commoner." She rose gracefully. "I have a selfish hope that you'll join the Irregulars. But it's a decision you must make for yourself."

As the other girl moved away, Tory twisted the fringe of her shawl nervously. She was fortunate that her brother and sister still accepted her. She could easily have lost Sarah if Lord Roger had broken the betrothal.

Her father was already lost to her. So were Louisa and horrible Edmund Harford. Even if she returned home tomorrow, the damage was done. In the eyes of those who despised mages, she was hopelessly tainted.

Yet even though she knew she could never regain her old life, embracing magic went against everything she'd been taught for the first sixteen years of her life. Emotions in turmoil, she stood and moved closer to the other students.

Several of the girls were Elspeth's dining companions, but two she didn't recognize. From their dress, she guessed they were from the village. One looked like she might be Jack Rainford's sister. She recognized several Lackland boys from watching them play games through the fence that divided the schools.

Males and females, ages from perhaps thirteen to twenty. They were sitting and working together as equals. That seemed to be true of the two teachers as well.

That equality fascinated Tory. She might not be allowed to attend Oxford or Cambridge, but in this place, what mattered was talent and hard work.

Drawing a deep breath, she accepted that Lady Victoria was no more. The death of her old self hurt, but now Tory was free to become whatever she wished to be. The thought was as exciting as it was alarming.

A ripple of laughter moved through one of the circles of students.

A dark-haired fellow glanced up—and her gaze locked with Allarde, heir to the Duke of Westover. She drew a shocked breath. Surely he had more to lose than anyone else here!

Energy thrummed between them like a plucked harp string. His gray eyes were smoke and magic.

He turned away, and she knew beyond doubt that he'd felt that snap of energy, too. And he didn't like it one bit.

She made her decision. If the Marquis of Allarde could risk a great title and fortune on behalf of his country, so could she.

At least, she could try.

CHAPTER 13

Decision made, Tory took a seat at the edge of Miss Wheaton's group. The teacher smiled when she saw Tory join the circle. "I believe we have a new Irregular?"

Everyone in both groups turned to study Tory. She colored. "Yes, Miss Wheaton. I want to do what I can to help, even though it's only irregular."

The teacher's smile widened. "Let us all welcome Victoria Mansfield."

As swift applause echoed off the hard walls, Jack Rainford called, "Tea time! We shall celebrate our new member."

"Not yet," Miss Wheaton said firmly. "Practice your lifting exercises while I speak with Victoria." Leaving the group, she joined Tory and led them back to the corner where they'd spoken before.

"In your Lackland classes, I focus on how to control magic so it can be locked down. Now it's time to talk a bit about the theory of magic," the teacher said. "You know the exercises I teach about visualizing your power being bound with silver cords?"

Tory nodded. "It seems too easy. I thought there would be spells or potions."

"Magic comes from the mind, whether you wish to suppress it or develop it. Some mages use spells and rituals because it helps them focus their power and their will, but the English magical traditions teach visualization. Imagine the outcome you want, then channel power into that image."

"That's how I do my floating!" Tory exclaimed. "I think about rising, and I do. I hadn't realized that I was doing it right."

"You have good instincts," Miss Wheaton replied. "We like to say that power follows thought. The clearer and stronger your thoughts, the quicker and more effective the outcome."

"I found that out the first time I bumped my head into the ceiling!"

"A bump on the head is worth an hour of lecturing on theory," the teacher said with a smile. "No two mages in this room have identical abilities. With training, you will learn which are your abilities. Most mages are very good in one or two areas, and have more modest abilities in several others. As I told you before, most mages can do at least a little healing, but few have the healing talent that Elspeth and I do."

"Is it the same with weather working and Jack Rainford?"

"Exactly. Any mage can learn how to move a cloud or raise a breeze, but few can build or shift a large storm. Jack is our best, and we are developing techniques to feed him more power as he needs it."

"At least I can do that." Tory frowned. "Miss Wheaton, I have a question. Why do the well-bred despise magic so much when the lower orders embrace it?"

"It is claimed that magic is evil or dishonest or manipulative."

The teacher frowned at her linked hands. "But I think the real reason is that to become a mage, one must be born with talent and then work hard to develop it. Money can't buy talent. Men who are rich and powerful in worldly terms deeply resent that this is a kind of power they can't have themselves. Since they can't buy talent, only hire it, they condemn magic."

"So if wellborn parents tell their children magic is wrong, the children will grow up despising magic and pass that condemnation on to their own children," Tory said. "People of the middling sort who wish they were better born copy the attitudes of aristocrats to make themselves feel superior, so they sneer at magic, too."

"There are always independent thinkers who will come to different conclusions, but they are rare." Miss Wheaton gestured to encompass those in the room. "Most people accept what they have been told without thinking much about it. Going against the wind isn't easy. But sometimes it's necessary."

"What if the French don't try to invade?"

"The Irregulars will still have the skills they learned here. No one needs to use magic if she chooses not to—but it's good to have the choice." Miss Wheaton rose. "Time for the last exercise of the night, our joining circle. We all hold hands and share our power. It's a way of harmonizing and learning to work together. Usually we use the energy to start heating our tea water." She clapped her hands. "Circle time!"

With a shuffling of chairs, the students stood and arranged themselves in a circle in the open part of the room. As Tory tentatively moved into place, Elspeth arrived and took her left hand. "It will feel rather strange, as if all the notes of a chamber quartet are singing through you. In time, you'll be able to recognize everyone in the circle by the flavor of their energy."

Jack Rainford appeared and took Tory's right hand in a warm, strong grip. "After this, we have tea along with shortbread made by the mother of one of the village students. Some Irregulars claim they come here just because of her baking."

Trying not to show that she was flustered by Jack's touch, she asked, "No one will be able to read my mind, will they?"

Elspeth laughed. "No, you'll just be one more note in the symphony of the Irregulars. It would be noticeable if someone was very upset, but there are no mind readers here. Just close your eyes and breathe in and out slowly. You'll feel Jack and me most strongly since we're touching."

Once everyone was linked, including the teachers, Mr. Stephens said, "And so we beginnnnn . . ." The last word was drawn out into a hum.

Tory closed her eyes obediently and took a slow, deep breath. Then she exhaled sharply as power flowed through her. Though it wasn't really like music, she couldn't think of a better comparison. Surely Elspeth was that strong, pure note like crystal bells.

Jack's energy was deeper. Wilder. He held the power of storms.

She couldn't separate out the other energy threads, though she guessed that Miss Wheaton might be a low, true power that contributed stability and comfort. Tory had no idea what she herself brought to the group. It would take time to learn who was who, but the rush of power that flowed through her was exhilarating.

Tory wasn't sure how long they held hands before Miss Wheaton's soft voice said, "And slowly end. . . ."

As the circle broke up, a girl across the room said with surprise, "The tea water is boiling already!"

"You must have added a good jolt of energy to the circle, Vicky!" Jack said admiringly, not releasing his grip.

Tory pulled her hand loose. "Surely not that much. I'm a newcomer here."

"Perhaps Tory helps blend energies well," Elspeth said. "Like water allows salt and sugar to dissolve. Miss Wheaton has mentioned that there are such talents. Tory, come meet the rest of the girls." Deftly, Elspeth whisked Tory away from Jack.

As they headed to a corner of the room that looked like a kitchen, Elspeth said under her voice, "Jack is a good fellow, but he does like to flirt."

Tory grinned. "I noticed."

Mr. Stephens intercepted them. "Victoria, I'm so glad you've joined us. We are blessed to be able to contribute toward such vital work."

Though not particularly handsome, he had a smile that made Tory appreciate what Miss Wheaton saw in him. She hoped he couldn't tell that she still had reservations about embracing her magic. "I'll try to be useful."

The teacher studied her thoughtfully. "Elspeth is right. You have the rare ability to blend and enhance the energy of other mages. It's a very useful talent."

Tory wasn't sure whether to be glad or alarmed at having a special talent. As the teacher was called away by someone else, Elspeth resumed their progress toward the simple kitchen. There was a pump for water, cabinets to hold china and utensils, and several cats who watched with interest. Instead of a regular fireplace and hearth, there was a long, narrow slab of stone with two large kettles simmering on it. There was no fuel under the kettles, only the stone, which radiated heat.

A younger girl gazed intently at a stone oven that was open in front. Inside were platters of shortbread squares. Tory asked, "Is she heating that shortbread with magic?"

"Yes, Alice is our best at producing heat," Elspeth replied. "We can't burn fires down here because of the smoke, so her talents are really useful."

As Alice concentrated on the shortbread, two boys stepped forward to lift the kettles from their hot stone. They poured the boiling water into large teapots that had been prepared with dry tea leaves.

Alice stood and brushed the knees of her skirt. "You're the new lass," she said with a country accent. "As you can see, I come from a long line of hearth witches."

Tory laughed and offered her hand. "Such a useful skill! I don't think I can do anything half so helpful. I'm Tory."

"You're just beginning to learn what you can do," Alice said consolingly. "So daft that you aristocrats are punished for your magic! Such a waste."

Elspeth introduced her to the girls preparing the tea and putting shortbread on plates. A local girl who looked like Jack turned out to be his younger sister, Rachel.

Both village girls and schoolgirls welcomed Tory warmly. She began to relax in a way she hadn't known since she'd woken up floating over her bed. The Lackland students might be outcasts from society, but together, they were a community.

People collected cups of tea and pieces of shortbread and drifted off to join others. Tory saw clusters of boys, clusters of girls, and several mixed groups. They found spots around tables or pulled chairs together so they could chat. There was no sense of rigid division like what Tory had seen in the school.

There were even two couples who had found corners where they could be private. Tory saw faint glows of pinkish energy around both pairs. Romance in the Labyrinth.

Her gaze moved to Allarde. He was studying her with grave eyes that made her think of medieval warrior monks. Again there was that snap of connection. He looked away and she did the same, though she couldn't shed her prickly sense of awareness.

She joined Elspeth, Alice, and several other girls at the long kitchen table. The hot, sweet tea was very welcome. After a swallow, Tory tried a piece of shortbread. "Lovely!" she said appreciatively. "Do study sessions always end with such treats?"

"Learning to master our magic burns a lot of energy." Elspeth tossed fragments of shortbread to two cats who had stationed themselves under the table. "After classes, we need to build up our strength again."

Tory took another piece of shortbread. "What a fine excuse to eat more."

She was just biting into her second piece when Allarde approached the table, his gaze fixed on her. Tory almost choked on her shortbread. She'd seen him only at a distance. Close-up, he was even more handsome, with softly waving dark hair and compelling eyes. His quiet intensity made him seem older than his years.

"Welcome to the Labyrinth," he said. "Are you related to Geoffrey Mansfield? Now Lord Smithson? He was called Mansfield Major because there was a younger Mansfield at the school."

Allarde was *tall*. Tory scrambled to her feet so he wouldn't loom over her so much. "Geoffrey is my brother. The young one was cousin George, from the Shropshire branch of the family."

"Mansfield Minor," Allarde said with a nod. "I was one of your brother's fags, and glad of that. He was the best of the senior students."

Fags were first-year students who were required to act as servants to the older students. "Geoffrey has always been a good brother," Tory said. "I shouldn't think even Eton would make him a bully."

"Eton doesn't always bring out the best in boys." He shifted from one foot to the other. "I'm Allarde, by the way."

"I thought in the Labyrinth we use first names?"

"Mostly yes." He shrugged. "For some reason, I'm always called by my title."

"I'm usually called Tory." She clenched her hands into fists to resist her desire to touch Allarde. If she did that, surely sparks would shoot into the air. "Do you have a particular talent, or shouldn't I ask? I don't know all the unwritten rules yet."

"One is allowed to ask." A whisper of a smile touched his eyes. "I'm good at moving objects"—a piece of shortbread swooped gracefully from the table and hovered in front of Tory—"and also at drawing conclusions from fragments of information."

She blinked and accepted the shortbread. "Both useful. Piecing information together would be a good military talent, I think."

His eyes brightened. "My family tree is full of soldiers and sailors. I think a fair number of them must have had magical ability, but there's no evidence. They were better at concealing their talents than I was."

"You may well have your chance to prove yourself in war," Tory said.

"We all will." He inclined his head. "I look forward to . . . working with you."

As he left, Elspeth gave a soft laugh. "Interesting. Very interesting indeed."

CHAPTER 14

Interesting indeed. When Tory turned to Elspeth, the other girl said, "We should leave now. People trickle out a few at a time so there's less chance of being noticed."

Tory noticed that the group was getting smaller, with students going off in different directions. She lifted the shawl she'd draped over her chair and prepared to leave. "Will it be the same route I used to get here?"

"No, I'll show you a different way."

As they headed for a tunnel, Miss Wheaton intercepted them and offered Tory a small, water-polished stone that buzzed with magic. "Carry this stealth stone when you come to the Labyrinth," the teacher said. "It will help prevent you from being detected."

Tory studied the stone. It was translucent white, made from quartz, perhaps. "How does it work?"

"The stone is charged with a spell that makes people less likely to see or hear you. You won't be invisible, but roommates probably won't realize that you've been gone, and if someone sees you, they won't question why you are where you are. Without these stones, it would be impossible for us to come and go unnoticed."

"Who bespells the stones with stealth magic?" Tory asked.

"Mr. Stephens. He has a gift for concealment." Miss Wheaton handed over a small drawstring bag made of raw silk. "You can store the stone here. The silk helps keep the spell strong."

Tory slipped the stone into the bag and tucked it in her pocket. "I have to wait two days before I can have more lessons?"

The teacher laughed. "Time will pass soon enough. Sleep well. I send energizing magic through our closing circles to make up for the late night, but you'll still probably be tired tomorrow."

"It's worth it!"

As Elspeth led the way toward the tunnels, she said, "We'll take the silver tunnel, which leads to the cellar below the refectory. I like it because it's covered all the way."

"I looked in that cellar and didn't see anything when I was searching."

"Doors to the Labyrinth are all bespelled so they're easy to over-look. Even when someone is looking, they're hard to find." As they headed into the blue tunnel, Elspeth pointed at a nearly invisible square opening in the ceiling. "That's one of the vents that keeps the air down here fresh. On the surface, most are hidden in the old out-buildings."

She turned into a tunnel that crossed the blue tunnel. Tory touched the small patch of color above into silvery brightness. "Why did you think it interesting that Allarde talked to me? It was only because he knew my brother."

"I've never known him to talk to a girl without a reason related to lessons. He's always the soul of courtesy, but he never flirts." Elspeth gave her a sidelong glance. "He didn't come speak to you because of your brother, no matter how fine a fag master Lord Smithson was. I saw energy pulsing between you. Surely you felt that."

"I felt a twang like a harp string," Tory said hesitantly. "What does that mean?"

She half hoped the other girl would say such a connection was powerfully romantic, but Elspeth replied, "There is a link, which could be for any number of reasons. Maybe you and Allarde have talents that will blend well."

Tory had to admit that seemed more likely than a grand love affair. "If I start eating at the table with you, will Nell Bracken and her friends stop talking to me?"

"Probably, but you don't have to turn away from them. Nell is very kind. She always takes new students into her group so they won't feel so alone and frightened when they arrive." Elspeth smiled wistfully. "We were friends until I visibly embraced my magic. Nell told me very politely that she was sorry, but she couldn't jeopardize her chances to leave as soon as possible by spending time with a known magic lover. She wished me well, and we haven't spoken since."

"It isn't fair that we should have to choose between friends!"

"It isn't fair that we're here at all. I don't mind being ostracized by most of the girls, but you might prefer to act like Mary Janeway. Did you notice her tonight? She's part of Nell's circle as well as an Irregular."

"That's right! I knew she was familiar, but she's very quiet at the school meals. Tonight she was laughing and talking."

"It feels good not to hide one's own nature. That's why I flaunt my wicked ways for all of Lackland to see," Elspeth said ironically. "But you might prefer being like Mary and quietly blending in."

"You won't mind?"

Elspeth shook her head. "You can cut me aboveground as long as you don't turn into a snob in the Labyrinth."

Tory didn't like the idea of ignoring Elspeth, but neither did she wish to be cut by Nell and the others. The rest of the short walk was in silence.

The tunnel ended in a stone wall. Elspeth touched the last patch of silver, and a door-shaped panel of stone pivoted open silently.

"As soon as we pass through the door, the mage lights will dim to less than a candle," Elspeth said softly. "After our next study night, I'll show you a different tunnel. You'll know them all soon enough. Can you find your way to your room on your own?"

There was just enough light for Tory to recognize the sacks of potatoes and turnips and other foodstuffs. A tabby cat ghosted silently by her ankles as it moved from the tunnel to the refectory cellar. As it leaped into action after a rustling sound, Tory said, "I'll manage. I can also find my way down to the Labyrinth again in two days. Thank you so much for all your guidance."

Elspeth gave her a fleeting smile. "You'll have your chance to help others in turn. Mages help mages. Go along now. Carefully."

The mage light faded just as Elspeth had predicted. By the time Tory was out of the cellar, it had disappeared entirely. But she could still feel the power of the stealth stone in its silken pouch. Lackland Abbey allowed more magic than its reputation suggested.

She moved through the school like a shadow, out of the refectory, into the dormitory, up the stairs. Outside her door, she hesitated. She couldn't risk the sounds of undressing inside since that might disturb Cynthia. Quietly she stripped down to her shift, which she usually slept in anyhow, and bundled her clothing and shoes into her shawl. Then she turned the knob and crept into the bedroom.

Cynthia made a sound and rolled over in her bed. Tory froze, not moving until her roommate began breathing regularly again. Cynthia had taken the bed by the window because it had a better view, which was convenient now since Tory didn't have to pass her roommate to get to her own bed.

After tucking her bundled garments in the corner between the wall and her wardrobe, Tory straightened out the lumped covers she'd left in her place, then slid into her bed. Now that she was back, she was bone-deep exhausted, but also exhilarated. What a night! She had discovered a whole new world, and a community of mages that accepted her warmly.

And a handsome young lord who never talked to girls . . . had talked to her.

Bong . . . bong . . . BONG!

The wake-up bell yanked Tory from sleep. She opened heavy eyes, wondering if she'd dreamed her visit to a school for magelings below Lackland Abbey.

Her gaze fell on the bundle of clothing tucked against her wardrobe. Her adventure had been real.

She swung her feet to the floor, glad that her mother had sent the small carpet Tory had requested. She was less tired than she should be after staying up half the night. Miss Wheaton's extra energy had helped. In fact, she felt invigorated.

Cynthia was already up and struggling with her gown. "Fasten up the back," she ordered. "Lucy has a streaming cold and I don't want her near me."

"Poor Lucy. You're a hard taskmistress," Tory observed as she moved behind her roommate to fasten the tie of the pretty blue poplin. "Have you thought of ordering gowns that you can put on without help?"

"I won't lower my standards!" Cynthia snapped. She smoothed out the skirt of her expensive garment. "You dress like a servant."

"I see you're in your usual cheery mood," Tory said with a laugh. She had the satisfaction of seeing Cynthia scowl. Good nature was the best shield against her roommate's bad temper. "Do you need any other assistance?"

Cynthia touched her hair, as if considering asking for help, then shook her head. "No, but thank you." The politeness was grudging, but at least she'd said thank you.

Tory finished dressing, collected her shawl, and headed out to the chapel. On the stairs she fell in with Nell Bracken and two other girls. One was Mary Janeway, the other Irregular. Mary's eyes were watchful, as if she feared Tory might give her away.

Tory greeted the other girls in her usual fashion, paying no special attention to Mary. Nell Bracken said, "You're looking happy this morning, Tory. Good news?"

Acting as if nothing had changed might be harder than Tory had expected. "I'd asked my mother for a rug to put by the bed, and it arrived yesterday," she explained. "Amazing how much nicer a day looks when your feet aren't icy."

The other girls laughed. Nell added shrewdly, "You're also adapting to Lackland, aren't you?"

Tory nodded. "I had a good governess, but I find I like going to school." She smiled at the others. "It's nice to be with other girls like me. I even like most of the classes. With one exception."

The other three groaned in unison. "Anything with Miss Macklin," Nell said succinctly. "She's making me hate Italian."

Tory felt the same way. She sat in the back of Miss Macklin's classroom and spoke very little and did her best not to be noticed. Sometimes it worked.

The other dark spot was the chapel services with the horrible curate. Tory had become adept at tuning out his rants and concentrating on energy exercises. This morning, though, she found herself thinking about the Irregulars. Enlisting with the other magelings to defend England had seemed romantic and right the night before.

Now, back in the normal world, she had doubts. What could a group of students do against Napoleon's armies?

And, selfishly, she wasn't yet ready to give up the dream of returning to a fairly normal life. Her brother and sister would still accept her if she left Lackland cured, but would that be true if she embraced magic? That might stretch even their tolerance.

She didn't think Geoffrey and Sarah would cut her entirely, but if Tory was publicly known as a mage, she might not be as welcome in their homes. Particularly after the memory of Jamie's rescue faded with time.

The decision was too large to make now. She bent her head as Hackett intoned the final prayer of the service. She would join the Irregulars and learn more about magic, and if the French came soon, she would do what she could to stop them.

But mentally she reserved the right to forswear magic if she changed her mind.

CHAPTER 15

Despite her misgivings, Tory loved her evenings in the Labyrinth. She learned interesting things in every session. From Miss Wheaton, she learned how to bring her thoughts and emotions to the center of her being when they were out of balance. And she learned how to focus her power to greater intensity once she was centered.

From Mr. Stephens, she learned illusion spells. She hadn't great natural talent in that area, but learning how to conceal things she preferred to keep private was useful.

She also liked getting to know the other Irregulars. The Lackland students like Nell were pleasant and they made good friends, but Tory discovered there was a stronger bond with boys and girls who were using their magic rather than denying it. Perhaps it was the risks they were taking together that made the friendships deeper.

The only activity all the Irregulars did together was the final joining circle. Otherwise, students studied in small group tutorials led by the adult teachers or advanced students. She learned the elements of weather work from Jack Rainford, healing from Miss Wheaton and Elspeth, how to warm or cool from Alice Ripley, the best hearth witch, and how to move objects from Allarde.

Tory's ability to blend the energies of others made her very popular in group exercises where students practiced working together. A week after she discovered the Labyrinth, she got the chance to help with some very practical magic.

Drenching rain had started in late afternoon. A few of the Irregulars had the ability to repel raindrops, but several village students arrived looking like drowned mice. Alice had to warm up the cook stones to dry wet clothing.

At joining circle time, Jack Rainford reported, "Upside is still wetter than my mum's washtub on laundry day. I didn't want to give myself a headache before class by trying to stop the rain, but if I can use the energy of the circle, maybe I can shift the clouds so we can be dry going home."

"Rather than the circle, take Tory's hand and see what you can do," Mr. Stephens suggested. "Alice, you join in, too."

Jack headed for Tory. "The best thing about these classes is the chance to hold a pretty girl's hand," he said. Then he reached for Alice. "Two pretty girls are even better!"

The female Irregulars groaned audibly. Jack was teased regularly about his flirting. Tory had never had classes with boys before. She found that the two sexes tended to treat each other like brothers and sisters. There were several romantic relationships, but much more friendly teasing.

Becoming relaxed with young men her own age would have been very useful if she was to have a London season, which she wouldn't. Girls who had attended Lackland were not presented to good society.

She found that she liked having boys as friends. She wasn't quite sure how to classify Allarde and Jack. Neither of them was anything as simple as a friend. Allarde didn't single her out for conversation again, but sometimes she felt his gaze on her. And Jack—well, he flirted with all the girls, but there seemed to be a special warmth in his eyes when he flirted with her. Though maybe all the girls thought that.

Tory, Alice, and Jack joined hands. "Just send energy to me," he said. "I'll use it to move the clouds away."

Tory closed her eyes and let the magic flow. Alice's power felt like the heat she generated so well, while Jack was his stormiest self. As their power flowed together, Tory found herself shadowing Jack as his mind reached into the sky.

After surveying the heavens, he summoned a wind from the north. And Tory was there, part of his magic! She was almost as exhilarated as when she floated.

After ten minutes or so, the rain clouds began to break up and blow away. "The rain has stopped!" Jack said triumphantly. "It was really easy. That was a big weather working, but I don't have any headache at all."

"I think that satisfies any remaining doubts about your ability, Tory," Mr. Stephens said. "Your connecting with two other strong talents made it possible for Jack to use his weather ability quickly and easily. Alice, will you heat the tea water now with the help of the other two?"

Alice obeyed, and the energy moving among them shifted from weather magic to a blaze of heat that didn't burn. It was better than walking on a sunny spring day.

"Enough!" someone called. "The water is boiling in both kettles."

Alice laughed. "That's the fastest I've ever boiled it! You're a useful lass, Tory."

Tory glowed with the praise. As the little sister in her family, she'd never been seen as very useful. This was much, much better.

"Does this mean that whenever strong magic is required, I'll be part of it?"

"Indeed it does," Mr. Stephens said with a smile. He gathered the Irregulars with a glance. "And now it's time for our regular joining circle. Let's see if Jack can bring us sunshine in the morning!"

Jack took Tory's hand again. "With us here, Lackland will have the best weather in England!"

By the fourth study session, Tory had developed a routine for slipping away from her room. She made up a bundle that included shoes and a sturdy, simple day dress that was easy to put on and take off. In the middle was the stealth stone and the whole was wrapped in her warmest shawl.

She used a bit of butter from the refectory to oil the hinges of the door and of her wardrobe. Her bundle she stored in the wardrobe, where it wouldn't be noticed among the other clothing. When it was time to leave, she removed the bundle and took it into the cold, dark corridor. There she dressed and headed downstairs, perhaps intercepting more Irregulars as they headed to the Labyrinth.

Studying with other magelings was energizing. When combined with the gentle healing power Miss Wheaton added to the joining circle, she never felt too tired for her regular classes the next day.

On the fourth night, Tory chose the tunnel that ended in the refectory cellar. It was her favorite route because the tabby she'd met there the first evening had become friendly and demanded petting. After scratching the cat's neck and chin, Tory opened the door to the Labyrinth, scooped up a mage light, and descended the steps.

Tonight she would have a tutorial on healing with Miss Wheaton and two other students who had started this term. This was another area where Tory had no special gift, but since healing was so useful, she was determined to get the most out of what talent she had. Since boys were always getting banged up playing their endless games, there was usually some young male to practice on.

More than half of the students had arrived by the time Tory reached the central hall. She looked around to find Miss Wheaton. Ah, there she was, talking to Mr. Stephens before formal classes started. By now, Tory was used to seeing a pink glow of energy between them whenever they were close. She wondered if they shared a few kisses after the students went home.

Tory was halfway across the hall when a familiar voice said waspishly, "What on earth is going on here?"

No, it couldn't be! Tory spun on her heel and saw Cynthia Stanton emerge from the same tunnel that Tory had used, looking as elegant as if she were going to tea. The witch had followed her!

"Miss Stanton." Mr. Stephens moved forward to greet Cynthia. "This is an unexpected pleasure. You won't remember, but you were here once before, shortly after you first arrived at Lackland. The Irregulars are students who have chosen to develop their abilities and form a magical militia to defend the country if Napoleon invades."

Cynthia frowned. "That sounds useful, but I don't remember being here before."

"You decided not to join us, so you were given a dream spell and sent back to your room." Mr. Stephens cocked his head to one side as he studied her. "What brings you here a second time?"

Cynthia pointed a long finger at Tory. "*She* has been sneaking out of our room. I thought she might have found a way to reach the boy's school, so tonight I followed her to see what she was up to."

"Studying," Tory said sharply. "If I can help keep England safe, I will."

"I care about my country, too!" Cynthia snapped back. Her gaze swung across the room. By this time most of the Irregulars had arrived and they were studying her with disgust or admiration, depending on whether they were girls who knew her or boys who saw only her blond good looks.

Cynthia's gaze halted. "Allarde?" she said with disbelief. "*You're* here? Your father will disinherit you!"

"If he does, so be it," Allarde said calmly. "Many of my ancestors gave their lives for England on the battlefield. A title is a small price compared to that."

"I'm as patriotic as anyone here," Cynthia said indignantly. "But why are you so worried that the French will invade? The Royal Navy will protect us."

"They will certainly try," Miss Wheaton said. "But some of our best foretellers believe that Napoleon will invade, and his forces have a good chance of success. If Lackland ends up a battlefield, we will be prepared to help fend them off."

Cynthia bit her lip and her gaze went to Allarde again. "If that is the case, I want to be an Irregular, too."

Miss Wheaton frowned. "We've never had a student who refused to join change her mind later."

Tory suspected that the teacher had seen Cynthia's interest in Allarde and was questioning the girl's motives. With justice. If Cynthia became an Irregular, she'd be able to get much closer to Allarde. But, blast the girl; she did have a powerful glow of magic around her.

"Let me speak with Mr. Stephens." Miss Wheaton and the other teacher moved to one side and started to talk in low voices. Tory suspected that the conversation was along the lines of "Lady Cynthia is selfish and mostly concerned with stalking Allarde" versus "but she does have a great deal of power, and we can always put a dream spell on her and send her away if she causes trouble."

After the consultation, Mr. Stephens put the Irregulars to studying while Miss Wheaton returned to Cynthia. "Your desire to serve is commendable," she said with a hint of irony in her tone. "Because you refused to join us before, we've decided that you must accept a special spell for the rest of this term. Are you willing?"

"What would it do?" Cynthia asked suspiciously.

"You won't be able to speak of the Labyrinth or the Irregulars when you're aboveground. That seems reasonable since you've changed your mind twice now."

Cynthia slanted another glance at Allarde. "I'll accept it," she said ungraciously.

"Very well. Tory, tonight you'll work with Elspeth on your healing because I will need to explain more about the Labyrinth to Miss Stanton."

"I suppose I must thank you for leading me here to join in such valuable work," Cynthia said with false sweetness.

"No need to thank me," Tory replied with equal falseness. Trying not to appear as if she cared, she turned to seek out Elspeth.

At least she would no longer have to dress in the cold, drafty corridor before heading to the Labyrinth.

CHAPTER 16

Elspeth and Tory escorted Cynthia back to the school when the study session was over. During the final joining circle, Tory had been able to identify Cynthia's energy, which was restless and unhappy. No wonder she was always so bad tempered. Tory felt a little more sympathy with her roommate but suspected that as an Irregular, Cynthia would be a disruptive force.

As they left the hall, Cynthia said waspishly, "Don't think that I'll treat either of you like friends just because we're studying magic together."

"Can we count on that?" Tory purred.

As Cynthia scowled, Elspeth asked, "I see an angry red glow around your lower abdomen. Do you have cramps?"

"What business is it of yours?" the other girl snapped.

"It might explain some of your bad temper," Elspeth said tartly. "If you like, I can take the pain away."

Cynthia hesitated, torn between misery and accepting help from a girl she despised. "What would you do?"

"Place my hand on your abdomen and send healing energy into the pain. It will only take a few minutes."

"She's really good," Tory said helpfully. "But you probably deserve to suffer, so I hope you refuse."

Looking daggers at Tory, Cynthia said, "Go ahead. My father always said that magical healing was just a hum."

"Then he's never experienced it. Hold still." Elspeth stepped close to Cynthia and gently rested her open hand on the other girl's lower abdomen. Cynthia flinched at the touch but didn't pull away.

Elspeth closed her eyes, her expression abstracted. Tory could see the flow of white healing energy moving from Elspeth.

After a minute or two, Cynthia gasped, "I feel better!"

"Give me another few minutes and you'll feel better yet," Elspeth promised.

The three of them stood in silence until Elspeth opened her eyes. "That should hold until your courses are done in another two days."

Cynthia said grudgingly, "Perhaps healing isn't a hum."

"Even the most stiff-necked aristocrats are usually willing to hire healers when ill," Elspeth said dryly. "A pity your father wasn't so flexible. Your mother might still be alive."

Cynthia turned white and spun around, almost running down the corridor. Elspeth sighed. "That wasn't kind of me, but she can be . . . trying."

"Be grateful you don't room with her," Tory replied. "Luckily, she mostly ignores me."

They reached a cross passage. Elspeth said, "I'll take this other route to the school. That's cowardly of me, but I can tell myself that

I'm being considerate of Cynthia's feelings since she probably doesn't want to see me again."

"Definitely cowardly," Tory agreed. "Sleep well, and thank you for the healing lesson. I'll never be as good as you, but I was able to provide some help for two of the boys who were bruised from playing football."

Elspeth turned left while Tory followed Cynthia at a slower pace. She found her roommate at the end of the passage muttering oaths as she tried to open the door to the refectory cellar. She turned to scowl at Tory. "I thought you two had abandoned me down here."

"I wouldn't do that to anyone." The words *even you* hung unspoken in the air. Tory stood on her toes to touch the silvery patch that controlled the door. Silently it swung open.

"How did you do that?" Cynthia demanded.

"The tunnels have color keys to guide people through the maze down here. This one is silver"—Tory touched the colored patch again and the door closed—"which is the hardest color to see against the white chalk. Only those who have magical ability can see the colors and use them to open doors."

Cynthia touched the silvery glow, smiling involuntarily as it opened, then closed again with a second touch. "This is rather fun. How many tunnels are there?"

"A lot. I'm beginning to know the ones that start on the girls' side of the school, but there are at least as many to the boys' side, and others that start outside the abbey. That's how the village students come."

Cynthia's scowl returned. "I never thought I'd be associating with village hearth witches! You seem to like magic even though it's destroying your life. You'll never make a decent marriage if you let the world know you're a mage."

"You are joining the Irregulars yourself," Tory pointed out.

"If I can help drive off invaders by using my magic, I will," Cynthia said. "But I'm not going to proclaim myself a mage to the world!"

At least Cynthia was honest about her mixed feelings. Though Tory's feelings were similar, she didn't talk about them. "My idea of a decent marriage is changing. Perhaps no lord will want me, but there are other good men in the world. Lots more than there are lords."

Cynthia's elegant nose wrinkled. "You mean disgusting commoners like that blond boy from the village?"

"Jack Rainford? He's a commoner, but he's not disgusting," Tory said cheerfully. "He's intelligent, amusing, a powerful mage, and good-looking. A girl could do worse."

Cynthia snorted her disagreement and opened the door to the basement again. "Thankfully not all the boys in the Irregulars are . . ." her voice disappeared as she stepped through the door. Astounded, she turned to Tory. After clearing her throat, she said, "I lost my voice for a moment!"

"The spell," Tory said. "You can't talk about the school on the surface."

Cynthia looked ready to explode. She stepped back into the tunnel and snarled, "This is *damnable!*"

Then she stamped into the cellar by the light of her fading mage light. Tory followed at a slower pace. How long until Cynthia quit again?

Not long, Tory suspected. Not long at all.

But Cynthia came to the next class, and the one after, and the one after that. Her expression was grim and the silk gowns she wore seemed too fancy for studying magic, but she came. Though her magical ability was untrained, she had a definite talent for weather working. That meant she had to practice with Jack, the "disgusting commoner."

Naturally, Jack flirted with Cynthia constantly. Tory was amused but also felt a certain grudging respect for her roommate's tenacity.

By mid-October, there was winter in the cold winds from the sea. Luckily, Tory had learned a spell from Alice, the hearth witch, that helped keep her warm. Alice could control temperature so well that she was always comfortable. Tory wasn't as good, but at least she didn't feel like she was freezing when she went out at night.

Not much disturbed the routine until the evening when she came to dinner to find Elaine Hammond, one of Nell Bracken's group, bubbling over with happiness. Elaine was nineteen, a fair, pretty girl with a sweet disposition. She was surrounded by other girls who were squealing with pleasure and offering congratulations.

Tory asked, "What wonderful thing has happened, Elaine?"

Elaine beamed at her. "Miss Wheaton says I'm ready to leave now! My sweetheart says regularly that he still wants to marry me, and finally I can say yes!"

"How marvelous!" Tory hugged the other girl. "When will you leave?"

"By Friday, I hope."

"Your sweetheart's parents don't mind that he's marrying a girl who has been in Lackland?" Tory asked with interest.

"His family loves me. They *like* the idea that our children might have magical ability. Harry's father owns mines in Yorkshire and is in quite a good way of business."

Tory laughed. "Let me guess. Before you came to Lackland, your parents disapproved of you marrying a man whose family is in trade, but now they're glad that a young man from a prosperous family is in love with you."

Elaine nodded vigorously. "My parents forbade me to see Harry before my unfortunate talents were discovered. They said he wasn't good enough for me. Now they've resigned themselves to the fact that I'm lucky to get him even if his family is in trade, so the banns will be read right away. In a month we'll be married!"

"I'm so happy for you," Tory said sincerely. She stepped back as another girl approached to offer congratulations. Elaine's situation gave everyone hope since her magical talent had actually removed the obstacles to marrying the man she loved. Tory didn't think Elaine had a great deal of power, and she didn't seem to have any regrets about having it locked down. She was lucky.

A servant approached and handed Tory a letter. "For you, Miss Mansfield."

The letter was franked by her father, which meant "Fairmount" was scrawled across the upper right corner in his bold hand. Peers of the realm like her father had franking privileges, so they could send letters for free. Tory never used to wonder why rich men had free use of the Royal Mail while impoverished scullery maids and farm laborers had to pay, but it now struck her as unfair.

Lord Fairmount hadn't written to Tory in the two months since he'd banished her to Lackland. This letter was from her mother, who wrote weekly with news of the estate and the neighbors. Tory's situation was never mentioned. Though not very satisfying, at least the letters proved that she hadn't been entirely forgotten.

After a paragraph of which tenants were ill and how her mother had taken jellies and syrups to the invalids, her mother turned serious.

Darling, I know how much you've been looking forward to coming home for Christmas and Sarah's wedding. Unfortunately, your father has forbidden it. He feels that the more time you spend at Lackland, the sooner you'll be cured. I shall be very sad not to see you, but I will write every detail of the wedding. Study hard, my dearest girl.

Tory almost wept with disappointment. She wanted so much to return to her home and sleep in her own bed, even if was only for a fortnight. How could she miss Sarah's wedding?

She reread the letter as if that might change the words, and realized what her mother was too tactful to say: Her father didn't want other guests at the wedding to see the disgraced daughter who had been sent to Lackland.

Though the earl hadn't officially disowned her, he was ashamed of her. Perhaps he would never allow her to return to Fairmount Hall. How long would it take for people to forget that the Lord Fairmount had a younger daughter?

She was disappearing already.

CHAPTER 17

Tory's mood was bleak when she headed into the Labyrinth that evening. At least she was welcome here, if not in her own home.

Not wanting to deal with Cynthia, she let the other girl go first and followed a few minutes later. Tonight she was scheduled for a tutorial with Miss Wheaton. When she reached the central workroom, she found the teacher writing notes at a table. Approaching, she said, "Good evening, Miss Wheaton. What am I to learn tonight?"

The teacher looked up with a smile. "How to husband your power carefully so you won't use it up too quickly and become exhausted."

"I can definitely use that!" Tory said, taking a seat at the table.

"It's one of the most valuable skills a mage can have." Miss Wheaton pursed her lips thoughtfully. "I must talk to Mr. Stephens about holding a drill on how to behave if the Labyrinth is raided. There hasn't been a raid in some time, so we've become rather lax. But half a dozen or so new Irregulars have joined us, so we need to make sure everyone knows what to do."

Tory frowned. "What does one do if the authorities raid us?"

"Basically, run," Miss Wheaton said with a laugh.

"Like chickens when a fox enters the yard?" Tory asked doubtfully.

"No, there are prefects for the three groups," the teacher explained. "Allarde for the Lackland boys, Elspeth for the girls, and Jack Rainford for the local students. They make sure all their people are moving out safely. There's time to get everyone organized because magical sensors on the entrances let us know when a raid is beginning. When the alarm sounds, most of the mage lights will go out, so the raiders will have a hard time recognizing anyone. There is just enough light left so people won't run into walls. The tunnels are such a maze that it's easy to avoid raiders. If a tunnel or exit is guarded, there are always other choices."

"What happens to a student who is caught? Or has that never happened?"

"It has happened, though rarely. The student is caned, which is bad enough. What's worse is that anyone caught down here practicing magic is locked in every night for as long as he or she remains at the school."

"How dreadful to be cut off from the rest of the Irregulars!" Tory exclaimed, thinking how her fellow mages had become her friends and her community.

"Most students find some way to compensate. Several become good at picking the locks to their doors. Others slip down to the Labyrinth during the day so they can practice their magic. But it's not the same as regular sessions, of course."

An understatement. Tory vowed to spend more time learning the tunnels to ensure she'd never be caught. Lackland was enough of a prison already. Being locked into her room at night would be a prison within a prison.

"Good evening, Victoria."

A tingle rang down her spine as she recognized Allarde's voice. She turned and greeted him with a smile, hoping she wasn't beaming like a madwoman. "Good evening to you, Allarde. Are you part of Miss Wheaton's tutorial this evening?"

"Yes. So is my friend Colin here. Have you two worked together before?"

"Not really," Colin said. Medium-sized and red-haired, he had freckles and an infectious smile. "Only in the joining circles."

"It's time to remedy that," she replied. "Do you have a magical specialty, Colin?"

"I'm a good finder if something or someone is lost." He chuckled. "It's not a glamorous skill, but it's useful."

"Splendid!" she exclaimed. "Can you tell me where I lost a silver brooch that my sister gave me? Or do you have to search for an item yourself?"

He cocked his head to one side. "Did you lose it about three days ago?"

When she nodded, Colin closed his eyes. "The catch broke when you were crossing the cloister garden. The brooch is on the west side, about a yard from the fountain. You'll have to poke around in the grass a bit. I think someone stepped on the brooch after rain and it got pushed into the earth, but you should be able to retrieve it without too much effort."

"Thank you!" she exclaimed. "I was very sorry to have lost it."

"As I said, my talent is a useful one." Mary Janeway joined them, and Colin's attention shifted. "Good evening, Mary. I'm glad we're working together tonight."

Mary gave him a bashful smile. Tory saw a soft pink glow between the two, and guessed that romance was budding.

As the two began to talk, Tory turned and found Allarde study-ing her with disquieting intensity. Feeling a little reckless, she said, "Is it my imagination, or do you often watch me in a way that is not casual?"

His gaze dropped. "It's not your imagination. I'm sorry. I am not usually rude, but there is . . . something about you. Ever since you first came to the Labyrinth, I've felt a connection that I don't under-stand. Do you feel it, too?"

"Yes, and I don't understand it, either," Tory replied. "But El-speth observed us that first day, and she says that connections are of many types. Perhaps our energies will blend together particularly well when we work together."

Allarde's expression eased. "That must be it. I can't imagine what other sort of connection there might be between us."

He certainly was eager for that twang of energy to be about magic, not romance, Tory thought regretfully. But Elspeth's expla-nation made him look more relaxed with her, and that was good.

Miss Wheaton said, "Time for this tutorial to begin. Colin—"

Before she could finish, a horn blared and most of the mage lights extinguished, leaving the hall dim and shadowed. Miss Wheaton caught her breath. "Raiders!"

After a frozen moment, Mr. Stephens stepped up onto the dais and raised his voice to carry through the room. "The raiders are us-ing the blue tunnels on both sides, the green tunnel on the boys' side," he hesitated, concentrating, "and the red tunnel on the girls' side. Prefects, look to your charges. There are only about a dozen raiders and since they're using just four tunnels, you can all escape easily. We'll meet again next week."

Despite the teacher's calm words, anxiety swept through the hall like a cold wind. Chairs scraped and voices rose as students headed for the exits. Allarde hesitated, his expression torn. "I must go. Just do as Elspeth says and you'll be all right."

"I will be fine," she assured him. "You have your duty. I shall see you at the next study session."

He touched her hair for an instant, then whirled and went off to collect the boys he was responsible for. Surprise held Tory still for a moment. Allarde was not acting like a mere colleague in magical study.

Setting that aside to consider later, she swung around and spotted Elspeth briskly marshaling the Lackland girls. Tory headed for the group that was gathering, telling herself that this happened regularly and the raiders almost never caught anyone. Mostly they just wanted to disrupt the classes and perhaps scare away the most timid.

"I'll go first," Elspeth called, rapidly scanning the girls gathering around her. "If I see a raider, I'll throw an illusion at him and call a warning to split into smaller groups and take other routes. There will be mages among the raiders, so your stealth stones won't help, but don't worry. They haven't caught a student in the years I've been here."

Most of the other girls had done evacuation drills, so there was no panic as they followed Elspeth into the green tunnel. Tory and Cynthia were the last to arrive, so they were at the back of the group. The other girl had lost her usual languid elegance and was visibly distraught. "If my father finds out I'm studying magic, he'll kill me!"

"He won't find out," Tory said soothingly. "It's not chance this is called the Labyrinth. We'll avoid the raiders and be safe in our beds in a few minutes."

"What if I get lost down here?"

"You won't. If we have to split up, just use the color codes to take yourself to the surface. I'll keep an eye on you." Tory dropped back and let Cynthia go ahead of her.

The girls were all moving as fast as they could, but most wore light slippers that weren't designed for running. Tory's anxiety increased as she heard the pounding of heavy feet nearby. A man shouted, then others joined in, bellowing like a pack of hounds after a fox. The furious voices echoed through the tunnels, harsh and threatening.

Wishing she hadn't thought of hunters galloping after their prey, Tory had to force herself to stay calm. If only the other girls were faster! Being last was making her nerves crawl.

As she whisked past a cross tunnel, a hoarse voice shouted, "There's one of the chits! Grab her!"

Her pulse spiked with fear. Realizing she was the only girl to have been spotted, Tory spun around and headed back the way she'd come, hoping to lead the pursuers away from the group. In her sensible shoes, she was able to run full speed, which felt good.

Her ruse worked. Far too close behind her, the same voice shouted, "This way!"

How far to the next cross tunnel? Too far, too far!

She reached a cross tunnel and darted to the left.

"She's gone left!" the hoarse voice called.

Damnation, the raiders were close enough to see her! They had good lights, too, so strong and steady that they had to be mage lights. That confirmed that there were mages with the raiders. Traitors! Elspeth said that mages didn't hurt mages, but the ones down here didn't seem to know that.

The men could run faster than she could, and they were gaining on her. Panting, she shot into another tunnel, then bolted into another. She didn't bother with the color codes. What mattered was losing the devils pursuing her. She could figure out where she was after she was safely away.

"There she is!" Once more they had her in their sights.

Desperate, she raced into another passage. She wished she could douse the dim mage light she carried, but without it she risked running into a wall and cracking her skull. They'd have her then.

Another turn—and to her horror, she saw that this passage came to a dead end. There was nowhere else to go.

She wanted to cry. Scream. Pray. She closed her eyes for an instant, trying not to think of spending the rest of her years at Lackland locked into a cell every night.

No! She opened her eyes, and saw that the tunnel now ended in a full-length silver mirror. Where the devil had that come from? She would have sworn that it wasn't there a moment ago. The mirror was almost as wide and tall as the passage, and the shining surface reflected her and the dim light in her hand as she pounded toward it.

"She must've turned down that one!" the hoarse voice shouted.

Tory slowed as she approached the mirror, reaching out in the hope she could move it to one side and hide behind it. She touched the surface, it turned black as an abyss . . .

. . . and she fell into hell.

CHAPTER 18

Lackland, WWII

Tory tumbled helplessly forward into darkness. She was falling, falling, being torn into screaming pieces. . . .

She slammed hard to the ground and the world turned dark.

Awareness returned with patchy slowness. Cold, damp stone under her belly. Absolute blackness. Shivering and disoriented, she tried to understand what had happened. Where the devil was she? She could no longer hear sounds of pursuit. There was only darkness and silence.

She must still be in the tunnel. The ground beneath her had the slightly irregular texture of chalk, and the air held a familiar damp coolness. So she must be in the Labyrinth. If she'd been unconscious for a while, the raiders might have left by now.

There had been a mirror, and touching the surface seemed to have transported her to this place. Was the mirror a magical portal to safety? Slowly she pushed herself to a sitting position and felt around. Her fingertips brushed a chalk wall, but she couldn't find the mirror.

Her stomach was queasy, and she'd have some dramatic bruises in the morning, but no serious damage had been done despite those horrifying moments when she thought she was being ripped apart. She closed her eyes and pulled her jagged energy into her center. When she had her balance, she used the heat magic she'd learned from Alice Ripley to warm herself to a more comfortable temperature.

Since there was still no sound from the raiders, she created a mage lamp, keeping it dim just in case. The light confirmed that she was in a Labyrinth tunnel, though this one looked as if it hadn't been used in years. Dust made a gritty layer on the floor and no footprints marked it. There was no sign of the mirror.

The portal must have moved her into a disused passage. She prayed it wasn't sealed. No, she could feel a faint current of air moving through. She got to her feet and moved toward the source of the air, all senses at full alert.

She was relieved to come to a cross tunnel, but she couldn't see a color code patch. This passage must not be part of the main Labyrinth.

She kept moving ahead. At the next intersection, she looked for the color code again. Nothing. This time she stretched up and touched the spot where the colors were usually found.

A glow appeared, so faint that she wasn't sure of the color. It might be blue, gray, or even silver. The magic had faded to almost nothing, but even so, it was comforting. She sent power to the patch, renewing the color to a recognizable blue so she could find her way back later.

She turned into the cross passage since it had the color code. She was still moving through undisturbed dust, leaving small, neat tracks. If anyone followed, she would be easy to find. But she didn't have the feeling there was anyone down here.

She was relieved again when the tunnel ended in a flight of dusty steps leading upward. The steps looked familiar, yet the dust proved it wasn't a passage that her fellow magelings used regularly. She climbed to the landing and touched the color coding area.

There was a dim glow of color and the door creaked, but it didn't open. Tory frowned. There had been mages among the raiders; they'd proved it by having mage lights. Could they have performed some great sorcery that sucked most of the magic out of the Labyrinth? She'd never heard of such a thing, but the early religious orders had managed to concentrate Lackland's magic below the surface, so perhaps the process could have been reversed.

She touched the magical patch again, this time pouring her own power into it. Groaning horribly, the heavy door opened in a series of small jerks. She darted through as soon as the gap was wide enough. She didn't want to be in the Labyrinth if the magic failed entirely and the door closed again.

She stepped into what seemed like a stone cellar, except there was no roof overhead. It was still night, so she hadn't been unconscious for too long. Cool moonlight illuminated piles of rubble on the floor. The cellar didn't look at all familiar. Perhaps she'd come up on the boys' side.

She looked up into the sky and frowned. Wasn't the moon only starting to wax? It should have been just a crescent, but the moon over her head was nearly full. She must have been so busy with school and the Irregulars that she'd lost track of the moon phases.

Still, it was convenient that the moon was bright enough to light her way out of the cellar. She let the mage lamp fade out. Since she didn't know where she was, it was best not to draw attention.

Carefully, she picked her way around the fallen stones that cluttered the cellar. This building hadn't been used in a very long time.

The steps on the other side were stone and solid, so she started to climb. The air was warmer than when she'd come down at the beginning of the evening.

Halfway up, she stopped in her tracks, her skin crawling with unease. The air didn't smell or feel like October. The wind was scented with new growth, not the dying leaves of autumn. This night smelled of spring.

She remembered tales of fairyland, where mortals slept years away after being enchanted. But she hadn't been enchanted, she'd been chased. Trying to keep her imagination in check, she resumed climbing. At the top of the steps, she looked around.

Lackland Abbey lay in ruins.

She caught her breath in disbelief. How could this have happened in a matter of hours? The general shape of the buildings was recognizable, including the tower of the chapel, but the roofs had caved in and walls had tumbled. It looked as if she'd come up through the cellar of the old refectory, though it was hard to say for sure.

Panic rose in her, swift and paralyzing. She forced it down. There was no obvious threat here. There was *nothing* here.

But the moon and the season and the ruins could not be denied. She was in a different time.

Fighting to master her fear, she headed toward the main gate. She would walk to the village. The school might have closed down and its stones been cannibalized for use elsewhere, but surely the village still existed. Even if years had passed, Jack Rainford or the other local Irregulars would remember her and offer help.

She almost stumbled into a jagged pit that had taken a huge bite out of the main drive. The moonlight saved her by revealing the danger just in time. She stared down, wondering what could have created such a large, raw hole. The scent of the earth was fresh.

Dear heaven, had the French invaded and this crater was from the impact of cannon? What had happened? Where in time was she? Lackland village. She prayed she'd find answers there.

The long drive was mostly overgrown with grass and the lock on the small door set into the large front gates was broken, so it was easy to get out. The walls were still formidable, though the spikes looked rusty. Cautiously, she stepped outside.

The road was still there but was now covered with a hard, dark substance. In towns, main streets were paved with cobblestones or perhaps bricks, but country roads were usually grass and mud and ruts.

If enough years had passed for the abbey to crumble, there was also enough time for roads to change. She knelt and touched the surface. The texture was a little coarse but overall smooth and hard. Excellent for carriages, though not as good for horses' hooves.

She stood, brushing off her hands. How many years had passed? Would there be anyone still alive who remembered her?

She almost leaped from her skin. Something white and ghostly was coming toward her with heavy feet. She clamped a hand over her mouth to smother a scream and backed toward the school gate, her gaze locked on the *thing*.

It mooed at her. Weak with relief, she conjured a mage lamp bright enough to show a cow with broad white stripes down its side. The pattern looked too regular to be natural, but why would anyone paint stripes on a cow?

The cow gave her a bored glance as it clopped past. She swallowed hard and crossed to the footpath she'd taken with Miss Wheaton. The path was much more direct than the coast road, and a pleasant walk through what were certainly spring woods.

English footpaths were ancient, and it was comforting to learn that this one hadn't changed much. Trees had grown, fallen, and new greenery had appeared, but the path was much the same as when she'd walked it before.

At the end of the path, she rejoined the road that ran down into the village. Nerves taut, she walked along the edge. Horses would be easy to hear on the hard surface, and one would expect travelers on a night with good moonlight. But she heard only the usual country sounds: the wind in the trees and shrubbery, the occasional rustling of animals, and the roll of the sea when she drew close enough to the shore to hear it.

She paused to listen to an unfamiliar low roar. It seemed to be coming closer. . . .

A huge beast with triple slits of light for eyes roared around a corner and straight at her. Tory gasped and dived off the side of the road to conceal herself in the bushes. The beast slowed for a moment, as if sensing her presence, then continued down the road, leaving an unpleasant scent that reminded her of burning lanterns.

She lay shaking on the ground for long minutes as she wondered what sort of world she'd fallen into. Another of the beasts rushed past. Had those smelly monsters killed all the people? She shuddered at the thought.

She must continue to the village and hope she would find people—and answers—there. Learning about this time and place might help her find her way home again.

She rose and brushed off the dirt and grass, then resumed walking. Now she stayed off the hard road surface. The beasts must have laid that dark strip of material for their convenience. They roared along as quickly as a horse at full gallop.

She reached the edge of the village sooner than she expected. New houses had been built using materials different from the usual stone. But all the buildings were dark. Not so much as a single flicker of candlelight showed in the windows.

Where were the people? If the rushing beasts hadn't killed everyone, had a lethal plague swept through the area? She shivered and walked faster.

The harbor below looked reassuringly normal, with fishing boats moored for the night. The road beasts surely couldn't use fishing boats.

A distant rumble was growing louder. The sound reminded her of the road beast, but the roar was even deeper and more ominous. Louder, louder, *louder,* the menacing growl boomed from the sky until it reverberated in her bones. She wanted to scream and run, but there was no place to run to.

A menacing creature like a huge, rigid bird flew high over her head and the sound dropped away quickly. The creature was following the coastline to the south.

She really had fallen into hell.

After the rumbling died away, she resumed walking because she didn't know what else to do. She supposed it wasn't unreasonable that all the villagers were in bed at this hour, but the unmitigated blackness was disturbing.

Ahead she saw one of the road beasts sleeping in a yard. Her first instinct was to flee, but it was motionless, with no glimmer of light from the monstrous eyes. Cautiously, she approached. Ah, the thing had wheels, so it was some sort of carriage.

She drew close enough to touch its hide, and found cool metal. Definitely some kind of carriage, one that didn't need horses. Maybe a steam engine inside made it move? Her father owned mines in the north that used steam-powered carriages that ran along tracks to move the coal.

She circled the carriage, which had glass windows all around. What had looked like eyes were some sort of glass lanterns on the front of the machine. But why were the lamps masked so that only slits of lights came out? Maybe the lanterns were too small to send more than narrow lights.

It was another mystery, but at least she no longer thought these beasts had killed all the people. They were just a strange carriage that could move fearsomely fast. The seats inside were deep and comfortable-looking, like the seats in her father's carriages. There was no coat of arms painted on the doors, though.

She bit her lip. She must have traveled into the future since nothing like this carriage existed in her day or in the past. But how far in the future? Surely many years had passed. Probably so many that none of the village Irregulars were still alive.

She was heading down to the harbor when she passed the parish church, Saint Peter's by the Sea. She felt a rush of relief at how solid and familiar it looked. Saint Peter might be the patron saint of fishermen, but maybe he would respond to prayers by a desperately lost student mage.

She climbed the steps and found that the heavy oak door opened smoothly under her hand. The interior was dark, but a surprising amount of light came through the stained glass windows.

Except they weren't stained glass anymore. The windows had been replaced with clear glass. They did a good job admitting moonlight, but they wouldn't fill the interior with brilliantly colored light during the day.

Even without the windows, the small church radiated peace. Feeling better than she had since the raid on the Labyrinth, she walked up the aisle to the altar. The very same cross, the same carved bench ends to the pews. She exhaled with pleasure. If the church had changed dramatically, she would have feared that God had died.

Vases of fresh flowers were set beside the altar. She brushed them with her fingertips. The flowers of May, not October. If there were still flower guilds decorating churches, the world hadn't changed beyond recognition.

The vicar's house had been right next door. Dare she knock on the door at this hour? Vicars were supposed to help people, and she certainly needed help. If she looked as young and confused as she knew how, he might not ask too many questions until she had a better sense of where she was. She suspected he'd be more cooperative if she didn't wake him up in the wee hours, so she'd spend the rest of the night in the church.

Before she could get settled, the door swung open and a narrow but fierce beam of light slashed across the church. A gruff male voice barked, "Who's there?"

CHAPTER 19

Heart pounding, Tory dived under the front pew before the light could find her. As the man walked down the aisle toward the altar, she lay as still as a terrified rabbit, hoping the stealth stone would keep him from noticing her.

The fellow muttered under his breath as he flicked the light about, keeping it low. It must be some form of mage light, though she'd never seen one that created such a narrow, powerful beam. As she opened her inner senses, she felt a soft buzz of magic.

The man hunting her was a mage. She was doomed..

He drew closer and closer, pacing back and forth as if he knew she was here. It took all her will to lie still when she desperately wanted to stand and run. But then he'd see her for sure.

"You!" He stopped by her hiding place, his shoes directly in front of her face. "You come out from under there. And don't try anything! I have a gun."

Looking as harmless as she knew how, Tory crawled out from under the bench and stood. The fellow's light was so bright that she couldn't see him clearly.

He said with surprise, "You're just a girl!"

His voice became lighter, and she realized that he sounded young, as much boy as man. He must have been lowering his voice to sound older.

She narrowed her eyes, trying to see him despite the glare. Tallish, broad-shouldered, fair hair. In fact, he looked rather familiar. "Jack?" she asked incredulously. "Jack Rainford?"

"I'm Nick Rainford. My older brother is Joe. Do you know him?"

His trousers and shirt and knit vest were unlike any garments she was familiar with, but he did look something like the Jack she knew in the Irregulars. Like a cousin, maybe. "I only know a Jack Rainford," she said cautiously. "Does he live around here?"

"I don't know any Jacks. Joe is away training to be an RAF pilot." Nick ran the light beam over her. "Who are you and why are you out in your nightgown?"

What was the RAF? "I'm Victoria Mansfield, usually called Tory, and this dress is perfectly respectable," she retorted. "Stop pointing that light in my eyes! What is it?"

"Just an electric torch." He pointed the beam down so it didn't glare. "That dress might be respectable, but it still looks like a nightgown. Where do you live?"

Irritated by his manner, she asked, "What business is it of yours?"

"It's my business because I'm part of the Lackland volunteer patrol. The local council formed it because we're on the coast and would be the first to be invaded."

Too much had changed for this to be the war against Napoleon, so it must be a different war. The English and the French had been fighting for centuries. "Why can't England and France learn to be friends instead of fighting all the time?"

"We're not fighting France," he said with surprise. "The French are our allies. The enemy is Germany, just like it was in the Great War." He shook his head. "How can you not know we're fighting the Nazis? Have you been living in a cave? That would explain the dirt stains on your nightgown."

"It's not a nightgown!" Exasperated, she plopped down on the pew. "Don't girls wear dresses around here?"

"Not ones that reach their ankles." His eyes narrowed. "You're a runaway. You can't be more than thirteen or fourteen. Shouldn't you go home? Or maybe I should take you to the police station."

"I'm sixteen, and not a runaway," she snapped. "Not that it's your business."

"There's a war on. Spies are everyone's business. That's why I've volunteered to patrol one night a week. I saw you come in here, so I followed, thinking you might be a Nazi spy." He sounded disappointed that she wasn't.

"Is Nazi a nickname for a German?"

He shook his head at her ignorance. "The Nazis are a political party. Their leader is Hitler, a tyrant who wants to conquer the world."

"He sounds like Napoleon, only German. Do you catch many spies?"

He grinned. "You would have been the first."

"Do you really have a gun?"

"I lied," he said cheerfully as he sat down on the other end of the pew. "But a spy would be armed, so I wanted to scare you. You still haven't said where you come from." His eyes narrowed. "Maybe you really are a spy. A pretty little girl would be a great choice, actually. No one would suspect you. You're probably really twenty-eight, a champion marksman, and you speak six languages flawlessly."

"You certainly have a good imagination! I speak French, but I'm no spy." She scowled at him. "If you must know, I've been staying out at Lackland Abbey."

His voice hardened. "The abbey has been in ruins for donkey's years. Just the sort of place a spy would hide."

"Would you stop this foolishness about spies!" But maybe this was a chance to learn more about the abbey. "How did the place get ruined?"

"I don't really know. It's been abandoned since maybe my grandparents' time. During the Great War, a German ship shelled it and that knocked down a lot of the buildings. Then a few weeks ago, an RAF plane dropped a bomb or two there by mistake." His voice changed. "They say once it was a school for sorcerers."

He sounded wistful. And he did have that glow of power around him. "Do you believe in magic?" she asked experimentally.

His expression turned wary. "Magic is just superstition. But . . . I've heard stories that once there was magic in the world."

He wished magic was real, she needed help and information, and because he was young, if he told everyone she was a lackwit, he might not be believed. It was time to take a risk. "Turn off that torch thing and I'll show you something interesting."

"You'll run away!"

"How far do you think I'd get before you caught me?" She raised her hands. "See? No weapons. Nothing in my hands. You'd hear me if I tried to escape."

"Very well." He turned off the torch with a small click.

Thinking she wanted to look at the torch more closely later, she concentrated and created a ball of light in her right hand. "If you want to believe in magic and haven't been able to, take a look at this mage lamp."

"What . . . !" In the gentle glow of the light, his face was startled. "It's some kind of Nazi trick that we haven't figured out yet!"

Nick Rainford certainly had spies and Nazis on the brain. "It's magic, Nicholas," she said patiently. "Here, put out your hand and take it."

Warily, he extended one hand. Tory rolled the mage lamp onto his palm. The light didn't dim at all, confirming her guess that Nick had magical ability.

He stared raptly at the ball of light. "It *tingles*."

"Brace yourself, Mr. Rainford," Tory said. "Magic is real, and you have some power, though it's undeveloped. Otherwise the mage lamp would fade out in your hand."

"This could be science, not magic." His gaze remained fixed on the light.

Tory took the lamp and brightened it to show his face better. "What is science?"

He looked baffled for a moment. "It's . . . it's studying how the world works and using that knowledge in practical ways."

"That sounds like natural philosophy." It was Tory's turn to be baffled. "Give me an example of science. Is your torch science?"

He nodded, raising the torch for her to see. "Electrical power is stored in batteries in the handle. When I turn the torch on, they send electricity into a little wire in the bulb. That makes the wire glow and give light. At least, until the batteries run out of power." He shook the torch, which was dimming. It brightened a bit. "Science in action."

So the world had learned to harness electricity. In Tory's time, it was mostly an intriguing novelty that didn't do anything useful. "Very handy, especially for people who don't have magic. Shall I give you another demonstration?"

"It had better be something better than a light," he said, still unconvinced.

Floating might not be of much practical use, but it was showy. She stood, closed her eyes, and visualized herself moving upward.

Her control was improving, because she glided upward at a reasonable speed, also drifting a dozen feet across the church to preserve her modesty. Then she created a fistful of tiny mage lights and tossed them into the air to float around her like candle flames. "Is this good enough?"

"Hey!" His exclamation was a strangled squawk. "It's . . . another Nazi trick!"

"You really are the most pigheaded boy." She floated down gracefully in front of the altar as the lights faded out above her. "Do you think your Nazis could have kept something like this secret? And if they could—why reveal it to you now?"

"I . . . I *want* to believe in magic." His face worked. "Family stories say the Rainfords were very good at it. But everyone knows that magic is just superstition."

"What happened to the magic?" she asked, puzzled how something that was so much a part of life had faded away. "When did people stop accepting it?"

"I don't know," he said slowly. "Maybe as science grew, there was less reason for magic and it faded away. These days, magic is considered to be either superstition or parlor tricks." His fingers whitened on his torch. "But . . . but there have been times when I've felt something inside me that might be magic, if I knew how to use it."

"You do have power. I can feel it." She sat again. "What year is this?"

His brows arched. "Did you fall on your head out in the abbey? Maybe the ghost of a sorcerer pushed you down some of those old steps."

"Perhaps, but *what year is it?*"

"1940, of course." He shook his head. "You are the strangest girl."

She sucked in her breath. Assuming England still used the same calendar, she'd traveled—one hundred and thirty-seven years into the future!

Wondering if there was any chance he'd believe her, she said, "I was a student at Lackland Abbey, but the school tried to eliminate magic, not teach it. In my time most people liked magic, except for the nobility. Wellborn children with power were sent to Lackland to be cured so our families wouldn't have to disown us. Students who wanted to learn more about our abilities would meet at night in the tunnels under the abbey."

"Easier to believe you're a Nazi spy!" he scoffed. "What year do you claim to be from?"

"1803."

"So you danced here through time from over a hundred years ago?" he exclaimed. "You're not just strange. You're *mad*."

"I didn't *dance* here!" she snapped. "It was more like being galloped over by a team of wild horses." She caught his gaze, willing him to believe. "Last night I went to the Labyrinth, the tunnels below the school, for tutoring. We were raided by the school authorities. I was trying to escape when I ran into a tunnel that ended in a tall mirror. I touched it and fell through, and here I am. I . . . I have no idea if I can go back."

Nick's expression changed. "Merlin's mirror. It really exists!"

"This makes sense to you?" She stared at him. "There's a legend that Merlin built the tunnels under the abbey, but I've never heard of his mirror. What is it?"

"Like I said, my family has stories of magic. There are lots of old Rainford journals. I've read them all, and several times there were mentions of Merlin's mirrors." He frowned, remembering. "There were seven mirrors. They looked like polished silver, and they could be used to travel through time and space. But that's all I remember."

Her brows arched. "So now you believe me?"

"I . . . I think I have to. The mirror must be like the device in H. G. Wells's novel, *The Time Machine,* but that was science, not magic."

"Maybe H. G. Wells was a mage?"

"No, he was a writer who lived about halfway between your time and mine." Nick made an impatient gesture with his hand. "He doesn't matter except that because I read his story about a time machine, it's easier to believe that the mirror is a time machine." His brows knit as he remembered. "The journal said Merlin's mirror doesn't work for everyone. You're just lucky."

"Luck I could do without!" She crossed her arms on the railing of the pew in front of her, so tired and confused that she was on the verge of tears. "If you don't take me to the police, I'll spend the night here. I won't steal anything."

"Then what?"

"I don't know," she said bleakly. "The mirror was gone when I woke up here. Otherwise I would have gone back through it and taken my chances with the raiders. Perhaps the vicar can help me. In my time, clerics were often mages."

"This vicar isn't." Nick got to his feet. "Come along, time traveler. I'm going to take you home."

CHAPTER 20

Even exhausted, Tory said firmly, "I am *not* going home with you!"

"You need food and rest," he said. "Tomorrow we can decide what you need to do next. My mother might have some ideas. She's read the family journals, too. She and my dad are both teachers and know all kinds of things."

As long as his mother was there, Tory supposed she'd be safe. More tired by the minute, she got to her feet. The problems she'd faced at Lackland Abbey seemed trivial compared to the difficulties she faced now. "I hope she can help."

"She's a better choice than the vicar or the police." Nick led the way down the aisle. "Doorways work in both directions. If you can come through one way, you should be able to go back the other way."

Hoping he was right, she followed him outside, extinguishing the mage light as she left the building. As they turned into the road, she glanced back at the church. Voice low, she asked, "What happened to the stained glass windows?"

"Lackland is on the front line for invasion, artillery, bombings—anything the Nazis might throw at us. That's why the council asked for volunteers to patrol the streets." He glanced back at the church. "As soon as war was declared last September, the vicar decided to removed the stained glass for the duration. The windows are stored somewhere out in the country. Probably in a cellar under a barn."

"That makes sense. But the church isn't the same without them."

"Nothing is same as it was before war was declared." Nick took Tory's arm as clouds drifted over the moon. "Careful, it's easy to trip over things in the dark."

She was grateful for his support in this strange world. "Is the war why Lackland is so dark? I would think there are lamps that work the same way your torch does."

"Yes, these days most houses have electric lamps, but blackout regulations are in effect." He steered her around something set by the curb. "All windows must be blocked so no light can get out. That's the biggest thing the Lackland patrol does, actually. We let people know if they accidentally violate the blackout regulations."

"It must be disappointing not to have Nazi spies," she said rather dryly.

"Not really. I want them to stay on their side of the channel," he said with a chuckle. "Travel at night is difficult. Motorcars originally couldn't use their headlights, but so many people were getting killed in accidents that now slits of light are allowed. Some farmers paint white stripes on dark cows so they won't be hit if they get loose."

"I saw one of those," Tory said, glad one mystery was solved. "Very odd."

Nick's gesture encompassed the dark village. "If the Germans start bombing, we don't want to make easy targets."

Tory tried to sort through all this information. Motorcars must be the road machines with the lamps masked to allow only slits of light. "Bombing?"

"Bombs are like—like exploding cannon balls." He drew her around the corner into a street that headed up the hill. "Airplanes are flying machines. They can cross the channel and drop bombs on our cities and factories. That hasn't happened yet, but it probably won't be long now. I'd rather they didn't drop bombs on Lackland because they see lights here."

"I think I saw a flying machine earlier. A horrible thing!" She shivered. "Tell me more about this war of yours."

He sighed. "Britain declared war last September when Germany invaded Poland. At first not much happened. People called it the phony war. But now there's bad fighting and Hitler seems to have taken over half of Europe."

"Which countries?"

"He grabbed Czechoslovakia and the Rhineland a couple of years ago, and rolled over Poland." He thought a moment. "Denmark was conquered in about two hours. The Norwegians are fighting hard, but they won't last much longer. Finland did a good job against Russia, but they were run over, too."

Tory had never heard of Finland and she'd thought the Rhineland was part of one of the German states, but borders were always shifting. "So the German states ganged up together and now they're allied with Russia?"

"Yes, and Italy, too. Italy has a dictator called Mussolini who's almost as bad as Hitler. They're both fascists, which means they want to boss everyone."

Italy was also a country, not a collection of kingdoms? "I need to find a map of what Europe looks like today! Where is the fighting now?"

Nick viciously kicked a pebble that skittered across the smooth road surface. "A fortnight or so ago, at the beginning of May, the Nazis invaded the Low Countries and France. Holland lasted five days, which was pretty good, but now they've surrendered. The Nazis are moving so fast they're calling it a blitzkrieg. A lightning war. Belgium is on the verge of surrender, and the French and British armies are being shoved back toward the English Channel."

"So the French and British really are fighting together," she said incredulously. "It's hard to believe."

"They were allies in the Great War, and now they are again." He swallowed hard. "And . . . and my father joined the British Expeditionary Force. He's right in the middle of the fighting. If he isn't dead already."

Tory winced at the pain in Nick's voice. "Why did a man with children want to join the army?"

"My dad was in the Great War when he wasn't much older than I am now. He was a good soldier, a sergeant by the end. He said England needs men with experience, so now he's an officer." Nick's laughter was bitter. "My mother said he was needed here, too, but he thought we should try to stop the Nazis before they got out of hand. It's too late now, though. In a month, the bastards might be invading England."

"In my time, we're also waiting for invasion, though in our case the French are the enemy." Wait, Nick would know what had happened! Urgently, she asked, "Did Napoleon invade England? Did we defeat him?"

"I . . . I'm not good at history," Nick said apologetically. "He might have invaded, but in the end, we did beat him. I'm pretty sure of that."

She supposed that was some comfort. But she hoped that Nick's mother was better at history than he was.

Tory was fading fast by the time they reached the Rainford house on the bluff. In the dark she couldn't see much when they finally got there, but it looked like a rambling old stone farmhouse she remembered from her time. The building was well separated from the road and other houses by trees. It faced the channel on the far side and she could hear the steady rhythm of waves below the bluff.

"We never used to lock the door." Nick turned his key, then opened the door and ushered her inside. After the door was safely shut, there was a click and the room was flooded with light.

Tory blinked at the blaze of brightness. This was like the electric torch, but a thousand times better. "It would take dozens of beeswax candles to light a room this well," she marveled. "Or a lot of magc lamps."

They had entered by the kitchen, which was easy to recognize even though it was much smaller than the kitchens of Fairmount Hall or Lackland Abbey. Probably no more than two or three people could work at once, but there were cabinets and work counters, dishes and pans, something that was probably a cookstove, and a large table surrounded by wooden chairs. Heavy black curtains covered the two windows.

"Evening, Horace." Nick bent to scratch the head of a sleepy black-and-white dog who emerged from under the table to greet him. "Do you want to go straight to bed, Tory, or would you rather eat first?"

As Horace came over to sniff her hand with interest, Tory realized that part of her shakiness must be hunger. She had burned a lot of power since her last meal. "I'll feel better if I eat something."

"How about a bowl of hot soup, bread, and cheese?" a woman's voice asked. "Nick, who is your friend?"

Tory spun around to see a woman entering the kitchen from the opposite door. She was pretty and fair-haired and had tired eyes, a long blue robe, and a mother's air of authority.

"Her name is Victoria Mansfield and I found her in the church,

Mum. She says she's a sorceress from 1803. Tory, my mum, Mrs. Rainford."

Tory cringed. How could he just blurt it out like that? Mrs. Rainford would send Tory to Bedlam! But Nick knew his mother.

Mrs. Rainford came sharply awake. "So you're the one," she breathed.

Nick had said his mother knew things, and now that Tory looked more closely, she saw a glow of magic around the woman. "I'm the one what?"

"I've had a feeling that someone very important would come soon," Mrs. Rainford said. "I wasn't sure who or why"—her amused gaze moved down Tory—"and I assumed it would be someone older, but I know your arrival is of vital importance."

"I told you my mother knows things," Nick said proudly.

"It's a pleasure, Miss Mansfield." Mrs. Rainford's scrutiny seemed likely to scorch holes in Tory.

"Tory will do, Mrs. Rainford."

Nick announced, "Mom, Tory can fly!"

"Not fly, float. Though I'm so tired at the moment I don't know if I could even get off the floor." Tory sighed. "I can try if you need a demonstration."

"If you've come from 1803, you've had a long journey," Mrs. Rainford said. "You need food and sleep. We'll talk tomorrow." She used a match to light a blue-flamed burner on the small stove. As she moved a pot from the back burner to the heat, she continued, "Nick, will you put out bread and cheese?"

While Nick obeyed, Mrs. Rainford asked Tory, "I imagine you would like to wash up and refresh yourself?"

"Oh, please!"

Mrs. Rainford led her out of the kitchen and up the stairs. "The bathroom is here. You can use these towels, and here's a new comb." She moved something on the wall that turned on a light inside the room, revealing a giant tub and a washstand. She turned one of the metal knobs on the washstand and water started running from the spout. "The right tap for cold water, the left for hot water. That takes a minute or two to warm up. Use this plug if you want the sink to fill. The tub works the same way."

Tory turned the other knob and watched with fascination as water gushed out. "Housemaids must love these! No more carrying cans of hot water up to the bedrooms."

Mrs. Rainford laughed. "Girls who want work have more choices than going into service these days, so there aren't many housemaids anymore. We're lucky to have modern plumbing." She opened the next door along the corridor. "The water closet is this small room here. Do you need a bit of instruction?"

Tory glanced at the wall and found a switch like the one that illuminated the bathing room. Cautiously, she moved it. Light!

The small room contained a china commode. On the wall above was a tank with a handle dangling from a chain. "I've heard of water closets, but I've never seen one. After using it, I pull the chain?"

"Exactly, and one of the world's most useful inventions." Mrs. Rainford turned toward the stairs. "You can use any of those blue towels. Take your time washing up. The soup will take a few minutes to heat."

Using the water closet once was enough to convince Tory she must try to talk her father into getting several installed at Fairmount Hall. Assuming he ever spoke to her again. And the hot water in the sink was wonderful!

She doubted that King George himself washed in such comfort at Windsor Castle. At home, not only did a maid have to carry up the water, but she also had to carry it away later. Being able to pull a plug and have water swirl away in a pipe was luxury.

Tory eyed the tub longingly. It was four times the size of the largest hip bath at Fairmount Hall, and it had taps, just like the hand basin. Bathing in that great beautiful tub would be heaven. But if she tried now, she'd probably fall asleep and drown. Besides, she was ravenous.

After washing her hands and face and letting down her hair, Tory used the damp towel to brush the worst of the dirt from her gown. She looked in the mirror and saw that combing out her hair made her look even younger. A mysterious time-traveling sorceress ought to have more presence.

But for now, she really didn't care.

CHAPTER 21

Tory woke from heavy sleep with her wits scrambled. Such a dream she'd had!

Her gaze fell on a frail birdlike contraption hanging in a corner of the small room. A model airplane, one of many built by Joe Rainford. Memory returned with a rush. God help her, she really had fallen through time into a future war-torn England.

During her late-night supper, where she almost fell asleep in her soup bowl, she'd learned that the RAF was the Royal Air Force, the military branch that operated those strange flying machines. Joe Rainford had joined as soon as he was old enough. Since he was away in training, his bed was available for Tory.

When Mrs. Rainford took her yawning guest up to the small room under the eaves, she said, "See all the model airplanes Joe built?

He was always mad for flying. I suppose it was inevitable he'd go into the RAF." Her voice was bleak.

There were at least a dozen models scattered around the room. Tory studied the nearest. Amazing that anyone would trust his life to such a rickety device. Airplanes would be easy targets in wartime. Mrs. Rainford certainly thought so.

But even though Nick's mother was quietly terrified for her husband and older son, she was a welcoming and efficient hostess. She'd found a nightgown and robe that belonged to her thirteen-year-old daughter, Polly, who'd slept through Tory's arrival. Polly was about Tory's height, and the soft, clean nightgown had been very welcome.

Part of her was tempted to hide under the covers, but that wouldn't help her find her way home. The thought of being stranded in this England with no friends or family was terrifying. Even if she returned to the exact time she'd left and was taken by raiders and locked up every night until she left Lackland, at least she would be in her own time, where she belonged.

Mrs. Rainford had opened the black curtains after Tory was in bed and the lights were off, so sunlight streamed in the window. She'd slept well into the morning.

She rose from her bed and padded over to the window. There was a fine view of the channel, and the village was just visible on the far right.

Tory gazed across the channel, glad that at least the eternal waves hadn't changed. On a peaceful morning like this, it was hard to believe that armies with monster machines were tearing at each other in France and drawing ever nearer.

When she went into the corridor on her way to the bathroom, she heard Nick's voice downstairs. Probably everyone was waiting for her to appear. She dressed and combed her hair out hastily, tying it back with a ribbon Mrs. Rainford had provided.

Then she headed downstairs. She liked the Rainford house. Though not grand, it was pleasant and welcoming, and there were comforts rare or unknown in Tory's time.

She followed the voices to the kitchen, which seemed to be the center of family life. The night before, Mrs. Rainford had worn a long robe, but now she was in a dress that barely covered her knees. Her ankles were visible! The young blond girl at the kitchen table was similarly dressed. No wonder Nick had thought Tory's ankle-length gown was nightwear.

Tory became the object of everyone's attention as soon as she stepped into the room. Nick's sister said doubtfully, "This is the sorceress?"

Tory didn't know whether to be amused or exasperated. "I am merely a mage in training. 'Sorcerer' usually means someone who practices dark magic, which I most certainly do not."

"Whatever she calls herself, she has power, Polly," Nick said. "Tory, this is my skeptical little sister. Polly, meet Victoria Mansfield."

As Polly acknowledged the introduction, Tory noticed that the girl had the glow of power. The long blond hair that flopped over her forehead and shoulders didn't disguise her burning gaze. Nick and Mrs. Rainford watched their guest with matching intensity. Even the shaggy family dog under the kitchen table was watching Tory.

"Good morning." Feeling like a mouse surrounded by cats, Tory bobbed a curtsy to her hostess. "Last night, you said you might be able to help me go home?"

"I hope so. I've studied the family journals as well as some old books that have come down with them." Using a quilted mitt, Mrs. Rainford drew a plate from the oven and set it on the table opposite where Polly and Nick were sitting. "We can talk after you have breakfast. Be careful of the plate, it's hot. I hope you like eggs and sausage."

"It looks lovely, thank you." Tory sat with enthusiasm. She hadn't seen such a good breakfast since she was sent away from Fairmount Hall. "But please tell me now what you've found. I can eat and listen at the same time."

Mrs. Rainford poured tea for Tory, then topped up everyone's cups. "Very well. I teach English and Latin, and the Latin helps with the older books. Nick said you described a silver object that sounds like Merlin's mirror."

Tory glanced up from her eggs. "I've never heard of that, but I wasn't a student in the Labyrinth for very long. What did the book have to say about the mirror?"

"The book that describes it is the oldest we have, but as Nick told you, the mirror was a portal for taking people through time and space. The chronicle translates as 'Merlin, he did make seven magical mirrors and he scattered them through the realms that men might travel to all times and places,' but that might be more poetry than fact."

"I moved in time, but not in space," Tory said thoughtfully. "How is the portal activated? I certainly didn't cast any spells. I just ran toward it and touched the surface, wondering if I could hide behind it. The next thing I knew, I was sprawled on the floor of the tunnel in this time."

"Apparently one needs a particular kind of magical talent to use one of the portals," the teacher replied. "Also, there must be a powerful need to be someplace else. Apparently you have the talent, and you also had the need."

Remembering her fear as the raiders chased her, Tory saw how she'd fulfilled the requirements. "Well, now I have a powerful need to go back. Do you think I can go home if I find the mirror again? It vanished after I'd passed through it."

"I wish I had the answers," Mrs. Rainford said with a sigh. "The chronicle suggests that the portal exists in another space and appears only when it's summoned."

"It sounds as if summoning is done through need and magic. So if I return to the tunnel where I came through, I might be able to make the mirror appear again if I consciously will for that to happen." Excited, Tory pushed the plate away and stood. "I might be home tonight!"

"No!" Polly exclaimed. "You must teach us how to use magic!"

As Tory blinked in surprise, Nick, who'd been silent until now, said, "We hoped you'd give us lessons before going back. All of us have some power, but we don't know what to do with it."

"Bad times are coming, and we need all the skills we can muster," Mrs. Rainford said quietly. "Very bad indeed. I have nightmares of bombs falling and cities on fire."

Her children stared at her. "You never told us that," Nick said.

"I didn't want to alarm you, but I need to persuade Tory to help us." Mrs. Rainford smiled wryly. "I've had a strong feeling that a powerful person would come and would help in some way. I just didn't expect a time traveler the age of my children."

"I don't know how to teach magic," Tory said uncomfortably. "I just started to do magical things without intending them and got caught and sent to Lackland."

"You know more than we do," Nick said. "Surely you can offer some guidance!"

As Tory hesitated, Polly said scornfully, "She's no mage. She just scrambled your wits because she's pretty."

"Yes, she's pretty," Nick retorted. "But she really did fly!"

Tory was glad they thought she was pretty, but it seemed like time for a demonstration. She concentrated until she felt the internal click, then gracefully rose a yard, which put her head near the ceiling. As Polly and her mother gasped, Horace came alive and leaped into the air to snap at Tory's toes. "Sit!" she ordered.

The dog sat, tail wagging furiously. Tory glided down to the floor next to him. "Are you persuaded, skeptical Polly?"

The girl's eyes were as round as saucers. "Can you teach me to do that?"

"You have to have the particular talent needed for floating, and it's rare." Tory gazed at Polly, letting her eyes drift out of focus. "I think your greatest strength will be weather working, which is a skill that runs in the Rainford family."

"I've always loved watching the weather, especially storms," Polly said bashfully. "Sometimes I . . . I feel the storms and winds. I can really be a weather mage?"

"You have the right kind of talent, and my guess is that you also have enough power." Tory frowned. "Though I'm no teacher, I could explain basic techniques. A lot of it is practice. I can't stay too long, though. I need to go home."

"Today is Sunday, which is why none of us are in school," Mrs. Rainford said. "Will you stay a week to get us started?"

Seeing Tory's uncertainty, Nick said, "Maybe you could spend two or three days here, go home, and then come back later?"

Tory shuddered. "Going through the portal is beastly. Once I leave, I won't be coming back."

"Then stay longer now," Polly said flatly.

"Three days," Tory said. "No more. Unless you plan to hold me prisoner?"

"Of course not," Mrs. Rainford said. "Three days should give us a good start. But you'd best finish your breakfast. We're going to work you hard!" She set a plate of toast in the center of the table, then added a jar of marmalade.

As Tory finished her eggs, Polly said, "It's time for the news."

She reached across the kitchen table and turned a switch on the decorative wooden box that sat against the wall. A male voice boomed from the box, "Newly selected prime minister Winston Churchill will be addressing the Labor Party conference in Bournemouth today. . . ." Polly turned a knob and the volume dropped.

"Good heavens!" Tory exclaimed. "Is this more of your science?"

Nick laughed. "Yes, it's a wireless. It works from electricity and receives electromagnetic waves through the air."

"And how is this not magic? Can you see or touch one of those waves?"

He started to reply, then stopped. "Not exactly, but I know they're there, or the wireless wouldn't work. Science has rules."

She grinned. "It sounds a lot like magic to me. So does your electricity. And your flying machines. Magic."

Mrs. Rainford laughed. "Most of us don't really know how things work, just how to operate them. So yes, they could be magic."

"Magic has rules, just as your science does." Tory spread marmalade on a piece of toast and took a pleasurable bite. "I've told Polly something of her talents. You already know what you are, Mrs. Rainford. A foreteller."

"I've thought that." The older woman bit her lip. "I have feelings, but I'm so often wrong. I think there will be food rationing, so I put up many preserves last summer, and we're planting a big vegetable garden now. While these things might be useful later, I can't even tell if my husband is alive in France! I have two images of him in my mind. One of him coming home safely, the other—" She drew a shuddering breath and shook her head.

As her children flinched, Tory said, "That's because the future is not absolute." She tried to remember what Miss Wheaton had said. "The future is a map of possibilities, not a single straight road. Our personal paths are more easily altered than the great events that affect whole nations."

"Like war?" When Tory nodded, Mrs. Rainford closed her eyes, her expression anguished. "Bombs will fall on London. The Houses of Parliament will burn."

Tory shuddered at the image. "I don't think seeing the future can change something so huge and dreadful."

"Perhaps not. But the more clearly I can see, the better my chances of keeping my family safe," Mrs. Rainford said with determination.

"What about me, Tory?" Nick asked. "Do I have power, or have I been fooling myself? You say Rainfords are often weather workers."

Tory closed her eyes again, seeing Nick as a swirl of differently colored lights. "You have some weather magic, though not as much as Polly. You have other powers, but I'm not sure what they are. You have finding ability, and you're very good at reading people, I think. Knowing what is in their minds and how to persuade them."

"That's true, but I don't think of that as magic." He scowled. "I was hoping for something that would make a difference."

"Don't take my words as gospel," Tory warned. "I'm just looking at what is readily visible. When you start to develop your talents, you'll discover for yourself what you can do."

Mrs. Rainford looked thoughtful. "Since your time here is limited, I think that Nick and Polly will suddenly be too ill to go to school."

"Will you also be ill?"

Mrs. Rainford made a face. "Since I'm a teacher, I don't think I can be."

"I'll start by explaining general principles to all of you," Tory said as she considered the best approach. "Since you must teach tomorrow, Mrs. Rainford, I'll tutor you privately this evening. Tomorrow, I'll tutor Polly and Nick during the day, then work with everyone in the evening. We'll have more sessions on Tuesday. We'll all need resting time mixed in—this is hard work."

Nick laughed. "For years I secretly dreamed of working hard at magic, but I didn't know where to start."

Tory regarded her three students. She'd thought the Irregulars were enthusiastic learners, but they weren't a patch on the Rainfords. "We start here and now. And don't blame me if you're exhausted by the end of the day!"

CHAPTER 22

For the next three hours, Tory explained principles, drilled her students on basic control exercises, and answered questions. About noon, Mrs. Rainford said, "We're all starting to flag, so my teacher's advice is that it's time for a break. Let's take a walk. You can see more of the village, Tory, and we can stop at the chippy for fish and chips."

"We can all use fresh air," Tory agreed as she got to her feet. "And I want to see what 1940 looks like in daylight."

As she pulled on her shawl, Mrs. Rainford said, "Tory, I think you should borrow some of Polly's clothing. You're about the same size. If anyone wonders who you are, we can say you're a friend of my goddaughter here for a visit. That's vague enough."

"I suppose you're right." Tory glanced at Nick. "I don't want anyone to think I'm wearing my nightgown outside."

Nick grinned. "That dress still looks like a nightgown to me."

"Come along to my room and I'll fix you up." Polly bounced to her feet. "It will give me a chance to be the expert."

"That's only fair," Tory agreed as she followed Polly upstairs.

The girl's bedroom was also tucked under the eaves but neat as a pin. She opened the doors of her wardrobe and studied the contents. "Here's a skirt, blouse, and cardigan that should suit. I'll go out so you can change."

Tory held up the indecently short blue skirt. "Don't your knees ever get cold?"

"It's not that short! At least I don't trip over a long skirt."

Before Polly could leave, Tory asked, "What is this strip of metal bits?"

"A zip. I suppose you didn't have them." Polly demonstrated how moving a metal tab opened or closed the skirt.

Tory pulled the tab up and down with delight. "This is certainly better than using pins and ties!" Setting the skirt on the bed, she asked, "What about undergarments? I suppose my stays will do, but my shift is too long for this skirt."

"Stays?"

"Short stays are padded supports for the upper body," Tory explained. "There are long stays that go over the hips, but I'm wearing a simple style that ends at the waist and laces up the front."

Polly made a face. "Are stays the same as a corset?"

"Yes, though there are many styles. What do females wear now?"

"I'll show you." Polly opened a drawer in a small chest and took out several small folded garments. "You can have this new pair of knickers I've never worn. This is a clean vest for your top, and a slip to wear under the skirt and blouse."

Tory examined the undergarments, thinking the vest and slip were like a shift that had been divided into two separate pieces. "The fabric is a very fine weave, and the stitches are *tiny*. Who does the sewing?"

"Stitching is done by a machine. The needle goes up and down very fast and locks with another thread from below." Polly demonstrated with her fingers. "Mum has a sewing machine if you'd like to see it later." She pulled another item from the drawer. "Women wear something called a brassiere. I don't need one yet, but my mother bought me this for my thirteenth birthday. She said I could grow into it."

Tory studied the brassiere, which had two shaped cups and a strap that hooked in the back. "This looks like a horse's harness. The vest looks more comfortable."

"Corsets don't sound very nice, either. I suppose it's what we're used to." Polly's gaze went to Tory's feet. "Your shoes don't look like anything worn now. I think our feet are about the same size. Mine might be larger. Here, try this pair of school shoes I outgrew over last summer before I had a chance to wear them."

"Oh, I like these!" Tory turned the shiny black leather shoes over in her hands. The heels were about an inch and a half high, and a thin, buckled strap ran over the instep. "They'll make me taller, too."

"Here are the socks to go with them." Polly offered a pair of white knit socks. "That and a hat should be everything you need."

Tory surveyed the mound of garments. "I'll call for help if needed."

"Surely a mage can master underwear!" Polly said with a mischievous smile as she left the room.

Tory did manage, though she felt decidedly odd without the familiar support of her stays. She'd never worn a skirt this short, and the zip made the upper part fit closely around her hips. But she did like the shiny black shoes, which fit perfectly. The cardigan was a warm knit garment that buttoned over the white blouse. She liked that, too. She went back to Joe's room and combed her hair before tying it back with the ribbon again.

"You look just like a regular girl," Nick said when she came downstairs.

"I *am* a regular girl," she retorted. "A regular girl who can do magic." On mischievous impulse, she used the magic she'd learned in Allarde's tutorial to float a navy blue beret from the coatrack to her hand. "May I borrow this hat, Polly?"

"It seems to want to be with you." Smiling, Polly snapped her fingers at the dog. "Come along, Horace. Walkies!"

The shaggy dog, which had seemed nearly comatose under the kitchen table, surged to his feet and raced to the kitchen door, toenails scrabbling. Tory was equally eager to get outside after the long morning of work. The sunshine was pale, but spring flowers were blooming with color outside.

As the group headed down the hill, Tory said, "Still fishing boats in the harbor, I see." The sight was comforting proof that life hadn't changed entirely.

Nick said, "We have a boat and we go sailing whenever we can. At least, we used to." His voice was wistful. Unspoken was the knowledge that his family might never be together like that again.

For distraction, Tory asked, "Do Mr. Rainford and Joe have magic?"

"I'm not sure," Mrs. Rainford replied. "Tom has very good hunches. Intuition. Joe was always very good at games because he seemed to know what the other team would do before they did themselves."

"That sounds like a very good skill for a pilot," Tory said encouragingly.

"I surely hope so," Mrs. Rainford said softly.

Tory tried to drink in everything. So much had changed. "What are the ugly poles with wires running between them?"

"They carry electricity and telephone lines," Nick said.

"Telephones?"

"A telephone is . . . is rather like a wireless, but it carries voices over a wire instead of through the air," Nick explained. "If you want to talk to a friend right away, you ring them up and speak even if they're on the other side of town."

Tory considered that. "What is the rush to talk to someone right now? Not many things are that urgent."

Mrs. Rainford laughed. "Some things are urgent. Others are just convenient. Suppose I was ill tomorrow morning. I could call the headmistress at my school and let her know so she could find someone else to take my classes."

That did sound useful. Tory nodded at one of the hulking road beasts, which sat at the edge of the street. Horace was sniffing at one of its wheels. "These ugly, smelly motorcars of yours. Do they also run on electricity?"

"They have petrol engines," Nick replied. "The burned fuel causes the smell."

"What is petrol?"

"It's made from oil and processed into a form that will run engines."

"Oil?" Tory said, baffled. Every question she asked begat more questions.

"A bit like the whale oil that once was used in lamps." This time it was Polly who answered. "But the oil that is made into fuel is from the ground, not a whale."

Tory's gaze went to an airplane that was flying north over the channel. "Do your flying machines also burn petrol?"

"More or less," Polly said. "I think the oil is processed a little differently for aircraft, but it's from the same basic material."

"That is going to be a problem when the war intensifies." Mrs. Rainford was looking not at the airplane but toward France. "Our little island has many people. We import the majority of our food, all of our oil, most of our other supplies. The Germans have underwater boats called submarines that hunt supply ships coming to Britain. In the Great War—that was from 1914 to 1918, Tory—the Germans sank so many ships that by the end of the war, we had only a month or two of food left."

Tory sucked in her breath. "You think that will happen again?"

"I'm afraid so. Rationing already started here in January. Only bacon and butter and sugar so far, but if the war intensifies, many other things will also be rationed."

"As long as they don't ration fish and chips!" Nick exclaimed.

"Fish come from the sea and potatoes grow well in Britain, so they're less likely to be rationed than most foods," his mother said. "But tea comes all the way from Asia. I'd better stock up on that."

Polly looked horrified. "We might not have tea?"

"Mum made me dig a huge garden this spring. I had blisters on my blisters," Nick added. "We'll be drowning in vegetables. I expect a chicken coop next."

"That's not a bad idea," Mrs. Rainford said thoughtfully. "I have a feeling that soon we'll be grateful to have our own eggs and chickens." She chuckled when her children groaned. "And maybe a rabbit hutch."

"No," Polly said firmly. "I'm not going to eat a bunny that I've raised. It would be like eating Horace!"

"Very well, no bunnies." Her mother smiled. "I don't think I could eat our own rabbits or chickens, either, but I do like my morning egg."

The Rainfords were so much more relaxed with each other than Tory's family! She couldn't imagine teasing Lord Fairmount about anything. But the Rainfords were having this easy conversation that was fun while also discussing more serious questions. "You might also want to buy fabric to make up clothing. Just in case. And soap."

"I hadn't thought of fabric, much less soap," Mrs. Rainford said slowly, "but as soon as you spoke, I knew you were right. What else do you feel?"

"I'm no foreteller." Still, like most mages, Tory had some ability to sense what might come to pass. She opened her inner senses . . . and gasped.

"Did you see something dreadful?" Polly asked worriedly.

"Not a particular event." Tory shook her head, trying to clear it. "But when I listened, I was hit with a tidal wave of fear and anxiety. Though people might not be talking about the war, they're thinking about it all the time."

"I can feel that, too," Nick said. "It's like a smothering blanket."

"My cousin lives in London," his mother said softly. "She wrote me about the night the blackout went into effect. She stood in her top floor window and everywhere she looked, lights were blinking out, as if the city was dying."

Polly shivered. "When you read us her letter, I remembered what that British foreign secretary said at the beginning of the Great War. 'The lamps are going out all over Europe. We shall not see them lit again in our lifetime.'"

Their words made it all too easy for Tory to visualize the lights going out, and to feel the grief of that. "But he was wrong," she said firmly. "Though the world is changed by war, your lamps did come on again. They will this time, too."

"I'm sure you're right." Mrs. Rainford smiled wryly. "There was just as much to fear in your time, yet Britain survived."

Reminded, Tory asked, "What happened to Napoleon? Did the French invade England? I asked Nick, but he said he isn't very good at history."

"Very true," Polly said, "but history is my best subject. Napoleon—"

Her mother held up a hand. "Don't say more. I have a strong feeling that it's better if Tory doesn't know what is going to happen in her time. Too much knowledge might cause problems. Is it enough to know that despite wars and many other changes, Britain today is a powerful, independent nation?"

Tory wanted to protest, but she thought better of it. Knowing the future would inevitably change Tory's behavior if she made it home, and that could be bad.

As they headed for the harbor, people occasionally called greetings, but the Rainfords just waved back, walking briskly so they didn't stop to talk. Tory was grateful for that. She might be dressed for 1940, but she could easily say the wrong thing.

They reached the harbor and followed the shoreline around to the right. Nick pointed to a boat moored at the last pier. "That's our boat. *Annie's Dream.*"

It was a neat vessel, with a deckhouse and room to sleep the whole family, though quarters belowdecks must be tight. "Who is Annie?"

"My name is Anne. Tom likes to call me Annie," Mrs. Rainford said fondly. "He promised me a boat when he asked me to marry him. How could I say no? He bought the boat from his fisherman great-uncle and we fixed it up together."

"On my last birthday, Papa took my whole class sailing," Polly said wistfully.

Tory thought that for a boat that wasn't large, *Annie's Dream* carried a lot of memories. "How big a crew does she need?"

"In a pinch, Polly and I can sail her," Nick said. "But a larger crew is better."

"I'm thinking of having the boat taken out of the water for . . . for the duration," Mrs. Rainford said. "She won't be getting much use, and the channel could be dangerous with a war going on just a few miles away."

"Not when the weather is just getting warm!" Polly protested.

"I want to go sailing this weekend." Nick glanced at Tory. "Do you sail? It's wonderful. You could stay and learn to crew."

She shook her head. "Tempting, but I'll be gone by then."

"Very well, I'll delay taking the boat up," Mrs. Rainford said. "We'll see how thing go. But for now—fish and chips!"

As they headed to the chip shop, Tory asked, "What does money look like now?"

Nick produced some coins and dropped them in her palm. "Twelve pennies to a shilling, twenty shillings to a pound, and coins for the penny, ha'penny, thruppence, sixpence, and so forth. This one is a half crown, which is two and a half shillings."

Tory poked through the coins. "Not that different from what I'm used to."

"In other words, British money has always been illogical," Polly said with a grin.

"Logical money would be boring." When Tory tried to return the money to Nick, he waved it off.

"Keep that for souvenirs," he said gruffly. "So you won't forget us."

As if she could forget this journey to another time! Tory put the coins away, glad she'd have something tangible to take away.

The chippy had a walk-up order window, a sign over the top that said THE CODFATHER, and half a dozen hopeful cats lounging about in front. Mrs. Rainford ordered four portions, which were served almost immediately. The fried cod and potatoes were wrapped in cones of newsprint, and tangy malt vinegar was sprinkled over them.

"Do you have fish and chips where you live?" Polly passed a cone to Tory.

"No. This smells lovely, though." Tory bit into a piece of the crispy, deep-fried fish. "Wonderful!" She tried one of the golden wedges of potato and sighed blissfully. No wonder Nick hoped fish and chips wouldn't be rationed.

"This is walking food," Nick explained as they headed back to the high street, which ran up the hill. He tossed several flakes of fish to the cats. His mother, sister, and Tory all followed suit. No wonder the cats looked so sleek and well fed.

She would miss this time and these people, Tory realized. But this wasn't her home. The Rainfords would defend England in their time, and she would do her best in hers.

She prayed that all of them would be successful.

CHAPTER 23

Lackland, the long road home

"Is this the place?" Nick asked, eyeing the chalk walls dubiously. "All these tunnels look the same."

"I think so." Tory had used intuition to guide her to the dead-end tunnel under the ruins of Lackland Abbey. Though she'd made a number of wrong turns, now that she'd reached this spot, she could feel powerful magic pulsing just out of sight.

It was Tuesday evening, and the Rainfords had escorted her to the abbey to say good-bye. Teaching magic required a lowering of shields on both sides, and in three days a powerful bond had been forged between Tory and her students.

They had worked so hard. She was proud of how they'd transformed their raw, untrained powers and were becoming competent mages. They would continue to improve now that Tory had laid a foundation of knowledge and mage discipline.

Tory wore her own clothing again, her shawl wrapped close to protect her from the bitter chill of her passage through time. Her stomach knotted as she contemplated what she was about to do. On her first passage, she hadn't known what would happen. Now she did—and she was not looking forward to it.

Polly asked bluntly, "What if you end up in a different time than your own?"

"After I recover from that trip, I'll try again. Since I'll be even more desperate, the second passage will succeed." Tory tried to keep her voice light, but she wasn't entirely convincing. It was dangerous to use magic she didn't understand, but she had no other choice. Mrs. Rainford had gone though all her old texts and found no hint of any other magical devices or spells that could move a person through time.

Tory turned to her friends. "I made gifts for you." She pulled three coins from her pocket. "I charged each of these with a particular kind of magic. Polly, here's a ha'penny. I like the image of Britannia that's engraved on the back. Can you tell me what kind of magic it holds?"

Penny clasped the copper coin, which was about an inch across. After several moments of frowning study, she exclaimed, "It's for focus! Thank you! I need this." She grinned. "Which is why you gave it to me, of course."

"Nick, for you, a three-penny piece." She handed him the twelve-sided coppery coin. "Can you feel what magic is in it?"

He closed his eyes. "Discernment? To help me cut to the heart of a matter?"

"Exactly. It should be useful sooner or later." She turned to Mrs. Rainford. "For you, a shiny silver sixpence, except it's not really for you."

"A sixpence is considered lucky." Mrs. Rainford closed her fingers around the coin. "Protection," she breathed. "It's for protection, and you made it for Joe."

"I can't guarantee that it will perform miracles," Tory said shyly. "But I think the coin will help keep him safe. Give it to him when he finishes his pilot training."

"Thank you." Mrs. Rainford's voice was choked as she hugged Tory. "Travel safely, my dear, and if you can't return to your time, you'll always be welcome here."

"You could really help us with the Nazis," Nick said. "And I'd take you sailing."

"With two brothers, I've wanted a sister." Polly shrugged as if her words didn't matter. "If you change your mind and want to come back . . ."

"You're making it hard to leave." Tory tried to smile. She turned to the end of the corridor. "This is going to be a huge letdown if I can't summon the mirror."

She gazed at the chalk and let her emotions well up. She wanted, *needed,* her friends and family and home. Images of her life saturated her mind, along with her desperate desire to return. She stretched her hand out, palm up. *Home . . .*

Power blazed with a soundless roar. As the Rainfords gasped, a tall, shining silver rectangle appeared in front of Tory. She saw herself reflected in its bright, flawless surface. She was small and dark-haired as always, yet her image was . . . commanding.

Reflected behind her were the Rainfords, their arms around one another. "Good-bye . . ." Tory's voice wavered as she moved close enough to the mirror to touch the surface. Cool silver that burned with magic . . .

The mirror turned dark. Power sucked her into the abyss, ripping and repairing as she fell endlessly in a place where she could not scream.

Then she was wrenched back to normal space, falling hard to the ground of a lightless tunnel. As darkness descended, she heard a man shout. Damnation, she must have returned to exactly where she began!

"Tory, wake up! Please, wake up!"

The worried male voice was familiar. But surely it couldn't be . . .

Tory's eyes flickered open. Dear heaven, it really was Allarde bending over her! She had made it back to her own time. Hazily, she realized that he was kneeling on the tunnel floor and she lay across his lap as his arms supported her. His usual controlled expression had been replaced by vivid concern, and he seemed to have an angelic halo.

Not a halo—a mage light floating above him. Half-convinced she was dreaming, she whispered, "Allarde?"

"Thank God!" he exclaimed. "Are you all right?"

Though she was trembling and exhausted, Allarde's arms were driving off the chill of the abyss. "I'm not hurt. Just . . . shaken. When is it?"

"Three days ago you vanished when the Labyrinth was raided. At first no one realized you'd gone missing." Allarde glanced at the chalk walls surrounding them. "Did you manage to hide here in a tunnel? You seemed to come out of nowhere."

Rather than answer, she asked, "How did you find me?"

"Tonight was the first session of the Irregulars since the raid. I'd been worried about you, so when the session ended, I decided to look around before going back to the school." His brow furrowed. "I was drawn to this location without knowing why. Then you tumbled out of thin air. Did you develop some new invisibility spell?"

"Much more complicated than that." The mere thought of explaining her adventures made Tory's head ache. "I was traveling through time."

"Pardon?" His gray eyes looked doubtful.

"As I said, it's complicated. I'll save my explanations for when the teachers are present so I won't have to repeat myself." A thought struck her. "Miss Wheaton and Mr. Stephens weren't caught and discharged, were they?"

"No, everyone escaped the raid. Elspeth said you led the raiders away from her group. That must have been just before you vanished." He smiled. "You're a heroine."

That sounded nice, though Tory hadn't felt very heroic at the time. She sighed. Lovely though her current position was, she couldn't stay here. She tried to get to her feet but almost fell from dizziness.

Allarde caught her. "You're in no condition to walk." He scooped her up in his arms and headed back along the tunnel, his mage light gliding in front them.

After an initial squeak of surprise, Tory relaxed with her head against his shoulder. His scent, his warmth, his energy—being held by him felt like coming home.

An alarming and alluring home. The austere beauty of his profile entranced her, and his right arm under her thighs gave her shivers in places she'd never thought about. A good thing she wasn't wearing that indecently short skirt of Polly's!

But she was puzzled. "I'm grateful for your care. It . . . it goes beyond what one expects from one comrade to another."

"You are more than just a comrade to me, Tory," he said softly.

"Then what am I?" she asked, her voice equally soft.

"I'm . . . not sure," he said, not looking at her.

They were approaching the main hall, and she had only moments left for this unexpected intimacy. She didn't want it to end, but she didn't know how to prolong it. "You had best put me down. Carrying me in might give people the wrong impression."

Gently he set her on her feet, keeping an arm around her while she got her bearings. "The impression wouldn't be wrong." He cupped a hand around her face, his touch so light that it was absurd for her heart to accelerate. "Merely . . . impossible."

"Why impossible?" she whispered.

"In other times and places, I could behave differently." He dropped his hand, his eyes deeply sad. "Not now. Not here."

He seemed to be saying that he admired her but felt he could not act on that. She wanted to protest, to make him say more, but something her sister once said echoed in her mind. *"When seeking a mate, you may meet men who could be right under different circumstances, but they won't do now for any number of good reasons. It is best to smile a gracious farewell and tuck that brief memory in your heart."*

Tory hadn't really understood then. Now she did. Their circumstances here in Lackland changed too many things. At a guess, Allarde could not take a mageling wife if he wanted to keep his title and inheritance. Since there could be no good end for them, he refused even to make a beginning. He was wise, damn him.

Throat tight, she said, "I hope that most of the Irregulars have gone home. I couldn't face a large audience."

She walked the last steps into the hall. The remaining people were the ones who usually stayed late: Miss Wheaton and Mr. Stephens, who always left last. The prefects, with Jack Rainford's sister, Rachel, staying with him. If those two stood next to Nick and Polly, no one would doubt a blood relationship.

Off to one side was Elspeth. And—blast!—Lady Cynthia.

Allarde raised his voice. "The lost has returned!"

"Tory!" Her name chorused as chairs scraped and people swooped toward her.

"I was so worried!" Elspeth reached her first and grabbed her in a fierce hug.

Jack arrived a moment later and hugged them both. "You look like death," he exclaimed, "but even so, it's good to have you back."

When Tory emerged for air, Miss Wheaton clasped her hands. "Thank heaven you're all right! When I returned here after the raid, I could feel that very powerful magic had taken place and it involved you, but I didn't know what it was."

Cynthia, who was hanging back, said, "I guessed that Tory was hiding somewhere. I was hoping she wouldn't return so I'd have the room to myself."

Ignoring Cynthia, Tory asked, "Has anyone here heard of Merlin's mirror?"

Mr. Stephens sucked in his breath. "That's a legend."

"Actually, it's not." Tory hesitated. "Should I tell you and Miss Wheaton what happened privately?"

The teachers conferred silently with a glance before Miss Wheaton replied, "Everyone wants to know, so you might as well tell us all at once."

Tory folded down onto one of the worn sofas. It was harder than furniture of the future. "As I was trying to escape the raiders, I discovered a magical artifact that took me to the year 1940, and now home again. I was told it's called Merlin's mirror."

Cynthia broke the startled silence. "A likely story!"

"That is exactly how Merlin's mirrors are supposed to behave," Mr. Stephens said. "Few people can work the magic, but for someone who has the gift, they are a portal to different times. I assume you stayed at Lackland?"

She nodded. "The abbey was in ruins, so I walked out into the village. In 1940, they're also facing war and invasion, too, only from the Germans, not the French."

"Our kings are German and the German states are our friends," Jack said.

"Not in 1940." Tory accepted a mug of hot, heavily sugared tea from Rachel. "Thank you! Time travel makes me ravenous." After a bracing swallow, she continued. "I found future Rainfords. I don't know how they would be related to you and Jack, but they are certainly related."

"Really?" Rachel looked delighted. "Are they mages, too?"

"They have talent, but magic has largely disappeared in 1940.

The Rainfords—Nick and Polly and their mother—asked me to teach them to use their abilities, so I stayed for several days. They need magic for their war as we need it for ours."

Almost everyone present started throwing questions at Tory, but Miss Wheaton held up a hand to block the torrent. "We are all perishing to learn more, but now you need sleep. Be ready to answer questions at our next meeting!"

"I won't answer all of them." Tory thought about what Mrs. Rainford had said. "I think it's better we not know too much about the future."

"You may be right, but we'll still ask." Jack collected his sister. "We're off now, but at the least, we're going to want to learn about those descendants of ours!"

Tory smiled. "I'm not sure if you and Nick would be friends or hate each other."

He grinned. "A pity we'll never find out."

A pity Polly and Rachel wouldn't meet, either. Polly had said she wanted a sister. "I'm so glad to be home," Tory said. "I didn't know if I could come back."

Allarde had been listening quietly, and she saw in his eyes that he understood how frightened she'd been at the prospect of being marooned in another time. "But you're here," he said, "and for that we give thanks."

Elspeth stood. "Come along now. You look ready to drop in your tracks."

There was no point in dropping when Allarde was heading in the opposite direction and couldn't pick her up, so Tory rose and followed Elspeth toward the blue tunnel. Cynthia followed.

As they entered the passage, Tory touched the color code. As it flared brighter, she said, "These had faded to almost nothing. Both the extra magic of the Labyrinth and the magical suppression above the surface diminished with time."

"What was the future like?" Elspeth asked.

When Tory hesitated, wondering what to say, Cynthia said acidly, "I think she made it up so she'd sound interesting."

Tory pulled out the coins Nick had given her. "Did I make these up?"

The other girls stopped to examine the money. "This penny has the date 1901 and a queen on it, not a king!" Elspeth brightened a mage light to see more clearly. "It says Queen Victoria. Perhaps you have a distinguished future ahead of you, Tory!"

Tory laughed. "You can tell by the engraving that she's from the House of Hanover. Probably a descendant of our King George. I quite like the idea of a queen ruling. We haven't had one since Queen Anne, and that's been almost a century."

"This ha'penny says George V, 1935." Cynthia handed it back to Tory. "The Prince of Wales will be George IV when his father dies, so there must be some other names between now and then."

"Victoria, and maybe some Edwards and Williams," Tory said. "Royalty isn't very imaginative with names." She put the coins away, thinking she'd have to find a good hiding place for them.

When they left the tunnel and emerged into the refectory cellar, the suppression of her magic was smothering. After several days of having full use of her power, she missed it more than ever. The disadvantage of returning to the abbey. But worth it.

When the three of them reached the dormitory, Elspeth touched Tory's arm in a silent good night before entering her room. Tory and Cynthia continued on to the end of the corridor. A dim lamp was burning in the bedroom.

As Cynthia turned up the flame, Tory saw that the other girl's belongings were strewn over Tory's bed and chair. "I see you weren't joking about wanting all of the space," Tory said dryly as she started collecting garments from her bed.

"The room had to look occupied," Cynthia retorted. "I told the teachers you were sick and couldn't come to your classes, so no one would know you were gone."

"That was good of you," Tory said, surprised. "Less chance for trouble."

"I thought you might have run away and needed a head start," the other girl said in a low voice. "But when there was no word, I started wondering if you'd fallen off the cliff when you were trying to escape."

Heavens, the glittering Lady Cynthia had actually been worried! "Thank you," Tory said. "If you aren't careful, I might start thinking you have a heart."

"At least I'm used to you as a roommate," Cynthia said waspishly. She turned off the lamp, leaving Tory in the dark.

Grinning, Tory dumped Cynthia's clothes in the other girl's side of the room before undressing and sliding into her bed.

Home. Being here was so good she didn't even mind Cynthia.

CHAPTER 24

"It's strange to feel the mirror's energy but be unable to see or access it," Miss Wheaton said as she warily touched the blaze of invisible power that marked the mirror's position. She pulled back her hand hastily. The energy might have been invisible, but it gave an uncomfortable jolt like an electrical shock.

"One must have a compelling reason to summon the mirror. Curiosity isn't enough." Tory pulled her shawl closer around her shoulders. Being so close to the mirror's power made her nervous. "How often does one need to go to another time?"

In the week since her return, life had settled back to normal. No one in the school had questioned the story of her being ill, and she'd quietly resumed her regular classes and her sessions in the Labyrinth.

Miss Wheaton and Mr. Stephens had asked her many questions about her trip through time, and she'd told them what she knew of the magic if not the history. But they hadn't asked her to visit the site of the mirror until tonight. The regular session was over and the only people left in the Labyrinth were the teachers and prefects who stayed late.

"I suppose you're right that curiosity isn't enough," Mr. Stephens said with regret. His eyes were closed and he'd been trying hard to summon the mirror with no success. "But the portal surely would be interesting to study."

"Perhaps the problem is that only Tory has the right magic to invoke the mirror." Miss Wheaton glanced at Tory. "Would you be willing to try summoning it?"

"No!" Tory shook her head and retreated several steps. "I'm quite sure that the mirror wouldn't take kindly to being summoned merely to be studied. If it comes when I call, I think I'd have to use it. On both my trips through the portal, I felt as if I was being dragged through by the magic, and I do not want to do that again!"

"What did going through feel like?" Jack Rainford had accompanied them to the dead-end tunnel. He and his sister were particularly interested in the mirror because of the knowledge that Tory had met future Rainfords.

"Like being chopped into small pieces, boiled up in a laundry tub, and then put back together," Tory said tartly. "I do not recommend the experience."

"I'd like to see one of those flying machines, though," Jack said wistfully. "It didn't sound anything like a hot air balloon."

Miss Wheaton turned back toward the hall. "I found some interesting research, Tory. It suggests that a person who has mirror magic can take others through with her."

Tory thought of Nick's comment about dancing through time. "So I could take your hand and you could take Mr. Stephens's and he could hold Jack's hand and we could go through like a line of country dancers?"

"I think so, though that's a guess." Miss Wheaton smiled. "But we'd need a good reason. Come along now. Time we went home for the night."

As the small group returned to the main hall, Tory hoped that fascination with the mirror would fade soon. She was getting tired of talking about it. Though it was an interesting artifact, it was like her ability to float: not especially useful.

When Tory reached the hall, Elspeth and Allarde were putting away tea mugs under Cynthia's bored gaze. Most Irregulars helped with the chores of maintaining the Labyrinth whether they were aristocrats or the children of field laborers, since what earned respect in the Labyrinth was magical ability. But Tory had yet to see Cynthia turn her pale white hands to anything resembling work. Her roommate always stayed late because the prefects stayed and Allarde was a prefect. Apparently Cynthia continued to hope that his unwavering courtesy would someday become a warmer feeling.

Allarde was most relaxed with Elspeth because they were cousins and had known each other before being packed off to Lackland. But Tory he still avoided. He was very discreet about it. She was probably the only one who noticed. Though she told herself it was because he cared, it still hurt. Couldn't they be friends even if the time and place were wrong for anything more to develop? But no, he just watched her with grave eyes and kept his distance.

Elspeth covered a yawn. "I'm tired. Are you ready to go back, Tory?"

"Indeed I am." In the last two sessions, Tory had started tutoring less advanced students. She suspected that her energy-blending ability allowed her to transfer her own understanding of a magical act directly to the student, but the work was tiring.

Tory and Elspeth headed across the hall to a tunnel that led to the girls' school. They'd almost reached the passage when Tory halted and looked back.

"Tory?" Elspeth turned, her expression inquisitive.

"I thought I heard my name being called."

The cry came again, and this time the frantic words were intelligible. "Tory? Tory, are you here?"

Tory spun around. The voice was familiar, and it came from the tunnel that led toward Merlin's mirror. Everyone who'd stayed late was in the main hall or in the process of leaving, so who could be calling from there?

"Tory!" The hoarse voice was closer, almost to the main hall.

Surely it couldn't be . . . ! Heart racing, Tory darted across the hall to the tunnel.

A figure staggered out of the entrance holding a dim mage light. Fair hair, tan trousers, a brown tweed jacket, and looking like the next thing to a corpse. A very familiar corpse.

"Nick!" Tory caught his arm, thinking that if she looked this bad when she emerged from the mirror, no wonder everyone had been worried.

"Tory?" he said hazily as he sagged against her.

Then Allarde was at his other side, taking most of Nick's weight. Jack took over for Tory and the two young men guided Nick to the nearest sofa, helping him stretch out on the cushions.

Tory bent over him. "Nick, it's me, Tory. Are you all right?"

Mr. Stephens and Miss Wheaton arrived, Elspeth and Cynthia right behind. Nick blinked up at Tory. "I . . . I made it here. I wasn't sure if I could find your time."

"You're in 1803 about a week after I came back." She rubbed his cold hands, trying to warm them. "Could someone make him some hot tea?"

"I'll take care of it," Rachel said. She was almost as good a hearth witch as Alice.

Miss Wheaton brought one of the old blankets that were kept in the hall and spread it over Nick, who was shaking with cold. Tory thought his passage through the mirror had been even more difficult than hers. The hot tea came quickly, along with the last pieces of shortbread. When Miss Wheaton wrote notes on mirror magic for the records, she should list that hot, sweet tea helped with recovery.

As color returned to Nick's face, Tory knelt by the sofa, still holding his hand. "Why did you come, Nick? Has something terrible happened?"

He tried to focus on her. "Remember I told you the Nazis were sweeping across Belgium and France with their lightning war and the Allies were trying to stop them?"

She thought back. "Yes, and your father is with the army, in the British Expeditionary Force. Has he been hurt?"

"I don't know!" Nick looked ready to weep. "Tory, it's all fallen apart so fast we're having trouble believing it. The Allies are being crushed. They've lost most of their armor and a huge part of the BEF has been cut off from the army farther south. They're being pushed back to the channel at Dunkirk, a little French port that's almost in Belgium. Calais and Boulogne are under attack, and it's just a matter of time till the bloody Germans overrun Dunkirk, too."

"Has the British army become so weak?" Mr. Stephens asked in a hushed voice.

"No, but the Nazis have come up with new weapons and battle tactics the Allies weren't prepared for. They have Panzer tanks—great metal vehicles that move fast and are very hard to stop. They ran around the French fortresses," Nick replied. "Europe is a shambles. Holland has surrendered, Belgium is on the verge, France is falling, and England . . . England will be next. It's happened in a matter of weeks."

There were gasps of shock from everyone listening. More than any of the others, Tory was able to visualize the horror of what Nick was describing. "Is anything being done to counter the Germans?

Or is our whole army going to be captured so England will have no choice but surrender?"

"That's why I'm here." Nick's eyes screwed shut as he fought for control. "The Royal Navy will evacuate as many men as they can, but there are hundreds of thousands of troops trapped. We'll never be able to get them all out. The navy hopes to save maybe thirty or forty thousand men. Thirty thousand out of half a *million*!"

No wonder Nick had been desperate enough to come through the mirror! Tory asked, "Did you come because you think we can help?"

"Yes." His eyes were burning as he stared into hers. "You have a weather mage, don't you? One of my own ancestors?"

"That's me." Jack stood behind the sofa, looking like he was Nick's slightly older brother. "Jack Rainford."

Nick raised his gaze to Jack. "You live here in Lackland, so you know how rough the channel usually is in late spring and early summer. The navy needs smooth seas so troops can be loaded into ships and evacuated. Smooth seas and clouded skies so the German airplanes won't be able to sink all our ships. Can you do that?"

Jack was taken aback. "You want me to go to 1940 and control the weather?"

"Yes." Nick's voice was dead serious. "Otherwise, Britain is doomed."

"I don't know if what you ask is even possible," Jack said slowly. "You would need major weather control for days on end to keep the seas calm and the skies overcast. I'm good, but no one has that kind of power." He frowned for the space of a dozen heartbeats. Then his expression became determined. "But I could try. I *will* try."

"With more power, you can control the channel for a longer time," Allarde said quietly. "I'll come with you."

"This is madness!" Mr. Stephens exclaimed, his expression horrified. "You're students, scarcely more than children! The school has a responsibility to your families. I can't permit you to do something so dangerous."

Allarde's brows arched. "You can't stop us, sir. Even if you report us to the headmaster, we can be through the mirror before he could act."

As Mr. Stephens hesitated, torn between his responsibility to his students and his duty to his country, Tory said, "We've been training to help if England needs us. Maybe it's the future we've felt calling."

Miss Wheaton smiled, rueful but resigned. "We must bow gracefully to the inevitable, Lewis. These young people are mages. They might accept guidance, but they cannot be forced any more than you and I could be at their age. Besides, the danger should not be great. They'll be in England doing weather magic, not heading into battle."

Mr. Stephens exhaled roughly. "Miss Wheaton is right. Any young man who chooses to serve his country is a warrior in truth if not in years. Go with my blessing, and I wish I could go with you."

"Young man or woman." Tory's hands clenched as she remembered the horror of passing through the mirror, but she had no doubt of what duty demanded. "I'm going, too. You'll need me to blend and enhance magic, and I can help with the portal as well."

Mr. Stephens's expression looked even more horrified. Males might be warriors, but not frail, delicate flowers like her. She gave him an innocent smile. "I'm the only one who has made the trip both ways, so I know what's involved."

"You said you didn't want to go through again," Miss Wheaton said, frowning.

"I don't." Tory's mouth twisted. "But now there's a compelling reason."

"I'd better come, too," Elspeth said calmly. "A healer might be useful."

Jack nodded. "True, and you'll add quite a bit of power."

Rachel Rainford said, "I'll come also."

Her brother frowned at her. "Mum will go berserk if we both leave."

"She'll go berserk if one of us does, so how would both of us going be worse?" Rachel said stubbornly.

"It would be, and you know it," Jack replied. "Since I'm the one with weather magic, I need to be the one to go."

"I think he's right, Rachel," Tory said quietly. "Your mother has always been so helpful to all the Irregulars. It hardly seems fair for her to watch both of her children go into the unknown."

"I suppose you're right." Rachel looked ready to spit. "But you'd better come back and tell me all about it, Jack Rainford!"

"My word on it, Rach." Jack's attention returned to Nick, who was sitting up now, though still pale. "Tory said your little sister has weather-working magic?"

"Yes, but Polly hasn't much training or experience."

"I'll guide the magic, so that doesn't matter." His gaze went to Cynthia. "You've quite a bit of weather magic, Cyn. Do you want to join us for a great adventure?"

"No!" she said, aghast. "I'm not going through a hole in time to a war with horrid new weapons! You can't make me!"

"No one is trying to force you," Allarde observed. Cynthia flushed.

"We might as well leave now," Jack said. "Nick, are you up for it?"

"No," Tory said firmly. "It might be dangerous for Nick to go through the portal twice in such a short time. It's a wretched journey."

"I can manage," he said, but he didn't look happy with the prospect.

"Better to leave tomorrow night, I think," Allarde said. "Nick will have time to recover, and there are some preparations that could be useful."

As the others nodded, Cynthia suddenly blurted out, "I'll go, too! You need weather talent and general power, and I have both."

"You would be a great asset," Allarde said gravely.

Jack didn't look quite so certain, but he said, "If you're sure—well, you have the right kind of magic."

Cynthia preened under the male attention. "After Jack, I'm the strongest weather mage, so it's my duty."

"I . . . I don't know how to thank you all," Nick said, his gaze moving from one face to another. "I never expected so much help from people who don't know me from Adam."

Jack chuckled. "What kind of grandfather would I be if I didn't help my many times removed grandson when he needed it?"

Everyone laughed, but Tory felt somber as she and Elspeth and Cynthia left. It was the laughter before the storm.

CHAPTER 25

"You don't have to do this," Tory said to Cynthia as they headed to the Labyrinth the next evening. Tory wasn't looking forward to passing through the portal again, but she was resigned to the need, and at least she'd see friends on the other side.

Lady Cynthia, however, looked like she was heading to the gallows. Her face was white and she was strung so tightly that she might break if someone touched her. Tory's comment gave her an excuse to glare. "You can't tell me what to do!"

"I'm not trying to," Tory said mildly. "But you obviously don't want to go through the portal. Why torment yourself?"

"I'm going to be needed. I'm certain of that." After half a dozen more steps, she added in a low voice, "And I need to know that I can do this."

So Cynthia was testing herself? Tory understood that. For her, the magic that had once seemed like a curse had become her challenge. If her abilities could help rescue British soldiers from death or captivity, it would be easier to accept the way that magic had shattered her life.

They reached the main hall. It wasn't a regular class evening, so there were only a few people apart from those who were actually going through the mirror. Jack, Rachel, and Nick were sitting on a sofa. Jack greeted Tory and Cynthia. "Nick and I have decided to say that we're cousins."

"Many times removed," Nick said with a smile.

"That's sufficiently vague," Tory agreed as she looked around. She and Cynthia were the last to arrive. Tory would have left for the Labyrinth earlier, but Cynthia had been fussing about what to take, and Tory felt it would be discourteous just to walk out.

Miss Wheaton and Mr. Stephens had come, of course, and Jack's mother. Lily Rainford was a small, calm woman who was a hearth witch who'd studied magic in the Labyrinth herself as a girl. Without the fear of invasion, classes had been more relaxed then.

Allarde scanned the group. "Everyone is here, so I suppose it's time to be off." His voice was calm, but there was a spark of excitement in his gray eyes.

"I'm ready," Nick said. He'd spent much of the time since his arrival in the main hall sleeping and recovering from the ordeal of the mirror. Jaw set, he headed into the tunnel leading to the mirror.

Tory hoped she looked calm, but her stomach was so tied in knots that she hadn't been able to eat a bite at supper. Though she wanted to see her friends in 1940, first she must get through the appalling portal. She followed Nick into the tunnel, others falling in behind her. The group reached its destination, stopping a little short of the dead end.

The mirror wasn't visible, but Tory felt its magic burning. Waiting.

"Don't try to be a hero!" Rachel said as she gave her brother a fierce hug.

"I can't help it if I'm naturally heroic." After hugging her, he embraced his mother. "Take care of Mum, Rachel."

His mother laughed, her voice almost steady. "As if I needed taking care of, my lad! You make yourself useful and get on home quickly."

"Yes, Mum," he said meekly. "Are you going first, Nick?"

"It's my place." Nick took Tory's hand. "You next since you know the way."

She clasped his hand and stretched her other arm back. Jack's warm fingers locked around hers. Next came Elspeth, then Allarde. If Cynthia still had doubts, they were assuaged by being able to hold Allarde's hand at the end.

"I wish I was coming with you," Mr. Stephens said wistfully.

"We're needed here for our classes and the other Irregulars." Miss Wheaton smiled, her worry almost concealed. "Travel safely and come home soon."

Nick turned to the invisible veil of magic that marked the mirror's location and raised his right hand. He probably didn't realize how hard his left hand was gripping Tory's. She didn't blame him. He hadn't fully recovered from his journey the previous night, and now he had the responsibility of leading all six of them through time.

His need had been powerful enough to bring him here, and now he was equally determined to return home, if he could. She felt him collect his energy and summon the mirror. The air in front of him shimmered as if trying to coalesce. Tory braced herself for the passage.

Nick reached out to touch the coruscating air—and nothing happened. His fingers passed through the haze of flickering light and the mirror didn't materialize. Tory added her energy to his, along with her desire and her memories of 1940.

Still nothing! Magic swirled through the corridor, thick and menacing, but the portal refused to form.

Nick tried again and then again without success. He was shaking with fatigue and the hand holding Tory's was clammy when he said in a choked voice, "I can't make it work. I'm trying as hard as I know how, but *it won't work.*"

Under his words, Tory could feel the panic that he wouldn't be able to return home. Since they were all linked by touch, she could also feel Cynthia's relief along with varying degrees of disappointment from the others.

Time to test the theory that Tory had special mirror magic. "Let me try," she said lightly. "I think the mirror likes me better."

"I hope it does!" Haggard but relieved, Nick exchanged places with her.

Feeling the weight of everyone's expectations, Tory closed her eyes to clear her mind, then summoned images. Countless soldiers jammed together as they waited for ships, desperate to get home. Nick's father among them because he'd given up his comfortable life to serve his country against a growing evil.

Tory and her friends were needed. *Desperately* needed. She opened her eyes and reached out with her right hand and every ounce of her will. *Take us where we must go. Please, for the sake of England, take us there!*

Cool silver burned under her fingertips, and then she was dragged into wrenching chaos. Disorienting, painful, yet Nick's firm grip remained real even as she plummeted into the abyss. Through him, she could dimly sense the others, their fear and alarm but also their strength.

Abruptly she twisted into normal space and crumpled to the hard floor. This time she didn't lose consciousness, quite. Though she was dizzy and cold, she wasn't alone. Nick had made it through as well, his fingers locked in a death grip around hers.

Light. They needed *light*. She managed to form a mage lamp in her right hand and tossed it up to cling to the ceiling. Throat dry, she asked, "Is everyone here?"

"I think so." Allarde's voice was unsteady, but he pushed himself to a sitting position. "You weren't exaggerating about what an uncomfortable journey that is!"

"Actually, it was a bit easier than before." Creakily, Tory got to her feet.

Nick gave her a twisted smile as he stumbled up. "I really hope we came to the right time, because I do not want to do that again!"

"Just what we need," Jack said tartly as he lurched up, bracing one hand against the wall. "The reminder that most of us will have to do this again."

"Maybe it becomes easier with practice," Elspeth said as she rose.

There was one person who hadn't spoken up. Concerned, Tory moved along the wall to where her roommate lay huddled and apparently unconscious. "Cynthia?"

She knelt on one side and Elspeth on the other. Elspeth rested her hands on Cynthia's head and sent a rich flow of healing energy. "Cynthia, can you hear me?"

After a minute, Cynthia's lashes flickered up. "That . . . that was *ghastly!*"

Tory sat back on her heels, relieved. "I warned everyone."

"I thought you were exaggerating to make yourself sound braver," Cynthia grumbled as she sat up.

"She's being insulting," Tory said mischievously. "Obviously Cynthia is getting back to normal."

Cynthia gave Tory a scowl fierce enough to blister paint. Allarde offered his hand to help her to her feet. "But we all made it here, which is quite amazing. I suppose we must go outside to learn if we've reached our destination."

"This looks right. The amount of dust, the footprints." Nick started down the tunnel. "I marked the way in when I came with Tory, just in case I ever had reason to need the mirror. I didn't expect it to be so soon!"

"I'm ready for fresh air," Tory said as she collected her mage lamp and followed Nick. The others came after her with a bobbing of mage lamps.

She was relieved to see that the abbey looked exactly as she remembered from her previous trips through the mirror. There were gasps when the other Irregulars saw the ruins of their school. It was one thing to be told what to expect, another to see it.

It was a very dark night that felt like May. "We're here," Nick said quietly. "The abbey looks right and the blackout is in effect, or we'd see along the shore."

Tory hadn't known that when she'd emerged here before. Darkness had seemed natural since she'd never seen electric lights. "I hope there's lots of food at your house. Time travel makes me ravenous."

"I think the portal burns some of our own energy in order to work," Allarde said thoughtfully. "That would explain why the transit is so tiring and disorienting."

"A good theory," Elspeth said. "Perhaps we could travel with food so we could start rebuilding our energy as soon as we arrive."

"Next time, I'll carry shortbread." Tory dimmed her mage lamp to the barest of glows. "We need lamps to get out of the abbey without tripping and breaking our necks, but keep them very dim."

"What if we want to use more light?" Cynthia asked.

"Concerned citizens will come after us threatening to call the police because we're violating the blackout." Nick dimmed his light, then headed toward the gate.

The others fell in behind him. Tory waited and brought up the rear. At least on this journey, she knew what to expect.

The Irregulars' journey to Lackland was shorter than Tory's had been because they walked to Nick's house on the bluff rather than down into the village proper. Even so, there was plenty to intrigue the Irregulars who were seeing paved roads, power lines, and motorcars for the first time. Tory thought it was fortunate that the blackout hid their conspicuous group from curious eyes.

Jack whistled when they reached their destination. "This house belonged to my uncle. It was smaller then, though."

"The property has been in the family forever. We have several acres, so there's privacy and room for a large garden. And some chickens that my mother just bought," Nick said. "My dad says every generation has added something."

He bounded up the steps and swung into the kitchen. "Mum, Polly, I'm back!" As soon as everyone was inside, he flicked on the overhead light. There were gasps of surprise. Cynthia looked admiringly at the fixture above. "This would be a great help when one is dressing for a ball."

"Or reading a book," Allarde said.

"Or doing embroidery," Elspeth added.

Feet pounded down the stairs and Polly and Anne Rainford surged into the kitchen dressed in nightgowns and robes. "You're safe!" His mother hugged Nick with rib-bruising force. "When I found your note that you would try to find Tory by going through Merlin's mirror, I was ready to do murder!"

"She's not exaggerating. You'd have been in big trouble if you got yourself killed, Nick!" Polly gave Tory a fierce hug. "Oh, Tory, I didn't think I'd ever see you again!"

"Not only did I make it to 1803, but I've returned with help." Nick waved at the Irregulars, who filled most of the small kitchen. "These are classmates of Tory's who volunteered to come because they have talents that will be useful. Unless—has the situation in France become better so help isn't needed?"

Mrs. Rainford sighed. "No such luck. The government hasn't publicly admitted the magnitude of the disaster, but things are going from bad to worse."

Nick's face tightened. "Then it's a good thing I went for help. Mum, Polly, can you guess which one is our very distant relation Jack, the weather mage?"

Mrs. Rainford's gaze went unerringly to Jack, with his fair hair and handsome, wide-cheekboned face. "You must be the Rainford."

"Yes, ma'am. Jack Rainford at your service." Jack glanced at his companions. "Nick didn't have much time to learn names, so I'll do the introductions. This is Lady Elspeth Campbell, Lady Cynthia Stanton, the Marquis of Allarde, and, of course, you know Lady Victoria Mansfield."

Mrs. Rainford and Polly blanched. "Tory?" Polly said faintly. "You're Lady Victoria?"

Tory shrugged. "Students at Lackland Abbey are stripped of our titles. I've found I don't really miss mine."

Pulling herself together, Mrs. Rainford said, "I hope that none of you object to plebian potato and leek soup. I made a great pot of it in the hopes that Nick would return soon. There's enough for all, but I'm sure it's not what you're used to."

Elspeth smiled. "It sounds lovely. Don't think of us as a pack of aristocrats but as a group of hungry young mages."

"Just as alarming in a different way!" Polly said.

"I've been feeding hungry young people for years, so that I can manage." As on Tory's visit, Mrs. Rainford lit a gas burner on the stove and pulled a pot of soup onto it from the back burner. "Polly, you and I need to change. Lady Victoria, could you show your friends the facilities?"

"I'm still Tory, Mrs. Rainford."

"I shall try to remember." The teacher's brow furrowed. "I didn't expect five guests. I haven't enough beds. There should be enough blankets and pillows, but you won't have much comfort or privacy."

"I know this is a great imposition," Allarde said in his soft, deep voice. "But we shall manage. It will only be for a day or two, I assume."

"First, we eat. I'll make sure the soup doesn't burn, Mum," Nick said. "Then we hold our war council. There is much to discuss."

No sleep for the Irregulars tonight, Tory suspected as she led the others upstairs. She just prayed that they'd be able to help hold off catastrophe.

CHAPTER 26

Serious talk was delayed until everyone had eaten at least one bowl of the hearty potato leek soup. Nick wolfed down three bowls before setting down his spoon. "Let us know the worst, Mum. What's happening?"

"The Nazis are closing in on Dunkirk, and the Luftwaffe is doing terrible damage to the port and troops waiting for evacuation." Mrs. Rainford glanced at the Irregulars. "The Luftwaffe is the German air corps. They've bombed Dunkirk's huge oil storage silos, and fires are so fierce that you can see the clouds of black smoke from here."

"Maybe the smoke will confuse the Luftwaffe," Nick said, grasping for hope. "Anything that blocks the pilots' view will help the evacuation."

"I hope you're right," his mother replied. "A national day of prayer has been declared for tomorrow. Every church in the country will be praying for a miracle to save our troops, and none too soon. Tomorrow afternoon the Admiralty is going to start evacuating men from Dunkirk with passenger ferries."

The shocked silence was broken when Jack said jauntily, "Well, here we are, Mrs. R. Your miracle!"

The teacher smiled a little. "I surely hope so. Along the coast here, everyone is talking about how the Admiralty is requisitioning self-propelled pleasure boats. The Dunkirk harbor is being bombed to uselessness, so shallow draft vessels will be needed to get close enough to the beaches to pick men up."

"Has *Annie's Dream* been requisitioned?" Nick asked.

"I sent a letter to the Admiralty when they announced they were compiling lists of possible boats, but I haven't heard anything back yet." Mrs. Rainford's hands fisted. "I want to be doing something!"

"We will," Tory said firmly. "How have you learned so much about what's going on if the government is trying to hide the news?"

"Remember you showed me how to scry the future by looking into a bowl of water?" Mrs. Rainford smiled sheepishly. "I've been practicing, and sometimes I can see vague images of what's going on at the naval headquarters under Dover Castle. The Royal Navy has been moving destroyers to the southeast for days. They're planning on two days of evacuation, though they'll keep going if possible. They'll have to go longer to have any chance of getting most of the men out."

"How useful to have a view into headquarters," Elspeth said admiringly. "I have some scrying ability. If we work together, perhaps we can get clearer visions."

"And perhaps . . . we can locate my husband," Mrs. Rainford said in a low voice.

"We can try." Elspeth's gaze was compassionate.

"The small ships make weather work even more critical," Jack said thoughtfully. "Rough waves make it hard to stay afloat, much less pick up soldiers, especially if the piers have been destroyed and rescue will have to be from the beaches." He closed his eyes as he evaluated. "There's some bad weather threatening on the Continent. If we get to work right away, we can keep it from forming up, but there's no time to waste."

"This is what we came for." Cynthia had the distant expression that meant she'd also been evaluating the weather. She had recovered from her transit and was looking unnaturally serious. "This system isn't too bad, but if the evacuation goes on for days, we'll need a huge amount of power. Can we do that, Jack?"

"I hope so. Once we get rid of this pattern and stabilize the calm, maintaining it won't take as much energy." Jack's expression was less confident than his words.

"What can I do?" Polly asked. Though she was the youngest person present, her expression was not that of a child.

Jack studied her with unfocused eyes, reading her energy. "You've got a lot of natural weather talent. If you pay attention to what I'm doing as we work on this system, you'll pick up the basics of weather magic quickly. With three weather mages, we can set up watches later for maintaining the calm."

"How can we nonweather mages help?" Allarde asked.

"We need to do a full circle now to flatten that Continental weather pattern. It will also give us a chance to practice blending our energies properly."

"We do need that," Tory agreed. "There is such a wide range of ability and experience in this group and we don't all know each other. I assume we'll have general mages stand watch with the weather workers to supply power so no one burns out?"

"I hadn't thought that far," Jack said, "but it's a good plan."

"We won't need so many beds if we take turns sleeping." Allarde got to his feet. "Where shall we set up our headquarters?"

"The sitting room is largest, and it has the most comfortable furniture and a view out over the channel," Polly said. "At least, it does in daylight when the blackout curtains are pulled back."

"Good." Jack scanned the other mages. "Everyone wash up or whatever and meet me in the sitting room."

Tory headed for the stairs. It wasn't her first choice to embark on major magical work when already tired, but not having a choice might be the first lesson of war.

Jack was fidgeting with impatience as the others trickled into the sitting room. "Come along now," he snapped. "The longer it takes us to get going, the more power it will take to destroy that weather system, and we need to conserve our power."

"It's not our fault the house has only one water closet!" Cynthia retorted.

Jack wisely didn't comment on that. He began moving chairs into a rough circle that included the sofa. "I'll sit in the middle of the sofa. Polly, you sit next to me to make it easy to follow what I'm doing. You opposite me, Tory. That should be the best place for you to work on the energy blending. Elspeth on my other side, then Nick and Cynthia. Mrs. R. by Tory, Allarde on her other side. Make yourselves comfortable."

"You want me to join your circle?" the teacher asked, surprised.

"You've got power and we need it." Jack's usual laughter had dropped away and he was dead serious. "To become a team, we must blend our energies."

"Anything I can do to help." Mrs. Rainford took the chair next to Tory's.

Tory took her seat, thinking the dining room chairs would be uncomfortable in an hour or two. Jack was wise to take the sofa since he had the most demanding job.

212 · *M. J. Putney*

People settled and took each other's hands. The last link was when Cynthia reluctantly took Tory's left hand. They tried to avoid working together in the Labyrinth, and Tory was surprised at her roommate's power. And under the power, anger and pain. Cynthia had a bitter need to prove herself to someone.

Jack's gaze moved around the circle, spending extra time on his twentieth-century cousins. "No need to look alarmed. Think of this circle as a carriage. I'm the driver and the rest of you are my horses."

There was laughter, which eased the tension. "Mind you don't use a whip on us," Allarde said with a smile. "Irritated mages are worse than unruly horses."

"No whips unless you deserve it," Jack agreed. "Once I've started, Tory will harmonize the energies. Tory, do you have anything to add?"

"Just relax and let your power flow," she said. "If you have to get up, say so because leaving too suddenly would be disruptive. Link the hands of your neighbors because touching conducts the most power. Does everyone understand?"

The Irregulars all knew this, and the modern Rainfords were all intelligent, so there were murmurs of assent. Tory closed her eyes. She experienced energy circles like chords of music, each individual with a separate note.

"And so we begin. . . ." Jack's calm voice signaled the beginning of their work. He hadn't been joking about the circle being a carriage with horses, because the mages were out of step to begin with. But since joining the Irregulars, Tory had become adept at balancing and blending different energies.

Carefully she braided each individual note with the others to create a rope of power. She'd never felt such intensity in a circle, for never had the stakes been so high.

Jack's energy was strong and focused as he reached into the sky. Polly echoed him, eager to follow and learn. Allarde was as deep and powerful as the earth itself, Elspeth was a pure, strong crystal chime. Mrs. Rainford had a warm stability flavored by deep fear for her husband and the other stranded soldiers.

Jack's weather perceptions swept south over the Continent as he sought the shape and weaknesses of the storm that was trying to coalesce and turn dangerous. The circle soared with him, supplying the power he needed to split the system into smaller pieces and send them in different directions.

The work took time and care and power but didn't strain the circle to the breaking point. Tory learned so much about weather magic that she suspected she'd be able to teach it even though she'd never be a real weather mage herself.

After the storm had literally been scattered to the four winds, Jack centered his attention on the English Channel itself. With the help of the circle, he calmed the seas and laid a blanket of light fog to protect the evacuation.

Hours had passed and Tory's backside was sore by the time Jack exhaled roughly and said, "We're in good shape now. This favorable weather over the channel should last for two or three days with only moderate effort from us. Tory, nice work on the energy blending. We can release the circle now."

Tory released the strands of energy. There were sighs of relief as people stood and stretched. Jack covered a yawn. "I can carry on longer. Cynthia, can you get by with a nap and a meal now, then relieve me in four hours or so?"

Cynthia looked tired but pleased with herself. "I can do that. You can manage another four hours?"

"I'll need help from one of the nonweather mages. Any volunteers?"

"I'll do it," Nick said. "I'm the one who brought you here, after all." He looked tired but satisfied with the fact that he was doing something important.

Allarde stood wearily. "I'll get some rest and plan to be back in four hours with Cynthia." He moved to the nearest window and cracked the blackout curtains. Then he swept them back to let the morning light pour into the room. "I see black smoke on the French shore. Those burning oil silos, I imagine."

Everyone joined him at the window to look at the channel's calm waters and misty sky. "I imagine the national prayer services are going on now," Tory said. "I wish I could go to Saint Peter's by the Sea and pray with the rest of the congregation."

"There is nothing to prevent us from praying privately," Elspeth said quietly.

Tory gave a silent prayer for the safety of the stranded troops. So many elements would have to work together for a successful evacuation. The Nazis must be kept away from the Dunkirk beaches. The destroyers and passenger ferries and small private ships would have to work tirelessly, and calm weather would have to hold.

The only aspect the Irregulars could handle was the weather. But they would do their part. She could only pray that the other elements would fall into place as well.

"We've done a good day's work," Mrs. Rainford said. "And now, my brave young mages, it's time to organize the beds."

The Irregulars were so exhausted they'd have accepted piles of bricks for beds, so it was fortunate that Mrs. Rainford sorted her guests out quickly. She gave Tory and Elspeth the master bedroom while choosing herself to join Polly.

Allarde would have Nick's room until the current watch was over, while Cynthia received Joe's room. Tory guessed that years of teaching allowed Mrs. Rainford to detect who needed the most mollifying to keep the peace, and that was Cynthia.

The group scattered quickly. After her turn at the water closet,

Tory joined Elspeth, who was already burrowed into the double bed in the master bedroom. "Do you mind sharing the bed, Elspeth? I haven't the energy to make up a pallet on the floor."

"Sharing is fine." Elspeth was largely invisible except for a swath of flaxen hair. "Neither of us takes much space. At this point, I'd willingly share with an African lion."

"A lioness," Tory quipped. "We must observe the proprieties."

Elspeth was laughing when the door opened and Cynthia marched into the room, her blond hair loose and her expression exasperated. She tugged off her gown. "I need someone to unlace my stays."

Since Elspeth was already lying down, Tory circled around Cynthia and began to work on the long stays. "You didn't bring short stays that lace up the front?"

"I don't have any," Cynthia snapped. "You should have told me there would be no servants, Tory! The Rainfords in our time have them."

"The subject didn't come up before we traveled here." Tory pulled the single long cord out of the eyelet at the top. "Servants are less common these days. I'll help you this time, but you should probably abandon the stays while we're here."

"I'd look indecent and my gowns wouldn't fit properly!" Cynthia sighed with relief when Tory finished the unlacing and the stays could be peeled off.

"Perhaps Mrs. Rainford has an undergarment you could use," Tory suggested. "They have something called a brassiere that doesn't need a servant to fasten it."

Cynthia made a disapproving sound. "I'll get that girl Polly to help me."

If Cynthia thought Polly would become a worshipful disciple like her admirers at Lackland, she was wrong, but that wasn't Tory's problem. "I'm sure Nick would be happy to help with your stays."

"Or Jack." Elspeth's muffled voice came from the bed.

Cynthia dropped her gown over her head so she wouldn't walk the corridor in her shift. "As if I'd let one of those commoners touch me!"

"But you'd let Allarde do it?" Tory asked with interest.

"Allarde is a *gentleman*."

"Meaning he's not interested in you," Elspeth murmured.

"You two are disgusting!" Cynthia turned to the door.

Remembering how she'd felt deep pain in Cynthia when they were linked, Tory said, "I'm sorry for the teasing. It's been a very long day." She opened the door and peered into the corridor. "There's no one in sight, so with luck you can get back to your room without anyone seeing you sans stays."

"Even Lackland is more convenient than this place," Cynthia grumbled.

Just before Cynthia stepped into the corridor, Tory said, "You did very well in the circle. Strong and steady."

Cynthia flushed but ducked her head with what might have been pleasure before she headed off to rest. Tory didn't envy her having to go on watch again so soon.

Tory crawled beside Elspeth, aching with fatigue. She thought the other girl was already asleep, but as Tory settled into the mattress, Elspeth said softly, "I can feel them."

"Feel who?" Tory asked sleepily.

"The injured soldiers. They're only a few miles away, Tory, and there are so *many*. On both sides. Most are just boys, only a few years older than we are." Elspeth made a choked sound. "I'm a healer, and I can't do anything to help!"

Hearing the anguished frustration, Tory said, "Even if you were in France, there isn't much you could do. A good healer can help a few injured men, but not thousands."

"I could *try*!"

Tory placed a hand on her friend's arm. "You must shield yourself so you can rest, Elspeth. For now, working in the weather circles is the most any of us can do. If the evacuation succeeds, at least the armies will be on opposite sides of the channel so they can't kill each other for a while."

Elspeth sighed. "I know you're right. But I still feel that I'm failing in my healer's duty."

"My mother used to say that worry is throwing good shillings at trouble that hasn't happened yet. So for now, sleep."

"A wise woman, your mother." Elspeth sighed again, the tension flowing out of her. "It isn't Cynthia that Allarde would like to touch. It's you."

Tory stared at the ceiling as Elspeth's breathing evened out. What a thing to be told when she was ready to fall asleep!

But even with such interesting thoughts, sleep did come.

CHAPTER 27

When Tory woke from exhausted slumber, it was evening and supper was ready for the table. Mrs. Rainford had made two large shepherd's pies and followed them with warm black currant pudding and lots of custard. By the time the Irregulars were done, the baking dishes scarcely needed washing.

"I don't always eat so much," Tory said with some embarrassment as she finished off a second serving of pudding. "But serious magical work really burns up energy."

Their hostess laughed. "I put away my fair share of the meal, too."

"But we did good work," Jack said with justifiable pride. "The channel is flat calm with mist and some light rain. Good for evacuation, bad for the Luftwaffe."

Jack was right. The weather was so smooth that all the mages were able to dine together, though Tory was sure Jack was quietly monitoring the skies, alert for changes.

"You're right about magic making one hungry," Polly said. "Tomorrow will require a major visit to the market."

Tory frowned, reminded that this was not a great house that routinely fed mobs of people. "We're going to eat you out of house and home."

"I'd like to contribute to the larder, Mrs. Rainford," Allarde said. "I brought ten gold sovereigns with me. I'm not sure if they're still being used, but surely gold has value. A jeweler or antiquities dealer should be interested."

Mrs. Rainford stared at him. "You are helping to save thousands of British lives at the least, you should be fed by way of thanks."

"I'm British, too, so I'm merely doing my duty." Allarde smiled. "You are providing us with a place to stay and excellent cooking. We are all sharing the work, so why not share the expenses, at least a little?"

Tory guessed that their hostess was weighing her desire to provide for her guests with the practical reality of buying food for eight more than usually hungry people. Practicality won. "Very well, Lord Allarde, your contribution is gratefully received. I wish I didn't have to go to work, but it would be difficult for the school to replace me on short notice, and children need teaching no matter what is happening across the channel."

"Can Nick and I be ill again?" Polly said. "We're needed here."

"Indeed you are, but I will be picking up your lessons at school and making sure you don't get behind," her mother said.

Polly sighed piteously but didn't argue.

"The Irregulars will want to see what England looks like today," Nick said. "We can't take a whole group of strangers into Lackland where everyone knows us, so I'll drive to some of the other towns around here. Besides buying food, I can take people who aren't on watch so they can get a better look at the modern world."

"You have one of those motorcars?" Allarde was the one who asked, his eyes bright, but everyone looked interested.

"Joe and I fixed up a wrecked Morris Oxford Six." A shadow showed in Nick's eyes at the memory of easier days when two brothers worked and argued and laughed over a mutual project. He continued, "She runs like a champ now, though. Good for touring as well as foraging for supplies."

"Seeing more of the world will be lovely, and I look forward to comparing a motorcar with a carriage," Tory said. "We'll need modern clothes, though."

"Luckily we Rainfords come in all sizes," Mrs. Rainford said. "Lady Cynthia, you're about my height. My clothes won't do you justice, but at least you'll blend in."

She studied the others with a practiced eye. "Tory and Lady Elspeth are about Polly's size, and Jack and Nick are fairly close. Lord Allarde is about Tom's height. These days most clothing is made by machine, not hand, and we're not a fashionable family, but at least no one will guess you're from another century."

"It's so strange to know that I'm a time traveler from another era," Elspeth said slowly. "Traveling through time should be impossible. Yet here I sit, drinking tea and eating supper and talking with friends, and it's exactly as real as when I was at home."

"'The center of the world is where I place my feet,'" Polly quoted. "A teacher told us that was a Spanish expression." Her foot tapped the floor under the table. "This is the center of my world. Real is what we can see and touch."

"I also find it strange that I'm eating in a familiar house with family, even if they are cousins a century removed," Jack agreed. "Mrs. R., with your magical ability, do you have Rainford connections on your side as well?"

"Oh, yes. You know how it is in small communities. Tom and I are third cousins, and I'm sure our family trees crossed many times over the years."

Tory's gaze moved around the table. Even Cynthia looked relaxed and not displeased even though the food and accommodations were not what she was used to. Working together for a common goal had made the eight of them a kind of family. She lifted her glass of cider to the others. "A toast to the weather brigade!"

Cries of, "Hear, hear!" and "To the weather brigade!" were repeated with raised glasses and laughter.

Even Cynthia joined in.

The plans decided over Sunday supper went well on Monday. In the morning, Nick, Polly, and Allarde drove to a nearby town where it was market day and came back by midday with enough food to feed the weather brigade for a week. They returned with Allarde talking about an amazing and alarming creation called a railway, which seemed to be a sort of giant motorcar that ran on metal tracks. Tory thought it sounded noisy.

As a general mage, Tory was needed only six hours a day for magical support of the weather workers, but there was plenty to keep her busy in a house without servants. After her morning weather watch, she tutored Polly, then enjoyed a drive with Nick and Elspeth. After she managed to relax her knotted fists, she decided that motorcars had advantages over carriages, but horses were better companions.

She also saw her first railway. The train was indeed noisy but a good way to move large numbers of people.

Later in the afternoon, she and Elspeth helped prepare lamb stew under Polly's guidance. Tory had never cooked in her life and she suspected the same was true for Elspeth, but she found that she rather enjoyed kneading bread and cutting up vegetables. She surveyed her mountain of sliced carrots with pride. "I'm learning as much from you as you are from me, Polly."

The girl laughed. "You won't need to know how to make stew when you go home, but I'll be practicing magic for the rest of my life, I hope."

"I had no idea onions were so fierce!" Elspeth said as she wiped her eyes. "In the future, I shall be more understanding of cooks."

Polly turned over the pieces of lamb she was browning in the skillet. "I wonder what we'll be eating in a year or two, since Mum expects rationing to get worse."

"You'll be grateful to have your own vegetables and eggs," Tory predicted.

"We have fruit trees, too, so we'll be canning and drying. It's a lot of work, but at least we can still have nice puddings since we'll have our own supply of fruit." Polly transferred the browned lamb to the stew pot and began browning more pieces. "Of course, knowing my mum, she'll be giving food to others who aren't so lucky."

"And you wouldn't have her any other way," Tory said with a smile.

"Probably not," Polly admitted. "But I may change my mind if I have to go years without a proper pudding!"

"Your mother is right that rationing will get much worse," Elspeth said thoughtfully. "But after the war, Britons will be healthier from the more Spartan diet."

"Healthier, maybe." Tory sampled one of the delectable ginger biscuits they'd made. "But not happier!"

Mrs. Rainford was tired when she arrived home, and happy to find the house reasonably neat and a good hot meal waiting. The weather brigade had kept the seas calm and the channel foggy, so they were able to celebrate another successful day.

After eating, most of the group decided to practice scrying. Ordinarily Tory would join in, but at the moment she yearned for privacy. She slipped outside, draping her shawl around her shoulders as protection from the cool May evening. The fog was thickening as sunset neared and swirling mists made the war seem mercifully far away.

She strolled out to the public footpath that ran above the sea and turned left. The fog muffled the sounds of the waves far below. She felt as if she were walking on the edge of the world.

Only a few months had passed since she'd walked along the cliff at Fairmount Hall during her mother's summer fete. Strange to recall how she'd been almost speechless with pleasure because the Horrible Edmund Harford was noticing her.

Most of her anger at his rejection had faded away. If she hadn't been a mage, she supposed he would have made an adequate husband, but magic was part of who she was and it couldn't be denied.

Now that she'd met more young men, she knew she could do a good deal better than Edmund Harford when the time came. Perhaps even a husband like . . .

"You look like a sea sprite newly born from the waves," a soft voice said, and Allarde emerged from the fog, sparkling crystals of moisture in his dark hair and magic in his mist-gray eyes.

CHAPTER 28

Enigmatic and more than earthly handsome, Allarde suited the mysterious atmosphere. Though Thomas Rainford's clothing fit his height and breadth of shoulder, the garments hung loosely around his lean, well-muscled frame. He'd still take Tory's breath away no matter what he wore.

A good thing he couldn't know what she'd been thinking!

Afraid her face might say too much, she bent to scratch Horace's ears. The dog had been at Allarde's heels and now he yearned for attention. "If I'm a sea sprite, you look like a legendary Celtic hero from ancient times."

Allarde chuckled. "The mist is wonderfully romantic. A time out of time."

"This entire visit feels like that." She straightened. "When we go back home, 1940 will seem like a fever dream."

He also bent to pat Horace. "Do you mind if I walk with you?" Foolish question. "Of course not."

Allarde fell into step beside her, altering his long stride to match her pace. "The white cliffs of Dover are famous for greeting travelers when they approach England, and here we are walking on them."

"I'm sure the men being evacuated from Dunkirk will never forget their first sight of the white cliffs as they come home." Tory shivered as the image struck her with such power that she must have picked it up from one of the evacuees. Passionately hoping that every last man could be rescued, she asked, "What do you think of modern England?"

"It's fascinating," Allarde replied. "Forever England and in many ways unmistakable, but so very different in other ways."

"I have mixed feelings about all the inventions people now take for granted," she said. "Many are very convenient. Others are just alarming. The locomotive I saw made me think of metal dragons. Where is Saint George when one needs a dragon slain?"

Allarde chuckled. "He's lost somewhere in the mists, I think. As startling as airplanes and motorcars are, I think the social changes are even more profound. In our England, aristocratic families have enormous power and influence. We are part of a small elite that runs our society."

Tory nodded. "When I found my way to the Labyrinth, I was surprised by the equality. I like that magical skill, not birth or breeding, is what matters in the Irregulars."

"I think England benefits from a more democratic society. There is greater fairness and talented men have many more opportunities." Allarde hesitated. "But it's not my England. I don't believe this era would ever feel quite like home."

"I feel the same way." She gazed toward France, which lay hidden by fog and darkness. "I'd miss my family, and I know I don't like living in a world that has such beastly weapons."

"The scryers say that with the calm weather, the evacuation is going on night and day." He also looked out to sea. "It looks as if our work in keeping the channel quiet will allow the evacuation to continue beyond the original two days they planned. Every day, thousands more men will be saved. Weapons and equipment can be replaced, but not the trained soldiers who are the core of the army."

"I wonder if we'll do anything more important in our lives?" Tory mused.

"Probably not, but this is enough. How many people ever have the chance to be part of a great and noble mission?"

"When you put it that way—not many." She smiled. "Especially not girls. Great and noble has usually been reserved for men."

"Not anymore. You're the heart and soul of our mission, Tory. We wouldn't be here without you." He gestured toward France. "Those men would be fighting without hope, facing surrender or death. Most of the world will never know what you've done, but we do." His gaze shifted to her. "I do."

She ducked her head, pleased but embarrassed. "I think it's fate that brought us all here. Or perhaps old Merlin himself. I'm just glad to be part of it."

"It's the most important work I'll ever do."

"Valuable as the weather brigade is, I hope it isn't the high point of my life," she said with a laugh. "There is so much more I want to do."

Allarde didn't smile, though. His face was grave, as if he were seeing something Tory couldn't. That was a drawback of socializing with mages. Often they *did* see things.

She and Allarde continued along in easy silence. Having him within arm's reach seemed almost too good to be true, yet in another way it felt entirely natural. As if they were meant to be walking through life as companions.

She would have been happy to walk with him forever, but eventually she said with reluctance, "We should return. Nick said this path runs along the bluffs for miles, but it's getting too dark to see our footing."

"You're right," Allarde said, sounding equally reluctant as he turned. "I'm on the next watch and need to get back."

"I'm on the late-night watch after yours, so I should get some rest." The otherworldly atmosphere made it possible for her to say, "I've enjoyed the walk, but why aren't you avoiding me the way you usually do?"

She thought he might ignore the question, or even vanish into the mists again. Instead, he said, "I've made my peace with fate, I think. And now that I have, it seems right to enjoy what time I have left."

A chill ran through her blood. "That sounds ominous."

"It isn't really." He took a dozen steps before continuing. "I think all of us have moments of knowing. Of absolute certainty that something is going to happen."

She thought about that, then shook her head. "I often feel something is likely, but certainty? No. You must have some foreteller talent."

"Perhaps. I've had this sense of certainty before, and it's always proved correct."

Interested, she said, "We're taught that the future is never fixed. Do you think that's not true?"

"I don't think that one can be certain about events involving other people because they can make unexpected choices," he replied. "As Miss Wheaton says, great events like wars that have the force of nations behind them are probably impossible to change except in relatively small ways, like what we're doing here."

"This is small?" she asked doubtfully. "So many thousands of people involved?"

"Small compared to the millions of people in the many nations that are already part of this war, and millions more who will be soon," he explained. "But I believe that there can be certainty about ourselves and our individual fates." His voice became very soft. "I've always known I would die young. Certainly before my eighteenth birthday."

She gasped as if she'd been struck a physical blow. "How can you believe that? Even the best foretellers can't see clearly about themselves or questions they care deeply about. That's why Mrs. Rainford can't see her husband."

"She can't because of her emotions, and also because the foretelling involves another person. It's not just about her." He walked another dozen steps. "For years I've seen myself lying drenched in blood, knowing I'm mortally wounded. Given that there's a war just a few miles away and modern weapons have a long reach, I'd say whatever is going to happen will probably happen here. Soon."

"Then go home through the mirror where it's safe!"

"If my time is up, running won't help," he said gently. "And I'm needed here. I'd rather die knowing I've done my best than possibly survive a little longer as a coward. Can you understand that?"

She took a shuddering breath. "The mage in me does. But the Tory who enjoys being with you most certainly does *not*."

"If death is inevitable, one should try to die well." His voice was wry. "I'd rather die as a man than a rabbit."

She'd always thought that he seemed older than his years, and now she realized that came from living with the certainty of his death. His calm belief and acceptance chilled her to the bone. "This is why you keep yourself from getting close to people? Why you always go by your title and never by your Christian name?"

"A title puts more distance between me and others." His voice was sad. "A Christian name is for the closest of family and friends, so I don't use mine. Why create more pain for people I care about?"

"That's very noble of you," she said tartly. "But also wrong-headed."

His brows arched. "How so?"

"Caring is always a risk because anyone can die at any time," she said intensely. "What a cold and lonely world this would be if everyone refused caring because they fear the pain of inevitable loss!"

"Though death is inevitable, most people don't know when it will arrive so it is easy to deny the future pain." He glanced down at her, his face a pale oval in the darkness. "Since I do know my end is near, I have some choice about how much to hurt those I care most about. I choose to minimize that pain."

She pulled her shawl tighter against the chill. "That makes sense, but I don't think I could be so honorable. I want to care and be cared for."

"I've had years to think about this," he replied. "I believe our spirits, the essence of who we are, survives. As for our bodies"—he shrugged—"at least I won't have to worry about gout and the other ills of old age."

He might have had time to become accustomed to the idea of dying, but she hadn't. She wanted to scream and beat her fists against his chest and tell him that the future wasn't fixed, he should fight to survive.

Yet what did she know about his life? Almost nothing. And she had no right to blame him for the bleak peace he'd achieved.

She drew a painful breath, wishing this walk would never end. She would call it a magical interlude except that she lived with magic every day. This was something quite different that she dared not name.

Horace dashed ahead of them. He was heading for the rambling farmhouse, which was a darker shape in the night. The white splotches of his fur showed his location when he flopped on the front steps to wait for them.

If Allarde chose to die well, she could choose to say good-bye well. "Thank you for explaining why you're reserved. It's better to understand." She just wished the understanding didn't hurt so much.

Allarde stopped and turned to place his hands on her shoulders. His touch affected her in every fiber. They'd never touched, except the time he'd carried her after she'd returned through the mirror. This affected her even more because she wasn't dazed from traveling through time. It was all she could do not to lean into him.

"Though I've accepted my fate," he said softly, "there is one thing I would like to do before I die."

Remembering his words about their mission, she guessed, "You hope to see the evacuation finish successfully?"

"Nothing so exalted." He gazed at her searchingly, as if trying to memorize every feature. "What I really want . . . is to kiss you."

She caught her breath, pulse accelerating. "That's easy then."

When she raised her face, he stroked back her hair and cupped her nape with one strong palm. "You are exquisite," he murmured. "So soft. So smooth. Like living silk."

He bent his head and touched his mouth to hers. In the cool night, his lips were warm on hers as he kissed her with gentleness, wonder, and regret.

Tory tensed with shock and delight. She'd never been kissed before, had never known how profoundly intimate a kiss could be. She slid her arms around his waist under the loose jacket, feeling the lean strength of his body, his warm aliveness. It was damnably unfair that they'd discovered each other when all they might have was a handful of days!

"Tory," he breathed as he buried his face in her hair. "My Lady Victoria. You look as fragile as thistle silk, yet you're strong, so strong. Like a tempered steel blade."

She wanted to weep. Instead she kissed him again, and there was nothing gentle about it. Her kiss was flesh and fire, mourning all their lost tomorrows.

Allarde responded with equal yearning. His embrace crushed her hard against him as his hands kneaded her back, molding her ever closer.

She'd thought she knew a little of love, but this was so much more. This was passion, hot and fierce, a hunger for closeness that ached inside her. She could feel his heartbeat as clearly as her own, could not tell where her emotions ended and his began. How could this embrace end when it was the deepest reality she'd ever known?

Yet end it they must.

Far too soon Allarde broke the kiss, though he didn't release her. "We'd better go in before I forget any claims I have to honor," he said raggedly.

"I wish you *would*," she said in frustration. This might be the last private time they would ever have together. She couldn't bear it.

"Don't tempt me!" he said ruefully. "I might not have much of a future, but you do, and I will not ruin you."

She wanted to be ruined, but she retained enough sense to realize she might feel differently when her blood cooled. "I suppose you're right." She made no attempt to move out of his embrace, where they fit together so perfectly.

"I've been selfish," he said softly as he stroked her hair. "I should not have spoken, but I found that I wasn't strong enough to let this chance go by. I don't want you to care too much, Tory. But . . . I'd like you to care a little."

She wanted to weep into the shoulder of Tom Rainford's tweed jacket, but she forced the tears to stay unshed. He thought she was strong, so she must live up to that.

Since he wanted so much to avoid causing pain, it would be selfish of her to show just how much she was hurting. Taking a deep breath, she stepped back, letting her hands skim slowly down his arms. "I do care, but I promise that you have not ruined my life. Quite the contrary. You have made it far richer. I will not forget you."

"I'm glad." He caught her hand and raised it to his lips, kissing the back of her fingers. "And now we really must go in."

She nodded agreement, and hand in hand they walked back to the house, almost tripping over Horace, who had been a quiet canine witness to their embrace. She was glad that none of the Irregulars could talk to animals. At least, none that she knew of. She wouldn't trust Horace not to gossip.

Quietly they went inside, still handfast. The kitchen was dark, but light and pianoforte music flowed from the living room. The sound was different from the pianofortes of Tory's time, richer and more resonant.

The warmth and beauty of the cascading notes caused Tory's throat to tighten. Just what she needed, she thought unevenly. More emotion.

"Elspeth must be playing," Allarde said softly. "She's a wonderful musician. That's one of her favorite Mozart concertos."

Tory felt a stab of envy for Elspeth because she'd known Allarde since they were in the nursery. When he was gone, Elspeth would have many memories of her cousin.

But Tory was the one he wanted to touch.

The concerto ended, the last notes fading gently away. "You're terrific, Lady Elspeth!" Nick exclaimed. "You could make a living as a concert pianist."

Elspeth laughed. "Not in my time, but it's a pleasant thought."

Tory was about to move into the sitting room when Mrs. Rainford spoke. "Here are copies of a song you might like. It's called 'Jerusalem' and the words are from a poem by William Blake, who lived in your time. Has anyone ever read him?"

After negative murmurs, the teacher continued, "That's not surprising. He was almost unknown until many years after his death. The poem was set to music during the Great War, and it's something of an English anthem. The song has been running through my head for days now. It seems very appropriate."

After a rustling of sheet music, Elspeth said, "The words are lovely. Do you want me to play it?"

"No, I will so you can concentrate on the words." There were sounds of the two of them trading places. "I'll play a verse of the music. Then we can sing it."

The music was haunting, and the words almost caused Tory to come undone when her friends began singing the hymn. She and Allarde stood with fingers laced together as they listened. The last lines brought tears to her eyes.

> *Nor shall my sword sleep in my hand,*
> *Till we have built Jerusalem,*
> *In England's green and pleasant land.*

As the poignant notes faded away, she wiped her eyes with her free hand. "I can see why Mrs. Rainford thought it appropriate."

"We are the sword carried in England's hand, Tory. One of the swords, anyhow." Allarde raised their joined hands and kissed her wrist on the pulse point, sending lightning flickers of sensation dancing through her.

Releasing her hand with obvious reluctance, he asked, "Would you like to go right upstairs so you can rest before your watch?"

Rest, and hide her raw emotions. She nodded. "Say good night for me." She slipped through the other door to the stairs in the hall.

As she started up, she glanced into the kitchen and saw Allarde's calm, grave profile as he walked into the sitting room. She might not have him for long, but they'd shared that kiss. Her first, and one she would never forget.

That would have to be enough.

CHAPTER 29

Tory was still awake when Elspeth quietly entered their room. "I'm not asleep, so you can turn on the light if you like."

Elspeth turned on the bedside lamp, which was less bright than the overhead. Tory still marveled over how easy it was to produce light. "How did the scrying go?"

"We were amusing ourselves more than scrying seriously, so I don't know if the results are any good. It does seem as if the evacuation will continue a few days longer, which means a lot more men will be rescued." Elspeth perched on the stool by the dressing table and began brushing out her long hair. "There's still no clarity about Mr. Rainford. Or rather, Captain Rainford as he is now."

Tory sighed. "Poor Mrs. Rainford. And Polly and Nick as well. I don't know how they keep going."

"I think they find busyness helps. In particular since what they're doing aids all the stranded troops." Elspeth stopped brushing her hair, frowning as she fiddled with the brush. "I think that maybe Captain Rainford is marching his unit from Belgium to Dunkirk and praying they'll be in time to catch a ship home."

"A lot of things could stop his men on the way," Tory said quietly.

"I know. So I kept my foretelling to myself." Elspeth resumed brushing. "I wonder what the headmasters will do to us when we return? It was possible to conceal your absence, but five students gone for days will be too many for them not to notice."

Tory covered a yawn. "They can't send us away to be cured since that's why we're at Lackland."

Elspeth laughed. "They may lock us up every night so we can't sneak down to the Labyrinth. That would be annoying."

Tory contemplated five years of being locked up every night without enthusiasm. "Grim, but endurable, I suppose."

"And worth every minute of being locked up. We were all able to scry the image of men pouring off ships at Dover. You've never seen such a sight!"

"I shall try scrying that tomorrow," Tory said. "I'd love to see the results of so many people working together to save the army."

"The numbers evacuated so far are only a drop in the bucket. Around eight thousand if Mrs. R. scryed the naval headquarters accurately. Hundreds of thousands are still marooned in France. But the evacuation is just getting started. With practice and a few more days, the numbers should be substantial."

"If the weather cooperates."

Elspeth frowned. "I'm worried about Jack. Cynthia and Polly are both talented weather workers, but Jack is by far the best and strongest, and he's pushing himself constantly. He's always monitoring and tweaking the weather, even when he's not officially on watch. If he doesn't get more rest, he could push himself to collapse."

Tory didn't like to think how much of a burden that would lay on Cynthia and Polly, who had nothing like Jack's experience. "The rest of us will have to keep the weather mages well supplied with power so they won't get overstrained."

Elspeth grinned. "Cynthia came the grand lady tonight and told Jack that he most certainly would get some sleep tonight, or *else*. He agreed very meekly to go to bed after the early night watch, so I think he's aware of the danger of pushing too hard."

"Cynthia?" Tory chuckled. "I wish I'd seen that. Is it my imagination, or has she been behaving surprisingly well?"

"It's not your imagination." Elspeth began braiding her hair for the night. "We've all been changed by coming here, and for the better. I can feel my magic growing stronger and more versatile. What about you?"

"I hadn't really thought about it." Tory considered. "My talent is helping others to connect. I'm not a great power in my own right."

"No?" Elspeth tied a ribbon around the bottom of the braid and tossed her hair over her shoulder. "You are connecting with people more and more easily, and I suspect that your range is increasing."

Tory frowned. "What would that mean?"

"That means you can send or draw power for some distance. If I needed more power for healing, you could send it to me. Or if you needed healing energy, you could draw some from me."

"I suppose that could be useful," Tory agreed. "I think it would have to be someone I know, like another member of the weather brigade."

"I wonder how we could test this?" Elspeth said thoughtfully. "Perhaps Nick could drive you to Dover and you could try to connect with me from there."

Tory groaned. "If I get to Dover, I'll try to reach you, but that's enough theory for one night. I need sleep because I'm taking the late-night-to-early-morning watch."

"Sorry to keep you talking." Elspeth slid into the bed and turned off the light. "Sleep well, Tory. Tomorrow should be a big day for the evacuation."

Tory knew that was true. But when she slept, her dreams were not of Dunkirk.

Tory's after-midnight watch was with Cynthia. The main problem was staying awake, but they managed, taking turns making tea and pacing around the sitting room, always maintaining the flow of magic. Cynthia monitored the weather over the channel and tweaked it now and then while Tory supplied a steady supply of power.

She yawned as she made them both a second cup of tea. "Have you seen the electric torch Nick has? It uses things called batteries that hold electricity that powers the light." She stirred honey into the tea since sugar was rationed. As she handed Cynthia the cup, she said, "I believe I have become a magical battery."

"And a good little battery you are," Cynthia said with tart amusement as she accepted the cup.

"I'm even picking up some weather magic," Tory said. "I'll never be as good as you or Jack or Polly, but it's a very useful skill."

"I like having my weather power valued." Cynthia rolled her eyes. "My evil talent was revealed when I kissed a handsome stable boy and liked it so much a storm blew up and flattened my father's best wheat fields. Ruined my favorite silk gown, too."

"Oh, my." Tory sat opposite the other girl, wondering if they might actually become friends. No, this was only a late-night lowering of barriers. "You control your magic really well now."

"My control is good, but I wish I had Jack's range. He can read weather halfway to the New World." Cynthia sipped at her tea. "Did you know that our former colonies in North America have prospered? The rebels went on to build a country that stretches from one side of the continent to the other."

"I didn't know that." Tory sipped her tea thoughtfully. "If they enter the war, I hope it's on our side."

"Mrs. R. says they want to stay neutral, but if that changed, they'd be with us, not the Nazis." Cynthia yawned again. "Isn't this watch over yet?"

"Almost." Polly was the speaker as she trailed into the room, blinking sleepily. "When Elspeth gets here."

"Cynthia, if you want to go to bed now, I'll work with Polly until Elspeth gets here," Tory offered.

"I think I will. This kind of concentrated work is really draining." Cynthia rose to her feet. "I'm eating like two hungry soldiers and have still lost a pound or two."

"Go on then. It's easier to be a battery. Polly, would you like some tea?"

Polly yawned hugely. "Please. Double honey. This late watch is the worst."

By the time Tory finished making the tea, Elspeth had arrived and Tory could go off to bed. This time she would certainly sleep.

The advantage of being a battery was that she stood fewer watches than the weather mages. She crawled back into the bed, thinking that in a week or so, she would be free to sleep the clock around. Dear God, but she hoped that Allarde would still be alive and well and able to do the same!

CHAPTER 30

"Damnation!" a voice bellowed through the house.

Tory jerked awake when she heard the oath. Jack? She scrambled into the robe she'd borrowed from Mrs. Rainford and darted downstairs, risking tripping over the hem and breaking her neck. It was very early, well before dawn.

The others were racing down, too. "Jack, what's the matter?" Allarde called, several steps ahead of Tory and taking the stairs three at a time.

Tory entered the sitting room as Jack swung around, blazing with rage. Polly was white and Elspeth was sending out calming energy without much success.

"There's a major storm moving in from the Atlantic. It will slam into here within hours today if we can't shift it." He glared at Polly. "The weather mage on watch was sleeping on duty."

"I'm sorry," Polly whispered, tears on her cheeks. "I wasn't really sleeping, but . . . but I wasn't paying as much attention as I should."

"How many men will die because you weren't doing your job?" Jack snarled, his fists clenched. Tory realized that under his fury was cold fear of the oncoming storm.

"Stop!" Nick intervened, stepping between Polly and Jack. "Don't you *dare* touch my sister!"

For a moment Tory thought the two Rainfords would come to blows. Then Cynthia grabbed Jack's arm, ruthlessly digging in her nails. "You know Polly hasn't your strength or range, Jack! Don't blame her for missing the early signs. Just tell us what to do so we can fix this."

"But Jack is right," Polly said as she wiped at her tears. "I wasn't trying hard enough. If I had, I might have felt the storm sooner."

Jack made a visible effort to master himself. "I'm sorry, Polly, I shouldn't have yelled at you like that. But we need to get to work on that storm system *now*! All of us. Get yourselves together and make the circle. Every minute counts."

"Do you want me, too?" Mrs. Rainford asked.

"I said all of us, and I meant it." Jack ran stiff fingers through his blond hair. "Please—if everyone can forgive me in advance. I'm going to be swearing and difficult and impossible until we head this storm off. *If* we do."

"Forgiven," Allarde said as he began moving chairs into a circle. "If you need help swearing, just ask."

That surprised an uneven smile from Jack as he dropped onto the sofa. "That part I can manage on my own. Now everyone *move*!"

Even with only one water closet, the whole group was assembled within five minutes. They took the same positions as the first time they'd done a weather circle, except that Polly traded places with Cynthia and sat next to Tory.

When the circle was complete, Tory said, "We're all upset, but energy will flow best when we're relaxed. Take a deep breath." She made her voice light. "I have a new image—not a driver and seven horses but an electric torch with seven batteries. Jack is the torch, and we're the batteries who will supply him power."

"And I lit up like a torch," he said ruefully. "Tory is right. Relax. Let your energy flow freely. We have maybe a one-in-four chance of deflecting this storm."

"Not bad odds," Allarde observed. "We can do this."

Tory felt the separate energy lines smooth out as people consciously relaxed. Voice low and controlled, Jack said, "And so we begin. . . ."

It took only a few minutes for Tory to decide that the torch and battery comparison didn't work. They were a team of horses and Jack was driving them hard, like Apollo hurling the chariot of the sun through the heavens.

But this was a chariot of storms, not light. They swept west over the Atlantic, riding the winds, diving into the waves and whorls. Passive but powerful, the circle fueled Jack's talent with their magic as he leaned into the fierce wheel of wind and rain. If they hadn't already worked together once with Tory braiding and maximizing the individual talents, they might have broken down from this strain.

Slowly, relentlessly, by sheer brute force, Jack built the air and winds he needed to deflect the storm as it drew nearer and nearer to the British Isles. Dimly, Tory was aware of the passing of time, of her growing exhaustion, of the numbness of her backside.

She was in a near trance when Mrs. Rainford said, "I should take a quick break to ring up the school to say I won't be in. Unless that would be too disruptive, Jack?"

"You can get up and even go to work if you have the energy, Mrs. R.," he said hoarsely. "We've just about mastered this beast. I'm putting the finishing touches on."

"I'm off then." Mrs. Rainford stood and put Tory's hand in Allarde's before leaving. Allarde squeezed her fingers, putting wordless intimacy into the gesture. Tory smiled, her energy lifting a little even though the circle was diminished by Mrs. Rainford's departure.

Now that she was alert again, she saw how Jack had shoved the storm into an amazing right angle turn that sent it northward over the Irish Sea between Britain and Ireland. They had achieved their goal, but at a high cost of magical and physical power.

After a few more minutes, Jack said wearily, "We've done what we can. Everyone can let go now."

The strands of Tory's energy braid unwove with startling speed as mages pulled back into themselves. There was a whimper from Tory's left and Polly's hand went limp. Tory opened her eyes to see the girl fold over like a rag doll onto Nick's lap. He put an arm around her. "Good job, little sister."

She didn't respond. He shook her shoulder, but she still lay limply across him. "She's out like a light," Nick said, worried. "She isn't hurt, is she?"

Elspeth was as fine drawn as silver wire, but she managed to lean over and rest her hand on Polly's head. After a long moment, she said, "No permanent damage, but she's going to sleep for a very long time."

Tory bit her lip, knowing how much the brigade would miss one of the weather mages. Polly's absence would also create additional pressure on the two remaining.

Allarde broke the silence to say, "I'll take her up to her bed."

He was the only one left with the strength to carry the girl, Tory realized. She looked around the circle with her inner senses open so she could evaluate their energy. Polly was a gray flicker, having pushed herself relentlessly to make up for what she saw as her failing. Most of the others were little better off.

Only Allarde burned a little more brightly. In this weary morning, she saw the full dimensions of his strength and his protectiveness. She would have given anything she owned to burrow into his arms and rest.

"The worst of the storm has been deflected, but it's going to require constant work to keep it from turning back," Jack said bleakly. "And in spite of our best efforts, there's going to be more wind and surf in the channel for the next couple of days. More waves to knock the ships around, fewer clouds to provide cover."

Tory made an effort to collect herself. "It's still better than a full-blown storm, which would have stopped the evacuation cold, probably for good."

Her voice barely audible, Elspeth asked, "Is the situation stable enough that we can all get some rest?"

Jack buried his face in his hands and exhaled roughly. "This storm can't be left untended. Cynthia, would you be able to take a watch while I rest?"

Cynthia made a sound perilously close to a whimper. It was hard to recognize her as the fashionable Lady Cynthia Stanton. Her hair was tangled, there were circles under her eyes, and her oversized nightclothes were badly rumpled. Tory thought she'd never looked more worth knowing.

"I can't right away, but give me four hours." Cynthia got to her feet wearily. "Can you manage that long? If you do, I think I can take a double watch after, if I have help from one of the general mages."

"I can manage four hours, but I'll need help," Jack said, his voice muffled by his hands. "I hate to ask when I've already asked so much of everyone."

"I'll be your second for this watch," Allarde said. "Tory, can you support Jack while I take Polly upstairs?"

If Allarde could keep going for hours more, she could manage a few minutes. "Of course. Take the time to splash some cold water on your face."

Nick said, "I'll second Cynthia on the next watch. Since I have a bit of weather magic, maybe I can help her with that as well as general power."

"That would be good," Cynthia said numbly as she headed out the door. "If I sleep through the alarm clock, will someone wake me? Someone female."

"A pity you just qualified that." Jack lifted his head from his hands, a trace of amusement in his eyes. "I was all set to volunteer."

Glad to know that humor hadn't entirely died, Tory got to her feet. By the time she finished stretching her cramped muscles, Allarde had gently lifted Polly from her brother's lap and everyone but Jack had left the sitting room.

Tory reached out to Jack with her energy and discovered that he needed to have his anxiety smoothed out as well as requiring augmentation for his depleted power. She sent calming energy and linked with him to help with the weather. The patterns over the British Isles and northern France were stable but filled with tension. It was easy to imagine the weather sliding out of control if it didn't have constant attention.

Not quite ready to sit again, she crossed to the window and parted the blackout curtains. It was morning, still early. Mrs. Rainford was pedaling toward the road on her bicycle, a two-wheel contraption that made Tory appreciate a nice horse. Tory didn't envy the older woman having to endure a long day in the classroom. But Mrs. Rainford had deep reserves. She'd changed her clothes, brushed her hair, and was looking somewhat revived as she pedaled off to her school.

It occurred to Tory that fresh air would be invigorating. She opened the window halfway and inhaled deeply before she subsided on the sofa cushion beside Jack. She took his hand and the energy flow between them increased. Wryly she said, "This isn't fun anymore."

"True, but I now have a better understanding of what it means to be a soldier." He leaned wearily into the sofa. "Thanks for the extra energy, Tory. Maybe I'll survive the next four hours after all."

"You will. Allarde is in slightly better shape than the rest of us." Reminding herself it was only for a few minutes, she managed to send Jack a bit more power. "You were splendid, Jack. I wouldn't have thought a storm that size could be turned aside."

"It couldn't have been done if the weather brigade didn't have so many powerful mages." He squeezed her hand a little, his touch comradely, not romantic. "I was overconfident because the first two days were too easy. I forgot that no matter how powerful a weather mage, he has to work with the raw materials the world supplies."

"And this time, the world supplied difficult weather."

Jack rubbed his face with his other hand. "I feel like a beast for the way I shouted at poor Polly. She might have picked up on the storm a little sooner if she'd been more alert, but her range isn't fully developed, and now she's temporarily burned-out. You must have felt how hard she was working."

"She was at her limit," Tory agreed. "When she wakes up, she'll realize you were shouting mostly because you were furious with yourself for not being able to work nonstop for days on end."

He sighed. "You're right, that was the real reason for my temper."

"Of *course* I'm right," she said loftily. "I'm a mage, you know."

He laughed a little at that.

Allarde returned and extended a hand to Tory to help her from the sofa. She came up lightly with his help, feeling the tingling power of his touch. "I'll take over now, Tory. Sleep well."

She gave him a private smile. "You do the same when Nick comes on watch. Even you need rest sometimes."

Jack said, "It's a godsend that you have such reservoirs of power,

Allarde. We couldn't have moved that storm if you hadn't been able to contribute so much." He covered a yawn. "I always thought aristocrats were worthless, not knowing how to do anything but gamble away their fortunes and give orders to people like me."

Allarde smiled. "A few of us have our uses." He settled down on the sofa, stretching his long legs out in front of him. "Time to tweak your storm again?"

Tory left them to it, profoundly grateful to be heading to her bed. But as she climbed tiredly up the stairs, she wondered how long the weather brigade could keep up such a grueling pace.

CHAPTER 31

Wednesday morning, Tory went down to breakfast feeling halfway human again. The frayed weather brigade had made it through Tuesday, though Jack and Cynthia were hard-pressed to keep the waters of the channel reasonably calm. The other mages contributed as much power as they could manage, since they couldn't afford to lose a second weather worker.

Most of the weather brigade was down for an early breakfast, and energy levels were near normal. Mrs. Rainford had scrambled up a very large pan of eggs with cheese, bread was ready for toasting, the eternal teapot was steaming hot, and the wireless was giving the latest news. By this time, Tory no longer marveled at the miracle of the wireless. She merely listened while she collected breakfast for herself.

She was shaking her head when she sat down between Nick and

Elspeth. "They keep saying the same things over and over. The BEF is trapped on the coast, the Belgians are thought to be close to surrender, and disaster is imminent. Mrs. R., have you heard anything more promising through your scrying?"

"In fact, yes." The teacher was seated at the table having a second cup of tea before heading to work. "I heard a discussion about Hitler's Panzer tanks. Several days ago they stopped before sweeping into Dunkirk, apparently because of marshy ground."

"A pity they didn't go forward and get swallowed up by the marshes!" Nick said.

"Sadly, the Nazis aren't fools." Mrs. Rainford spread currant preserves on her toast. "They were about to move again on Dunkirk, but instead they're heading south to join the fighting there. Bad for the Allies to the south, but good for the evacuation."

"That's good to know," Allarde said as he took a second serving of eggs. "I'm glad we have our private line into Dover Castle."

"I believe I've figured out why I'm able to eavesdrop there so well," Mrs. Rainford said. "A cousin of mine works in the naval headquarters. She and I grew up together, and I suspect she has some magical ability herself. Everyone from Admiral Ramsay on down is working nonstop, so as long as she's there, I can connect through her." She took a bite of toast. "The evacuation code name is Operation Dynamo."

"Any news about the small boats they've been organizing?" Nick asked.

"I almost forgot to mention that. The first convoy of small ships should leave Ramsgate this evening, with more to follow from the other ports. Most of the evacuees will go to Dover, Ramsgate, Folkestone, and Margate," his mother said. "But there are Lackland boats in the volunteer armada."

Nick was about to ask more when Polly appeared in the kitchen door, her face ghostly pale. Conversation stopped. It was her first appearance since her collapse after the storm circle.

"Polly, I'm so glad you're up!" Tory greeted her. "How are you feeling?"

The girl's face twisted. "My magic is gone! There's nothing left!"

Her words evoked gasps of shock and sympathy. Elspeth cut through the other reactions by saying firmly, "Your magic isn't gone permanently. Intense magical work is known to cause temporary paralysis, but the power does come back. It just takes time."

Polly caught her breath, hardly daring to hope. "How much time?"

"It varies," Elspeth said. "Probably several days. Perhaps longer."

"Too long for me to be able to help during the evacuation," Polly said glumly. "I suppose I should go to school."

"The whole southeast coast is in turmoil because of the evacuation, so classes aren't covering much," her mother said. "Though it's not a glamorous job, you could stay home and run the household. I would if I were here, but I'm not, so if you're willing . . ."

"Of course I am!" Polly said, her expression brightening. "You get on to work, Mum. I'll make sure everyone is fed properly and the house doesn't become a sty."

Tory guessed that Polly was grateful to continue as part of the weather brigade even if she couldn't join in the magic. Exhausting though the work was, the Irregulars shared a warm camaraderie unlike anything Tory had ever experienced.

"That's settled then." Mrs. Rainford stood. "I'm off now. Rule, Britannia!" She hugged Polly on her way outside.

Tory glanced at the clock. "Time I got to work. Cynthia, you're on watch with me, aren't you?"

"For my sins," the other girl said, but her insults no longer carried any sting.

Jack had been working his watch while having breakfast and listening to the news. With the weather steady and his energy recovering, he could do two things at once, at least for a short time. "Shall we hand over the watch in the sitting room?"

Cynthia nodded, but before they could move from the kitchen, Nick said, "Tory, Cynthia, after this watch, I'll drive you into Dover. I'll do another run later in the day. We all need some fresh air, a change of scenery, and a chance to see the results of our work at first hand."

"Will you buy me some fish and chips while we're out?" Tory asked.

He grinned. "It's a deal."

Tory went off to her watch feeling cheerful at the prospect of getting out for a bit. But by the time the watch ended, she was in need of a real break because they'd had to ride the weather hard. Despite their best efforts, sharp winds were blowing over the channel, causing more surf on the Dunkirk beaches and blowing smoke away from the town so the Luftwaffe could see to bomb the beach.

But they were able to keep the water calmer than usual for this time of year, which counted as success under these conditions. Tory had given up striving for perfection and was willing to settle for "the best we can manage."

Jack and Allarde replaced Cynthia and Tory. Tory had to fight the desire to wrap her arms around Allarde whenever they were in the same room, and from the light in his eyes, he felt the same, so probably it was just as well they wouldn't be confined in Nick's Morris Oxford for the expedition into Dover.

Cynthia claimed the backseat so she could doze on the drive into Dover. Tory sat in front with Nick, too interested in the journey to nap. The road was busy, with great lumbering army trucks moving in both directions as well as the usual autos and lorries.

Along the way, Nick pointed out a train racing along a track in the distance. "Southern Railway is running as many extra trains as they can put together to get the evacuees out of Dover. I think everyone in Britain is helping, or wishing they could."

She nodded. "It's fortunate that we're a seafaring nation and so many people have boats that can be used in the evacuation."

"I wish I could take *Annie's Dream* over," Nick said wistfully. "I keep thinking that if I was there, I'd be able to find my father. I do have finder talent, though I haven't had the time to develop it."

"Many people can sail boats to Dunkirk, but we're the only ones who can keep the weather tamed," Tory pointed out.

His hands tightened on the steering wheel. "I wish I could do both."

As they neared Dover, Tory remembered that Elspeth thought Tory might be able to connect with the other members of the weather brigade over a distance. The time was right to test the theory, so Tory closed her eyes, centered her mind, then reached out, visualizing a golden line stretching out to her friend. *Elspeth? Elspeth?*

She felt as if she were trying to identify fabrics by touch while blindfolded, but after several mental calls, she felt a surprised response from her friend. Nothing as clear as words, but a distinct sense of pleased recognition coming from Elspeth.

Delicately, Tory imagined drawing healing energy toward herself. After a moment, Elspeth began to help. Not wanting to tire the other girl, Tory closed that off and offered power in return. Elspeth accepted some, then politely ended it when they were in balance. Grinning, Tory thought, *Farewell,* and withdrew. This ability to send or receive power over a distance could prove useful.

"Why are you smiling like you were just handed a cream cake?" Nick asked.

"Elspeth thought that with my connecting talent, I might be able to connect with people over a distance. So I just tried and was able to reach Elspeth," Tory explained. "We couldn't actually talk, but we could identify each other and I was able to send and receive energy. I don't know if it would work over longer distances, but I was able to manage these few miles."

"We're all learning so much about what we can do!" Nick said. "These last days have been like a university course in mage craft."

Tory chuckled. "I used to wish I could go to Oxford or Cambridge, but of course girls can't, so this will have to be my university experience."

"Girls can go to Oxbridge now," Nick said. "Mum went to Lady Margaret Hall in Oxford."

"She *did*?" Tory asked with delight. "I must talk to her about it."

Since they were heading down into Dover, Nick said, "The harbor is going to be berserk, but I know a place to park that's high enough to give us an overall view of the port, plus I have two pairs of binoculars in the boot."

"Binoculars? Boot? I really need a 1940 dictionary!" Tory said.

"Binoculars are like . . ." He thought. "Two spyglasses bound together so you see for long distances. The boot is a compartment in the back of the motorcar to carry things."

"Are we there?" Yawning, Cynthia sat up and looked around.

Dover was electric with excitement, anxiety, and purpose. Tory felt it powerfully and guessed her companions did, too. The eyes of the world were on Dunkirk and Dover this week.

The side street Nick parked on led right down to the harbor, which was jammed with vessels and people. As she climbed from the motorcar, Tory glanced up at Dover Castle, which loomed over the town from the cliff. It was ancient, she knew, close to a thousand years old. "Strange to think that Admiral Ramsay and his staff, including your mother's cousin, are working away in the tunnels up there."

"And probably getting even less sleep than the weather brigade," Nick said.

"I hope the admiral's tunnels are more comfortable than the ones at Lackland." Cynthia shaded her eyes with one hand as she looked down at the harbor. Tory thought rather waspishly that it wasn't fair that Cynthia managed to look elegant even in the oversized clothing of a middle-aged schoolteacher.

Turning her attention to the harbor, Tory exclaimed, "You weren't joking about the craziness! Ships are parked three deep at the quay."

"Unloading as fast as they can so they can cross back again. The newspaper says they can't take the shortest route across the Straits of Dover because Nazi artillery along the French coast are shelling our ships." Nick opened the back of the motorcar and drew out two devices. "Here are the binoculars."

Tory peered cautiously through the device, and sucked in her breath when the turmoil of the port was abruptly right in front of her. "I feel like I'm on the quay!"

Cynthia looked through the other pair. "They're taking wounded men off the ships," she said in a hushed voice. "Some are being treated right there on the quay."

"Others are being given food. Supplies must be very short for the troops in Dunkirk," Tory added. "The ships look like they've been damaged. German flying machines, I suppose?" She passed her binoculars to Nick.

"There's a destroyer, and a minesweeper, and a passenger ferry," he said as he studied the docked vessels. "As you say, they're banged up, but at least they're still sailing." Soberly, he returned the binoculars to Tory.

"So many men," she whispered. One ship must just have arrived, because the decks were packed with soldiers as tightly as herring in a barrel. If the seas had been rough, they would never have been able to evacuate as many men.

Soldiers were pouring off the vessel that was docked right on the quay, most of them wearing filthy uniforms colored somewhere between tan and brown. Their metal helmets looked like inverted saucepans.

As she watched, a woman who'd been fighting her way through the crowd flung her arms around a battered, weary man. He buried his face in her hair and clutched her as if he'd never let go. Tory's throat tightened as she wondered if the woman had some finder ability that against all the odds had miraculously brought her to the right place at the right time. A lump in her throat, she said, "Thank you for bringing us here, Nick. This certainly illustrates the importance of what we're doing."

Cynthia nodded as she handed her binoculars to Nick. "I just saw a boy not much older than we are get off the ship, then kneel and kiss the ground."

"I'm going to need those fish and chips," Tory said. "I can't think of better fuel for more weather working."

CHAPTER 32

By the end of Wednesday, all the Irregulars had visited Dover and Nick was muttering that it was a good thing petrol wasn't rationed yet. Tory thought the expeditions were an inspired idea, though. Besides the pleasure of getting out, everyone returned from Dover with renewed commitment to their work.

Polly efficiently prepared breakfast the next morning. Tory envied her the competence she'd acquired because both her parents worked and the three children had all had to do chores. Today's breakfast was a steaming pot of oatmeal porridge liberally laced with dried currants and the golden raisins called sultanas. With milk and a bit of honey, it was delicious.

Having finished her breakfast, Mrs. Rainford said, "I have a little time before I need to leave for school. Shall I see if I can scry the small ships heading over the channel to help in the evacuation?"

"Yes," Nick said firmly. "You can tell us they're sailing smoothly because the water isn't as rough as usual and even sailors who've never been out of sight of land are racing to Dunkirk and no one is getting seasick."

"I'll get my scrying bowl." Mrs. Rainford took a small crystal bowl from a cupboard. "Tory, you haven't done any scrying with us, have you? This bowl was my grandmother's, a wedding gift that she passed to me when I married. I believe she had the same kind of foretelling magic I do, though I'm not sure she was aware of it."

She handed the bowl to Tory, who was surprised at how alive it felt in her hands. "There's magic in the crystal," she said as she set it on the table. "Perhaps it's been used so much that it's absorbed power from the users."

"That would explain why it works best of all my bowls." Mrs. Rainford filled the bowl with water halfway and placed it on the table, then added several drops of ink with an eyedropper. The ink swirled into the water, turning it blue-black.

"I didn't know ink was used," Tory said. "I've not done any scrying. I was about to study it in the Labyrinth when we were raided."

Sliding into teacher mode, Mrs. Rainford said, "The ink isn't necessary, but it's how I was taught, and it works for me. Scrying is just a matter of looking into something to see images, you know. It can be water, a crystal ball, fire, a candle flame, mirrors—anything that works for you. I don't always see the images very clearly, but sometimes I hear voices."

She cupped the bowl with her hands. "When you have your bowl or candle ready, it's just a matter of relaxing and concentrating on the water." She closed her eyes and slowed her breathing. Gradually her expression relaxed. "I'll start with looking at the evacuation headquarters under Dover Castle."

Opening her eyes, she gazed into the inky water, not focusing. After a minute or two, she said, "The evacuation is going well, but there are losses. A naval destroyer was sunk, I think. Maybe more than one. Others are damaged. But the work goes on."

"You're better than the wireless, Mrs. R.," Jack said. "Your news is more up-to-date. Can you see what's going on at Dunkirk?"

She closed her eyes, as if blinking away the vision of naval headquarters, then looked into the dark water again. "There's still smoke pouring from the town and the bombed harbor. There's a passenger ferry pulling up to the mole. That's a thin breakwater that wasn't designed to have huge ships berthing against it. Bad piloting could smash the mole to bits, but it's the closest thing to a pier that's still intact. The men are boarding the ferry so quickly!" She bit her lip. "Wounded men are being carried on."

Nick asked, "What about the small ships?"

Mrs. Rainford closed her eyes again, then gazed into the bowl. "Heavens! They're pouring across the channel, boats of all sizes."

Elspeth said, "If Tory added her special power, might you see even more?"

"It's worth a try." Tory moved to stand behind the older woman's chair. As she placed her hands lightly on Mrs. Rainford's shoulders, she asked, "Does this make any difference?"

"It *does*! The images just became much clearer. Can you see anything over my shoulders, Tory?"

Tory looked down, letting her gaze drift as she mentally asked for a sight of the Dunkirk beaches. To her surprise, she began to see vague images. Her heart constricted at the sight of mile after mile of stoic troops waiting and praying. She wasn't sure if the images were in the water or in her mind. No matter. They felt true.

She turned her attention to the evacuation fleet. "I see ships, lots of them, though that doesn't tell us anything we didn't know. Do you see anything new, Mrs. R.?"

Mrs. Rainford gasped, her hands spasming so hard that water

sloshed from the bowl and the smooth surface vanished into ripples. "Tom! I saw Tom!"

"Dad!" In an instant, Nick and Polly were beside her, staring into the bowl.

"Is he all right?" Polly demanded. "Where is he?"

"Give me a moment." Their mother's hands were shaking so badly she had to release the bowl so the water would smooth out.

When Mrs. Rainford regained her control, she clasped the bowl again, peering in anxiously. "He . . . he looks all right, except for a crude bandage around his left forearm. But so tired and filthy!"

"Is he waiting on the beach or by the mole?" Nick asked.

His mother frowned. "I don't think he's in Dunkirk yet. He seems to be marching with his unit. He's helping another man. I . . . I recognize the soldier he's helping. His name is George and he's a boy from Lackland that your father taught."

"Some of the BEF troops who were farthest from Dunkirk might still be marching there," Elspeth said. "But surely he's close now."

"That settles it." Nick straightened, his expression grim and very adult. "I'm going to go get him in *Annie's Dream*."

His mother spun around so quickly that Tory had to jump clear. "You'll do no such thing, Nicholas Rainford!" she said vehemently. "The *Dream* is too small for the channel and too large for one person to handle. You're not taking her anywhere."

"I'll go with him," Polly said flatly. "I might not be able to do weather work, but I'm a better engineer than Nick. The two of us can manage the trip."

"Neither of you is going anywhere! You can't be spared for what would probably be a wild goose chase, Nick." Mrs. Rainford stared down at the bowl. "Even if . . . if Tom makes it to Dunkirk, how could you ever find him in such a crush of troops? There are hundreds of thousands of men there! Let the Royal Navy bring him home."

"I've a talent for finding," Nick said stubbornly. "If I'm there by the beaches, I *know* I can find him."

"We need you here," Jack said. "With one less mage, any kind of emergency would break us."

"I'm *going*!" Nick said. "I'm sorry the rest of you will have to work harder, but this is my father. I'll only be gone a day or so."

Tory said slowly, "Elspeth and I experimented and found that I can reach people over distances. It worked between here and Dover. I might be able to keep Nick connected to the circle well enough to stand his usual shifts."

"I absolutely forbid it!" Mrs. Rainford's voice broke with anguish. "Your father and Joe are already gone, Nick, perhaps never to return. Am I to lose my whole family to this damnable war?"

The room fell silent until Allarde said quietly, "If Nick and Polly go, they will return, Mrs. Rainford. I'm sure of it."

Tears were bright in her eyes. "Do you have foretelling talent, Lord Allarde?"

"Some. It isn't consistent, but I have flashes of certainty, and I just had one. I believe Polly and Nick will make it to Dunkirk and back safely." He hesitated. "I also think they're the best hope for your husband and the other men in his unit. I'm not as clear about that, though. They may not be rescued."

Mrs. Rainford closed her eyes, her face twisted. "This isn't only my decision. Jack and Cynthia are already stretched to the limit. What if Tory can't channel energy from Nick, who won't be able to focus if he's being attacked by the Luftwaffe? Nick and Polly are both good sailors, but can they handle the *Dream* in a war zone?"

Jack bit his lip. "If there's a chance that Tory can connect with Nick when we need him, I'm willing to let him go. I'd do the same if it could have saved my father."

Cynthia sighed. "If working harder gives your husband a chance, I'll do my best."

"I'll sail with Nick and Polly," Allarde said. "I've been sailing many times. I wouldn't want to captain the boat, but I can follow orders."

Tory gasped in horror. Allarde had seen a bloody death for himself and now he was volunteering to go into a war zone? "No!" she cried. "Not you, too!"

His gaze met hers, sad but implacable. "I must do this, Tory. If I'm along, the trip will be safer for everyone. I'm sure of it."

"Do you see yourself coming back with Nick and Polly?" she asked, her voice edged. "Or doesn't your certainty go that far?"

He hesitated. "You know foretelling is almost impossible for oneself."

Tory realized she and Allarde were holding another conversation under the one everyone else heard. She wanted to cry out that he'd foreseen his own end so he must not go, but she could not betray the most private self he'd revealed to her.

But damn him! Because he wanted to die like a man and thought doom was inevitable, he was creating a self-fulfilling prophecy. Expecting death, he was hurling himself directly into harm's way.

Jack was frowning. "I think Cynthia and I could get by without Nick, but not without Nick and Allarde both. If Tory can't connect to you, this won't work."

Nick looked at Tory, his gaze pleading. "Do you think you could channel Allarde and me over a distance, Tory? You're the key to making this work. Maybe whoever is piloting won't be able to send power to the weather mage on duty, but with Polly and me both available to pilot, you could channel Allarde and me at different times."

"He's right," Jack said. "We can't let Nick and Allarde both go unless Tory can feed their power to us while they're away. Without them, Cynthia and I would be as burned-out as Polly before another day passed. So it all hinges on whether Tory can keep the mages on the boat in touch with the weather workers on land."

Tory stared at her pigheaded, heroic friends, wanting to wring multiple necks, yet she could understand everyone's position. Nick and Polly were willing to risk their lives in the hope of finding their father, Mrs. Rainford wanted her husband back but not at the cost of her children's lives, Allarde was convinced he was going to die and wanted to go heroically, and Jack was reminding the others that weather working was still their most critical task since it could mean life or death for thousands of men.

Anger faded, replaced by bleak despair. They were at war and there was no safe place. Even if she could persuade Allarde to stay here, the Luftwaffe could start bombing the English coast at any time. Giant cannon could bombard the ports from German ships. Even staying in Lackland was no guarantee of Allarde's survival.

Despair was replaced by clear, cool certainty. "I'm quite sure I can connect us between ship and shore," she said. "But I'll be able to do it better from *Annie's Dream*. I'm going, too."

There was an explosion of protest from Jack, Nick, and Allarde, with Allarde's voice cutting over the others. Aloud he exclaimed, "You can't risk yourself there, Tory! You *can't!*" while silently his eyes said, "*I might die, but I need to know you're all right.*"

"I am much less fragile than I look." Her lips twisted. "Someone once said I was as strong as tempered steel, and I am. I've also had some sailing experience, so I can help on the crew."

"Three people will be enough crew without you," Nick retorted. "You should stay here with the weather brigade."

Tory's gaze met Allarde's, and she hoped he could hear her thinking that there would be ice-skating in hell before she would let him join Operation Dynamo without her. "Allarde, do you have a foretelling about whether or not I'll come back safely, like Nick and Polly?"

She could see that he wanted to lie and tell her she'd be risking her life if she joined the crew, but he was too honest. Aloud he said,

"No. I have no idea either way." His eyes said, *"I care too much to be able to foretell for you."*

She didn't have any foretelling sense, either, nor any sense of destiny. Her feelings were primitive and undeniable: She needed to be with Allarde because she cared for him. Stronger than reason was the mad, superstitious belief that he couldn't be killed right in front of her, he *couldn't*!

"You can't go, Tory!" Jack exclaimed. "There would only be three of us left here, and I suspect you won't be able to channel as much power from the boat as we'll need."

"Mrs. R. can call in sick and help with the weather watches. She has the ability." Tory narrowed her eyes at Jack. "Don't waste time arguing with me. I can be just as stubborn as anyone else here—"

"—and that's pretty darned stubborn!" Nick muttered.

Ignoring him, she continued. "And if I'm going to link people together for the weather work, it will be from *Annie's Dream*."

"No," Allarde said softly, his heart in his eyes. "Please . . . no."

It hurt to hurt him, but she held her ground. "Yes."

Cynthia's bleak eyes revealed that she'd seen the silent dialogue between Tory and Allarde and realized that he would never be hers. Hiding her regrets with a bored shrug, she said, "If Tory wants to be a dead heroine rather than a live mageling, let her go. Maybe she'll be useful."

"Tory holds the winning hand," Elspeth said, her calm voice cutting through the tumult of emotions. "Nick needs Polly and Allarde on the boat, Jack and Cynthia need power from Nick and Allarde, and Tory is the only one who can supply it. So either she goes to Dunkirk, or no one does and Captain Rainford and his unit must take their chances with the rest of the troops."

The arguments continued awhile longer, but no matter. Tory had won, and they all knew it.

CHAPTER 33

Once everyone accepted that Tory was going to sail on *Annie's Dream,* preparations for departure moved quickly. Mrs. Rainford called her school and talked through a scarf to say she'd come down with her children's cold, she had laryngitis, and she'd be unable to teach today and tomorrow. Yes, surely by Monday she'd be recovered enough to return to her classes.

While her mother was busy spinning lies, Polly took Tory up to her room. "You're going to have to wear trousers to crew. You're a bit smaller than I, so I'll give you the boating outfit I've just about out-grown. The trousers were cut down from Nick's castoffs." She dug into her wardrobe. "Here's a shirt, also Nick's, and I'll get one of the family guernseys."

"What's a guernsey?" Tory asked. "Something from Guernsey Island?"

Polly nodded. "A fisherman's jumper. The design has been knitted by Guernsey islanders forever. Very comfortable and warm, and the wool is so tight it resists water." She tossed a dark blue knitted garment to Tory. "Women knit variations in the patterns so they can identify drowned bodies."

"Delightful." Tory examined the garment. "I trust no one drowned in this one?"

"Not that I know of. Guernseys last so long they get handed down in families. We have half a dozen different sizes from small child to my father's. I suppose Allarde will wear that one since it would be the best fit." She handed the other garments to Tory. "I just outgrew the blue guernsey and have moved into an olive green one."

"I've gone from wearing your clothes to wearing Nick's. Is this progress?" Tory stripped off her skirt and blouse. "The guernsey smells like a sheep."

"When it gets wet, you'll smell like a sheep, too." Polly knelt and groped under her bed. "I have a pair of old boat shoes that should fit if you wear thick socks. They're badly scuffed, but the rubber soles have tread cut in so they don't slip on wet decks."

Tory donned the worn white shirt that must date to when Nick was a child. The cotton was wonderfully soft. Next came faded tan trousers, equally worn. As she belted up the loose waist, she said, "If my mother could see me now!"

"I suspect the countess would not approve." Polly pulled on her own trousers. "My grandmother certainly doesn't like seeing me dressed like a 'scruffy little boy,' which is how she describes my sailing clothes. But they're so comfortable!"

Tory agreed. Comfort mattered if she was going to be wearing the same garments for a day or more. The dark blue guernsey hung halfway to her knees and should do a good job of protecting her from cold channel winds.

"You'll need a hat to warm your head and hide your hair." Polly briefly disappeared into the folds of the green guernsey as she pulled it over her head. Emerging, she said, "It's probably best if we don't look much like girls."

"The gentlemen were horrified at the idea of us crewing on the boat," Tory said as she sat on the floor to put on heavy socks and the boat shoes. "Not so much Nick, but Jack and Allarde."

Polly pulled on her own shoes. "Nick would be just as protective if he didn't need me to act as engineer and you to channel power back to the weather brigade. Have you ever crewed on a boat?"

Tory grinned. "Well—I've been a passenger on several sailing yachts."

Polly's mouth quirked up. "That's what I suspected. But an extra pair of hands will be useful, and you'll be busy with magic half the time."

Tory braided her hair quickly and began securing the braids to her head with Polly's clever modern hairpins. "Are you anxious about us going to Dunkirk?"

"Terrified," Polly said bluntly. "But I'd never forgive myself if I did nothing and my father doesn't . . . doesn't make it home."

"I know Nick is determined to find him, but . . . it may be harder to find a particular person than he thinks, even for a determined and talented finder," Tory said hesitantly, torn between realism and not wanting to crush hope.

"I know it's a very long shot," Polly said soberly. "But I feel . . . I guess it's superstition. I want to believe that if I help rescue other fathers and sons and brothers, there will be someone to rescue mine."

"If everyone feels that way and pitches in to help, a lot more of those fathers and sons and brothers will be saved." Tory stabbed in the last hairpin, hoping her braids would stay out of the way for as long as necessary. "Ready, honorary sister?"

"Ready." Polly flashed a smile that made her look very like Nick. As they headed to the stairs, she asked, "Are you frightened?"

"I will be when this starts to feel real," Tory said wryly. "Now it feels more like a really strange dream."

Downstairs Tory paused in the door of the sitting room, where Cynthia and Elspeth were working the weather. "We're off now. Wish us luck."

Cynthia scowled at her. "Make sure you bring Allarde back in one piece."

Tory hoped Cynthia wasn't sensing disaster. "We should all be back safely in a day or so with no damage done and stories to tell. I hope no more really dreadful weather systems come through to tire you and Jack out."

Elspeth rose from the sofa and came to give her a hug. "Be careful, Tory. There will be danger all around you."

"As long as it's around and not on top of us!" Tory hugged her friend back, adding under her breath, "I'm sure I can channel energy over distance, but I'm not so sure I can do it in a war zone. I'll do my best."

"I know." Elspeth stepped back, not quite controlling her expression. "I think you need to be on that boat, though I'm not sure why. We'll all do what we have to."

Waiting in the kitchen were all the other sailors plus Mrs. Rainford and Jack, who would go down to the boat and help prepare it. As Polly had predicted, Nick and Allarde wore the same kind of rough, practical clothing as the girls.

Nick's guernsey was brown, while Allarde's gray version brought out of the color of his storm gray eyes, not to mention setting off his fine broad shoulders. He looked more like a pirate than an eligible young lord. An appallingly handsome pirate.

Polly tossed a jaunty red knitted hat to Tory. "Here's a beret for you." She pulled on a similar one knitted in green. "Time to go?"

"It's not too late for you to change your minds," Allarde said, speaking to both girls but with his grave gaze on Tory. "Nick says he and I can handle the *Dream* without any more help."

"Nice try, Allarde," Polly said cheerfully, "but it's not going to work. You may know something about sailboats, but I know how to run the *Dream*'s engine, and I can pilot her as well as Nick. I'm more useful than you are."

When Allarde arched his brows, Nick said, "You're stronger, Allarde, but Polly's right about knowing how to operate the *Dream*. She's a good pilot and the best engineer in the family after my father."

"You don't know any more about mechanized boats than I do, Tory," Allarde pointed out. "If you stay here, there's that much more room for rescuing soldiers."

"I don't take up much space," she retorted. "Accept that I'm going, Allarde. I promise that I'll be useful."

"If you've finished arguing, it's time to go," Mrs. Rainford said. "I've packed cheese and crackers and biscuits in this bag. Enough to keep you going for a few days."

"Thank you, Mrs. R." Allarde took the bulging canvas bag from her. "You've taken very good care of us."

"If that were really true, I'd sink *Annie's Dream* so you couldn't join Operation Dynamo," she said tartly as she headed out the door.

The battered Morris was crowded with six passengers. Mrs. Rainford got behind the wheel while Polly slid across the front seat and was sandwiched cozily between her mother and Nick. Tory guessed that the Rainfords wanted to be as close to one another as they could, which in a motorcar seat was rather close.

Allarde climbed into the back. Tory said, "Short people sit in the middle, I think." She slid across the seat until they were touching shoulder to thigh. Jack sat on her other side, just as close.

Nick said, "That bag of food could go in the back, Allarde."

"It's a short ride so I'll carry it," Allarde said. "In case I get hungry."

Jack laughed, but Tory found why Allarde wanted to ride with the bag spilling over his lap. Underneath it, his hand locked on hers as if he would never let her go. His warm, strong grip made her want to turn into his arms and seek shelter. But that wasn't possible now.

She raised her gaze and again had the sense they were speaking without words. His *"I want you safe,"* met her *"I care for you, and I will not be left behind,"* and merged into mutual acceptance and tenderness. She turned her gaze forward again, but he was still a living presence within her.

All too soon they reached the harbor. Mrs. Rainford parked the Morris and they all piled out. The mournful cries of the gulls made Tory think of doomed spirits.

A white-haired man with a cane sat on a bench outside a weathered shed. His eyes sharpened when he saw them arrive. "Good day now, Mrs. Rainford, Nick. Planning on taking that nice little boat on a cruise to France?"

Nick grinned. "Hello, Mr. Dodge. How did you guess?"

"Who wouldn't want to go? Look how empty the harbor is." He waved his cane at the other piers, where only a handful of rowboats were moored. His face worked for a moment. "I have a grandson in your father's company. I'd be off myself if I was able."

"We'll bring back some BEF troops just for you, and maybe Danny will be one of them." Nick nodded to his companions. "Some friends are going to crew for me, but first we have to take off everything that isn't necessary and get more fuel."

Mr. Dodge fished a key from his pocket. "You can stash your bits and pieces in my shed here. There are cans of fuel you can take, too."

"Thank you! That will save us some time."

"Least I can do," the old man said gruffly. His gnarled hands folded on the head of his cane. "There's a rope ladder in there you might want to take. Could help men climb onto the boat."

The Irregulars all piled on board. Though small, it was designed as a working boat with an engine room and small cabin belowdecks and a tiny wheelhouse to protect the pilot from the weather. Tory estimated that if they packed every available space above and below and in the skiff that could be pulled behind, they might be able to carry twenty-five to thirty men.

As the boys started removing everything that wasn't needed, Polly and Tory cleaned out the galley, which was barely large enough for two small females. They kept tea, mugs, honey, and a kettle to heat water, which Tory could do without lighting a fire. Nick and Mrs. Rainford checked over everything on the boat that could be checked.

As they worked, onlookers gathered. One couple arrived bearing large, full water bottles. "Our boy came home to Folkestone two days ago," the man said. "He told us the troops got powerful thirsty as they waited. They'll want this when you pick 'em up."

Another woman brought two bulging bags of hard candy, a third contributed a large canister of tea, a fourth offered a first aid kit and a large box of bandages, "just in case." Two men pitched in to help load the heavy cans of fuel.

As the group enlarged, Mrs. Rainford muttered an oath under her breath. "The assistant headmistress of my school has just arrived. There goes my pretense of being ill."

"You're looking remarkably healthy for a woman with a streaming cold," the salt-and-pepper-haired headmistress said with dry humor as she approached Mrs. Rainford. "I don't know how you've managed to work at all, Anne. Do what you must, but we expect you back Monday after Tom comes home!"

Mrs. Rainford caught her friend's hand gratefully. "I'll be there, I promise."

There was little left to say, so the final good-byes were more hugs than words. As Mrs. Rainford held Polly, she said fiercely, "Allarde, you had better be right!"

"Don't worry," he assured her. "The *Dream* will be home soon, and you'll all be telling stories about this day as long as you live." He glanced at Tory, his eyes narrowed.

She scowled at him as she hugged Jack. "Do not even *think* of asking again if I'll stay here. Someone needs to chaperone Polly."

As Allarde smiled, Mr. Dodge said incredulously, "You're taking these two little girls to Dunkirk?"

"We're smaller targets," Polly said jauntily as she prepared to cast off.

"Damnation!" Jack kicked at the weathered planking of the dock. "I wish I was coming with you!"

"What you're doing is even more important," Tory said softly.

Jack sighed. "I know you're right. But I don't have to like it."

The old man quoted, "And gentlemen in England now abed / Shall think themselves accursed they were not here."

"Shakespeare," Mrs. Rainford said. "Henry the Fifth inspiring his troops before the battle of Agincourt."

"England won then, and we will again," Allarde said in a voice as compelling as Henry V's must have been.

Polly had gone below and now the engine caught, the roar drowning out the gulls. They pulled away from the dock and Nick turned the little ship toward the channel. As the onlookers broke into applause, Mr. Dodge rose painfully to his feet and saluted.

Engine roaring and Union Jack flying, *Annie's Dream* set off to war.

CHAPTER 34

Tory and Allarde joined Nick at the wheel as they cleared the break-water and entered the choppier waters of the channel. "This is a little late to ask, Nick," Allarde said with humor glinting in his eyes, "but are you sure you know how to run this thing?"

Nick laughed. "Mum would have burned the boat before we boarded if she didn't know how well we can handle her. All three of us spent our summer holidays working on or around the Lackland fishing boats. I know these waters well and this boat even better. She may be small, but she's stouthearted."

Giving thanks she was a good sailor, Tory clutched the edge of the wheelhouse as the boat rolled. "Do we have a particular plan?"

Nick nodded, his eye on the horizon. "We're going to head north to join the little ship convoy out of Ramsgate. There are Royal Navy officers on some of the boats, and they'll know how to avoid sand-banks and minefields."

"Minefields?" she asked, sure the answer wouldn't be good.

"Bombs floating in the water to sink ships unlucky enough to run into them," Nick explained.

"Wonderful," she muttered. "I hope your finder talent is good at locating such things before we become too well acquainted."

"I think it is." Nick stepped aside. "Take the wheel, Tory. I'm going to teach you and Allarde the basics of holding the boat on course."

Tory's first reaction was panic. Her, steer this boat, which suddenly seemed much larger?

"Don't worry, you'll be fine, Tory," Nick said. "The main thing to remember is that the wheel controls the rudder, so you have to turn the opposite direction from where you want to go. Once you get the feel of it, I'll explain the compass."

Reminding herself she couldn't get into much trouble in open water, Tory started to relax. "It takes a lot of strength to keep the wheel straight! You make it look easy."

"That's because you're just a wee bit of a thing," he said teasingly. "I wouldn't give you the wheel in a storm, but you should be able to steer in average conditions."

When Nick was satisfied that Tory understood the basics, he said, "Your turn, Allarde. You said you've done some sailing?"

Allarde changed places with Tory and took the wheel. "I'd do much better driving a coach and four, but I've had some sailing experience."

Tory decided it was time to go below to the engine room. Polly greeted her with a grin and a smudge of oil on her cheek. It was the happiest she'd looked since burning out her magic. "It feels good to be on the water again." Polly patted the noisy, smelly engine. "I want to study engineering when I go to university."

"Do many girls do that?" Tory asked with interest.

"Practically none." Polly laughed mischievously. "That means I'll be the only girl in most of my classes, and won't that be fun!"

Tory joined in. It was good to have something to laugh about.

The river of little ships sailing out of Ramsgate was impossible to miss. "I've never seen so many different kinds of boats," Nick exclaimed as he turned the wheel, arcing the *Dream* toward the convoy.

Equally awed, Tory asked, "Could you name them all?"

"Most. Not all." Nick shaded his eyes with one hand. "There are corvettes and minesweepers, and I think that's a fireboat. From London, maybe. That might be a Dutch barge. Some of the ships are smaller than *Annie's Dream,* too."

He fell silent at they saw a naval destroyer heading back to England. Tory raised the binoculars and saw decks jammed so tightly with men that she wasn't sure they could even turn around. Soon they'd be home, and the destroyer would return for another load. She sent a silent prayer for the ship's safety.

Allarde said, "It must be about time for me to go on weather watch with Jack. Are you ready, Tory?"

"It will be interesting to see how well this works." She took the steps down into the tiny cabin and sat on one of the padded benches that were also berths. The cabin was so narrow she could rest her feet on the opposite bench.

Allarde sat beside her and took her hand between both of his. "This part I like."

"As do I." She fluttered her lashes extravagantly. "I might need Polly to chaperone *me.*"

She was about to connect with his energy when she heard a distant rumble. The harsh, irregular sound caused her to freeze. "Do you hear that?"

His hands were still around hers. "Guns. From Dunkirk."

They had to be loud to be heard over the boat's engine. Telling herself to focus on the task at hand, she closed her eyes and tuned herself to Allarde. His energy was warm. Deep. Strong. Worried.

With Allarde connected, she reached out to Jack. Their minds touched and she felt his relief, though she wasn't sure if it was because he'd doubted if they could work this way, or that he was just glad they were well.

She linked the flow of energy from Allarde to Jack, and felt the stress on Jack diminish. She had to stay as part of the link to keep it flowing, but she contributed little power of her own. Better to conserve it for . . . whatever might come.

By the time Tory and Allarde had finished the weather session, the guns were much louder. Halfway up the steps to the deck, she stopped in her tracks, staring. The cool gray skies of the English Channel had been replaced by the fire and fury of a war zone.

They were nearing Dunkirk and smoke billowed from the burning port, black against the sky. An acrid stench bit Tory's nostrils, overwhelming the scents of the sea.

Ships were everywhere. Little ships moving in both directions, a destroyer berthed at the mole, and a boat burning in between. Perhaps a passenger ferry. Tory prayed it hadn't had been carrying passengers when it was hit.

Grim-faced, Nick stood at the wheel while Polly perched in the bow and scanned the water for mines and dangerous debris. Lesser debris—boots, a helmet, something Tory couldn't bear to look at— bumped the sides of the boat.

Ahead were the wide, sandy beaches of the French coast. Masses of men waited onshore and among the sand dunes, and ragged lines of soldiers had waded out into the water up to their chests.

Behind her, Allarde asked quietly, "Do you want to stay below?"

Shaking her head, she climbed to the top of the stairs and stood aside, keeping one hand on the railing. She'd listened to the wireless and studied the newspapers delivered to the Rainford house, but she was still unprepared for the brutal impact of war.

They were getting near enough to the soldiers to pick out individual faces when a hell-born Nazi airplane screamed straight down from the sky like a rabid banshee. Tory's instant of paralyzed horror was broken when Allarde grabbed her and hauled her down against the wheelhouse, shielding her with his own hard body.

An explosion shattered the air, so close her ears were numbed and debris rattled off the *Dream*. Moments later, a huge wave sent the boat pitching wildly as Nick grimly fought with the wheel to save them from capsizing.

Tory was overwhelmed by cacophony and fear. Allarde's heart hammered against her ear and she had to struggle for breath because he was crushing her, yet his closeness was the only thing keeping her from screaming.

Dear God in heaven, what if Allarde was killed while protecting her? What if he would have been safe if she hadn't insisted on coming? She bit her lip until it bled.

Fear ebbed, leaving Tory shaking. She was here now and it was too late for second thoughts. Though she felt fear in Allarde as well, his voice was calm as he released her. "Welcome to Dunkirk, my lady."

"What was that *thing*?" she asked, trying to match him for calmness, though she was less successful than he was.

"A Stuka dive-bomber," Nick replied. "Technically, a Junker 87. It's designed to stoop like a falcon and drop a bomb from about fifteen hundred feet up. Then it pulls out of the dive. This one sounded like it was going to crash into the *Dream*, but it was aiming at that destroyer over there."

Tory looked and saw that the destroyer's side deck was badly crunched, but the ship seemed seaworthy. "I'm glad we're not a large enough target to interest a Stuka."

Polly had poked her head out of the engine room, oil smudges black against her white face. "Think we'll get used to those things anytime soon?"

"Not used to them," Allarde said. "But next time we won't be quite so startled."

Startled. Tory almost laughed. British understatement in action. He was right, though. Next time one of those monstrosities hurled itself from the sky near her, she'd still be afraid, but not, she thought, panicky.

They continued toward the beach. She tried to identify the different forms of destruction. Bombs exploded with ragged booms, machine guns chattered, artillery shells screamed and then exploded. Other airplanes, fighters, not Stukas, swooped over the mole where the big destroyers were loading men, their machine guns blazing.

She squinted at the fighter. "They seem to be shooting fire. Is that the bullets?"

"Tracers," Nick said tersely. "Some of the bullets have an explosive charge in the base that burns as they travel through the air so the gunner can see where the bullets go."

So they could kill more efficiently. Feeling sick, Tory moved to the wheelhouse. There was a white line around Nick's lips as he tried to watch for danger from all directions. "How are you doing?" she asked.

"Sweet Jesus, Tory," Nick said in anguish. "How can I ever find one man in that mess of people? I thought I'd know where to find him!"

"It may not be possible," she said gravely. "There's so much fear and desperation swirling around Dunkirk that the mental channels are burning with emotion as much as those oil silos. Locating one individual will be difficult. But look at all of these other boats. Your father might already have been picked up and be on his way home."

Nick's face tightened even more. "He's not. Dad is out there somewhere."

"As long as he's alive, he can be rescued. If not by us, by another boat."

Allarde had come up behind her. "In the meantime, we have plenty of work to do," he said calmly. "We get as near the beach as we can and load as many men as we can and we take them out to a larger ship. Then we come back and do it again."

Nick exhaled roughly. "Right you are. I'll take her in now." He turned the boat toward the nearest line of men, who were standing chest-deep in the water. Tory scanned their faces. Most looked so *young*. Some were stoic, some exhausted, some frightened, and all watching the advancing *Dream* as if the boat were their one hope of heaven.

Polly called, "Hard a' port! There's something nasty down there!"

Nick obeyed and the *Dream* moved to the left. Tory sensed danger averted. Maybe one of those horrible mines Nick had described.

Allarde said, "Tory, could you bring up the rope ladders? Time to secure them to the cleats."

Silently she went belowdecks and returned with the armful of rope and bars. Allarde had already launched the skiff so it could be towed behind the *Dream*. Together they secured the ladders so that one hung over each side.

By then they'd reached the closest line of men, and Nick brought the vessel to a vibrating halt. Some of the soldiers could barely keep their heads above the low waves.

Nick halted the boat as Allarde called, "Use the ladder on the other side if you're strong enough. If you need help, come to this side!"

The soldiers split, and the *Dream* rolled to port with the weight of a large man scrambling up the ladder. Allarde called again in a voice of easy authority, "Take it slowly! We don't want the boat to capsize. We won't leave until she's full."

The men took the ladders more carefully. When the next soldier got his head over the railing, he said in an amazed London accent, "Crikey, you're all kids!"

"Yes, but we're kids with a boat," Nick barked. "Want a ride?"

"Too bloody right!" The man scrambled onto the deck and moved out of the way.

Allarde crossed to the side where men who needed help waited. He caught an up-stretched hand and helped lift an exhausted boy aboard.

Tory guided the men below and got them seated as tightly as possible. One ended up sitting on the toilet of the tiny water closet, and the main cabin had eight more, all jammed so tightly they could barely move. They murmured weary thank-yous, some staring when they realized she was a girl.

When the little cabin was packed to the limit, she collected the bandages and first aid kit and climbed onto the deck. Allarde had kicked off his shoes and stripped off the guernsey, and he was down in the water helping those who most needed aid.

She felt a buzz of magic around Allarde and guessed that he was using his lifting ability to make it easier to get the men on board. As he worked, he kept up a stream of soothing words, talking about how they were safe now and all England was cheering them on. A rough voice with a Scottish accent growled, "What about us bluidy Scots?"

Allarde laughed. "You're getting cheered on, too, Angus."

Polly was moving around the deck, dispensing water and hard candies to men who gulped both down thirstily. Tory summoned her modest healing abilities and called out, "Who needs some patching?"

"My mate here needs help," one man said gruffly. "Head wound."

Tory made her way through the press of bodies and set to work.

"I'm so glad I'll get a chance to practice my bandaging!" she said brightly.

That invoked laughter, but an older sergeant said disapprovingly, "Little girls shouldn't be out here."

She snorted. "Neither should big men."

"The little miss has a point," another voice said as Tory set to work cleaning the head wound. There were mutters of agreement. All too soon, the boat was so full that the crew could barely move. Allarde scrambled aboard again, calling, "We'll be back!"

He pulled his guernsey on over his wet clothing as the *Dream* turned slowly, careful of the skiff packed with more men, and headed out to one of the large ships anchored beyond the shallows. The boat handled sluggishly as they moved away from shore, and the large waves made it roll unpleasantly. Tory and Allarde kept an eye on the loaded skiff, where men held on to the gunwales and each other for dear life. But they made it safely to one of the smaller naval vessels.

"Minesweeper," Nick said tersely as he pulled alongside.

While navy sailors helped the evacuees aboard, Polly passed up her empty jugs and called up for more drinking water. By the time all the soldiers were on the naval vessel, the refilled jugs were lowered to her.

The *Dream* pulled away and headed back to the beach. Dusk was falling, but the flames of the burning town kept full darkness at bay. Polly took the wheel from her brother. "Get some rest, at least until we pick up our next load."

Nick nodded tiredly and slumped on the deck against the wheelhouse. Tory realized uneasily that only Nick and Polly had enough skill to pilot the boat under such dreadful conditions. But Tory could help them keep up their strength.

She made a pot of hot, sweet tea, serving mugs of it with chocolate-covered biscuits. By the time they were ready to pick up their second load, they all felt stronger. Less shocked by the horrors around them and the numbing cacophony of sounds.

Day slid into weary night as they worked nonstop, yet still the beaches held masses of men. On the third return to the beach, Tory reached out to Elspeth, with whom she had the closest bond. She hated to admit they would be unable to help the weather mages, but they had no strength to spare. Elspeth seemed to understand and was unsurprised, but Tory could feel her worry.

Once Tory felt magic from one of the men she helped on board. Dutch, she thought, but he spoke French and she was able to ask him his name and assure him that soon he'd be safe. God knew there was no safety in this hellish place where the air stank of fire and fuel and airplanes roared overhead spitting death and mines lurked below the surface, devastation in waiting.

They took turns resting on the benches in the cabin during the quiet runs back to the beach. Tory found sleep impossible. War zones were so *noisy*.

When dawn broke, the sky was dangerously clear and suitable for the Luftwaffe. Tory served a breakfast of cheese and crackers and more tea, knowing her ability to heat water would never be more useful. When and if she made it home, she'd fall on her knees and thank Alice Ripley for teaching her the trick of it.

Wearily, she sat and leaned against the wheelhouse. A beautiful morning in hell.

Polly, who had been leaning against the railing as she finished her tea, said, "Allarde, why not sit down and put your arm around Tory? Everyone knows you're wild about each other, so you might as well enjoy a few minutes together."

Tory wanted to sink through the deck and disappear. "And here I thought we were being so discreet!"

"Apparently not." Allarde sat beside Tory and wrapped an arm around her shoulders. "An excellent idea, Polly. Discretion doesn't seem very important just now."

Tory turned into him, draping her arm across his waist and burying her face against his guernsey. "You smell like a sheep," she said, voice muffled.

He gave a soft laugh. "So do you, my lady." He brushed his fingers over her braids, which had come unpinned. She knew she looked like a pigtailed street orphan, and at the moment, it didn't matter.

It didn't matter at *all*.

CHAPTER 35

Annie's Dream and her increasingly exhausted crew worked through an endless Friday, and the even more endless Friday night that followed. As Saturday dawned and the boat turned from delivering another load of soldiers to a navy corvette, Polly emerged from the engine room to say, "Time to go home. We're running low on fuel."

Tory felt them give a collected sigh of exhausted relief. Except for Nick. He hadn't mentioned his father again, but Tory had felt his desperate tension as he continually scanned the beaches every time they returned for another pickup.

"One more run," he said, his eyes bleak with the knowledge of failure. "A smaller batch because I'm not crossing the channel with more than maybe fifteen passengers, and we can't use the skiff safely."

Polly frowned. "We should go now. As it is, we'll be on fumes by the time we reach Lackland. If we get that far."

"One more run," Nick said flatly. "It would be a pity not to take a few more evacuees all the way home when we have the space."

"Don't be stupid!" his sister snapped, her temper as frayed as his. "Sloppiness like that could get us killed."

"There are so many ships going back and forth that we should be able to get a tow if we run out of fuel." His voice dropped. "Please, Polly. For Dad's sake."

Her eyes spasmed shut, her exhaustion and grief written on her gray face. "All right. One more run. But that will *have* to be the last."

Nick nodded and turned the boat toward the beach for the last time. Too tired to care if they ran out of fuel before they got home, Tory leaned against the wheelhouse just below the smashed corner where bullets from a Messerschmitt's machine guns had taken out chunks of wood. More bullets were buried in the deck. There were even ragged holes ripped through the Union Jack.

The crew wasn't looking any better. Nick and Allarde had developed shadow whiskers, which were particularly noticeable on dark-haired Allarde. Polly had oil smudges beyond counting and Tory was glad there were no mirrors on board because she didn't want to see herself with ragged braids and bloodstains from some of the wounded.

The worst moment of the endless day had been when the fighter had buzzed them. For a ghastly moment Tory had wondered if this was how Allarde would receive the mortal wound he dreamed about, but miraculously no one was hurt. They'd just dropped off a load of passengers, so the *Dream* was almost empty. If the decks had been packed, there would have been serious casualties.

Her spirits lifted at the knowledge that they were about to leave, and boat and crew were intact. She didn't take that for granted, not after seeing ships sunk or blown apart around them.

Nick sighed as they cruised toward the beaches, where countless men still waited for rescue. "It was pretty jolly foolish of me to think I would be able to find Dad here."

"But a noble foolishness," Allarde said. "If you hadn't decided to join Operation Dynamo, that's several hundred fewer men evacuated."

Tory got to her feet and moved behind Nick in the wheelhouse, placing a hand on his shoulder. "For your own peace of mind, do one last search for your father. Maybe my energy will help."

"You're a sport, Tory." He scanned the beach, using both eyes and magic—and halted as he looked north. "Wait! Allarde, can you link in?"

Allarde obliged, one hand on Tory's shoulder and the other on Nick's. The power increased, and Tory felt Nick's muscles tense. "Damnation!" he exclaimed incredulously. "Dad's right there. *He's right over there!*"

Polly darted up from the engine room, her face ablaze with hope. "Are you sure? This isn't wishful thinking?"

"He's there. To the north. His unit only just got here. They had to fight Nazis the whole way." Nick turned the wheel and they headed toward the upper end of the beach. Tory could barely breathe with excitement. If Nick was right, what a gift to take home to Mrs. Rainford!

As the masses of troops thinned out, Nick said, "I think he's in that group of soldiers there, at the end of that jetty made by running army trucks into the water. See?"

Tory squinted and saw a dozen or so men hanging on to the truck that was farthest out into the water. As they neared the jetty, a hoarse voice called, "It's a boat from home, the bloody *Annie's Dream*! Hey, over here! We're from Lackland!"

"Damned if you aren't right!" another man bellowed excitedly. "It's bloody well our turn!"

"Dad!" Polly screamed as she raced to the front of the boat. "Dad, you're here!"

As the *Dream* drifted up to the bedraggled cluster of soldiers, Allarde said, "I'll take the wheel, Nick. You help them board."

Nick didn't stop to argue. He bounded across the deck and started helping wet, tired soldiers aboard. Most of them greeted him by name.

In the babble of voices, Tory deduced that this group from Lackland had enlisted together, and watched out for each other on the long march from Belgium. They must have been one of the last BEF groups to reach Dunkirk, because most of the other troops still waiting for evacuation were French soldiers.

Tory had no trouble picking out Tom Rainford. Not only was the family resemblance strong, but he was the last one in line, making sure that every one of his dozen men was safely on board. He had a filthy bandage on his left forearm, just as Mrs. Rainford had seen in her scrying bowl. Tall, blond, and indomitable, he was Nick in another thirty years.

The last man to board was Captain Rainford. Wearily he took Nick's hand and scrambled onto the deck. He looked ready to collapse, but he managed a smile. "What took you so long, Nicholas?"

Nick threw his arms around his father with rib-bruising force. "Mum is really, really angry with you, Dad!" He held on to his father as if he couldn't quite believe that he had really succeeded in finding the one man he most wanted to save.

"I'm furious, too!" Polly hurled herself into the embrace.

Her father stared at her in shock even as one arm locked around her shoulders. "What the devil is my little girl doing here?"

"Saving lives," she said, tear tracks running down her oil-stained cheeks.

"Nick, you brought your little sister into the middle of a war?" the captain said, still incredulous.

Nick grinned, unabashed. "Polly is as stubborn as the rest of us, Dad. She insisted on coming, and I needed an engineer."

"I'm right here, so you don't need to talk about me in the third person," Polly said tartly. "If you hadn't been fool enough to enlist, Dad, I'd be home practicing my sums instead of dodging Stukas."

"Don't scold him too much, Polly," a younger man said with a grin. "If not for Captain Rainford, our whole company would have been cut up and captured."

Another man chimed in. "We're the rearguard volunteers who held off the Krauts while the rest of the company got away. A good thing the boat didn't leave without us!"

Polly buried her head in her father's ragged army jacket. "A bunch of bloody heroes!" she said, her voice muffled.

"Watch your language, young lady!" her father said in a schoolmaster voice. "You're not too old to be spanked."

She pulled her head back, her eyes narrowing like a furious cat's. "I am a heroine of Dunkirk. Would you *dare*?"

"Absolutely not." He rested his cheek on her head, tears in his eyes. Tory had never seen three people who were so filthy, exhausted, and desperately happy. Softly, Tom Rainford added, "I am so proud of both of you. Now, can we go home?"

"We're on our way, sir." During the Rainfords' reunion, Allarde had brought the boat around so they were facing the channel. "Nick, you'd better take over until we're clear of the debris and mines."

Nick nodded, reluctantly releasing his father. As he picked his way to the wheelhouse, the other soldiers began to settle into comfortable spots. With a smaller group of passengers, there was room to spread out. A sergeant said teasingly, "Sounds like your womenfolk are going to have your hide when you get home, Captain."

"They can have it," Tom said with a grin.

As he took the wheel, Nick said, "Danny, your grandfather Dodge sent us off and I'll bet you a shilling he'll be waiting when we bring you home."

"That's a bet I won't take. The gaffer spends most of his waking hours watching Lackland harbor," retorted a redheaded young man who sat against the railing with his helmet off and something squirming inside his jacket.

Nick blinked. "Danny, your chest is behaving oddly."

Danny unfastened the top buttons of his jacket and a scraggly little dog stuck its head out, eyes bright with interest. "Think my mum will let me have a dog now?"

"If you returned with an elephant, she'd let you keep it." Nick turned his attention to the cluttered waters as he worked his way out. The sea was even more dangerous than when they arrived because of the ever-increasing amount of wreckage.

Tory said, "I'll go below and make tea." She ducked down to the galley, giving the kettle a blast of power to heat the water quickly. She also put most of the remaining food in a bag, so within a few minutes she was distributing biscuits, crackers, and small pieces of cheese. There were enough mugs to go around, so the soldiers clutched the hot drinks with blissful expressions.

When Tory collected the empty mugs and went below to brew more tea, she found Polly and her father in the cabin. Polly must have been telling her father what had been going on, because he looked at Tory in disbelief. "This child can do magic?"

"I'm not a child." Figuring a demonstration was easiest, Tory floated one of the mugs from her hand to the galley counter. "This ship is crewed entirely by mages. Nick found you through magic, and I'm thinking you have some magical power yourself, Captain Rainford."

He closed his gaping mouth and thought. The man badly needed a haircut, but it was easy to see why Anne Rainford had fallen in love with him. "Maybe I do. Something to think about after I return home, take a bath, and sleep in a warm bed with my wife."

Polly sighed, her happiness fading. "You're going to leave again, aren't you?"

"I'm still in the army, kitten." He put an arm around her. "But I'll get a few days leave before I report back to duty."

Having made her tea, Tory took the mugs above decks again, leaving Polly and her father to talk. The *Dream* had cleared the port area and was heading out into the open channel, taking the northern route they'd used when sailing over. "Nick, do you want to visit with your father? Allarde and I should be able to carry on for now."

"Thanks, Tory." Nick let Tory take the wheel and made his way through the soldiers, half of whom were sprawled asleep by now.

Allarde had been talking to their passengers, putting simple bandages on wounds and charming the little dog, who was apparently named Fromage, the French word for cheese. When Nick went below, Allarde moved to the wheelhouse and took over the wheel. Tory relinquished it gladly. Even in fairly calm waters, steering the boat was tiring, and she did not need to be more tired.

The wheelhouse was tight with both of them in it, and that was just the way Tory liked it. She slid a discreet arm around Allarde's waist. "As Polly said, I do believe we're all officially heroes now, Allarde. And we're all hale and hearty."

"We're not home yet." His gaze was on the horizon, where ships large and small were strung in both directions. "The Luftwaffe is still up there, submarines could be lurking, and if we stray outside the channel that has been cleared of mines . . ." He shook his head dourly.

She studied his profile. "Wouldn't you say our circumstances are improving?"

"Indeed they are." He smiled back, but his eyes were shadowed.

Quietly she asked, "Do you foretell danger before we reach England?"

His brow furrowed. "I'm not sure if it's true foretelling or just general worry after two days in the middle of a battle."

"Probably just worry. For two days, war was our world," Tory said thoughtfully. "Now it's quickly beginning to seem like a bad dream."

"No doubt you're right." But his eyes were still shadowed as he gazed toward the white cliffs of home.

CHAPTER 36

As time passed, even Allarde relaxed. The skies were clear and sunny, which was bad in terms of being attacked by the Luftwaffe, but the soldiers were happy to doze on the warm deck. The ships heading across the channel moved at different speeds, some faster, some slower than *Annie's Dream*.

After Polly took over the helm, Tory and Allarde lounged in their usual position against the wheelhouse, discreetly holding hands. She squinted at the ship that was slowly overtaking them. "That's a hospital ship, isn't it? I think I see big red crosses on the funnels."

"Yes, it was converted from a passenger ferry." Allarde sat up straight. "Luftwaffe heading this way."

Tory narrowed her eyes. Two airplanes were flying high over the shipping lane. It wasn't the first time they'd seen Nazi aircraft, but she had a bad feeling about this pair. "Lucky we're too small to interest them."

"The hospital ship is a sizable target," Allarde said grimly.

"Surely they wouldn't attack a ship full of wounded men?"

He shrugged, his gaze fixed on the approaching planes. "They might not see the red crosses. Or they might not care."

With hideous suddenness, a hell-born scream tore through the midday sky as an airplane dived shrieking toward the sea. "Damnation!" Allarde leaped to his feet. "That Stuka is going after the hospital ship!"

Tory also jumped up, unable to do anything but watch in horror as the dive-bomber roared straight down at the ship full of wounded men. A fighter plane escort followed, diving at a less dramatic angle.

"Tory, link with me!" Allarde grabbed her hand with bone-cracking force.

Time seemed to slow as the Stuka dropped its bomb and pulled out of its dive. All Tory's anguished attention was on the bomb that sped toward the hospital ship with lethal precision.

The air almost burned as Allarde hurled all his magic at the bomb, struggling to push it away from the ship. As soon as she recognized what he was doing, Tory frantically joined her power with his, shoving at the evil bomb before it could slaughter hundreds of wounded men. Together they pushed, pushed, pushed, straining their power to the limits.

The bomb dropped just behind the hospital ship, exploding with a horrendous boom and blasting a huge wave of water in all directions. The ship rocked almost to the point of tipping over before it recovered, and the great wave surged toward the *Dream*. But they'd done it!

Tory was on the verge of cheering when the fighter plane swooped down till it was barely skimming above the water. Machine guns blazing, the fighter strafed the hospital ship. Tory winced, but it didn't look as if the attack had done much damage.

Then everything happened at once:

Allarde shouted, "Tory! Get down!"

The Messerschmitt swung toward *Annie's Dream,* still firing its machine guns.

Allarde wrapped himself around Tory and dived toward the deck.

Two of their passengers grabbed their rifles and began shooting at the fighter, shouting, "Murdering Nazi bastards!"

Tory hit the deck with numbing force, Allarde's weight crushing down on her.

Bullets struck the fighter plane's fuel tank and the aircraft exploded into flames.

The last bullets from the Messerschmitt raked across the deck of *Annie's Dream.*

The boat rolled wildly as the huge wave created by the bomb swept under them.

The Messerschmitt crashed into the sea as the BEF soldiers cheered.

And Allarde fell away from Tory, blood jetting from his throat.

Tory screamed in horror. No, *No!* She hadn't believed he could be killed right in front of her eyes, it wasn't fair, *it wasn't fair!*

He rolled onto his back and she saw that a bullet had struck the right side of his neck. The wound didn't even look deep, but a major vessel must have been ripped open. No one could survive long with blood pouring out like that, the brilliant scarlet saturating his gray guernsey.

Tory yanked out the crumpled handkerchief she'd found in Nick's old trousers and pressed it against the wound, desperate to stop the blood flow. As long as he was bleeding, he was alive, wasn't he?

Allarde's eyes flickered open, the misty gray almost black as the spark of life diminished. "I'm glad . . . we had some time, my love."

He drew a rattling breath and his eyes closed.

"Nooooo!!!!!!!!!!!!!!" Tory called out to the heavens, reaching across the channel to touch Elspeth, demanding all the healing energy her friend had. She also grabbed at Nick and Jack and Cynthia and Mrs. Rainford, ruthlessly pulling every shred of power she could find, even the small amount that Polly had recovered.

The healing magic burned in her hands with such ferocity that she thought the blood-soaked handkerchief might burst into flames. She let it fall and pressed her palm directly on the wound.

With Elspeth's power joined to hers, Tory had a clear sense of how the blood vessel had been damaged. A small wound, but large enough to kill in minutes. If she could repair that vessel, close the hole so the bleeding stopped before it was too late . . .

Dimly she felt hands on her shoulders, Nick and Polly both. And one of the soldiers, a man from Lackland who had some power and understood magic, joined them and gave what he could to Tory. There was even a trickle of untrained magic from Captain Rainford, who had taken over the helm.

She took that rush of power and fused it together, wielding the magic like a blade. As she flooded the damaged vessel with healing energy, the lethal little wound began to close. In her mind's eye, she *saw* it closing, a fraction at a time, until the vessel was smooth and solid, blood pulsing calmly through as it was supposed to. Then the protective skin, complete with dark bristles from two days without shaving.

"Tory," Nick's voice said gently. "Tory, I think he's going to be all right. The wound has stopped bleeding. Allarde's shoulder was grazed but nothing to worry about. You can stop now." He pried her hands away from Allarde. "Let go now, Tory. He's going to be all right."

Dazed, she sat back on her heels. Sure enough, the neck wound had closed and there was only a small mark left. All the soldiers had drawn back, respectfully leaving the healers room to work even if they didn't fully understand what was happening. Perhaps because they were Lacklanders, none of them even looked surprised.

Behind them, smoke rose from the sea where the German fighter had crashed. Furiously she hoped the pilot burned in hell as much as he had on earth.

Allarde's eyes flickered open, the spark of life bright again. His face was white, his only color the blood drying on his cheek, but he managed to whisper, "Tory, my love. Maybe . . . not all mortal wounds . . . are lethal."

"I *told* you that if I came I'd make myself useful!" she said stupidly.

He gave a small choke of laughter. His eyes closed and she felt how desperately weak he was, but he reached feebly for her hand.

Relief scalded through her. Tory grabbed his hand, then folded over and hid her face against his bloody guernsey.

And wept.

"Look," Tory said softly, tears stinging her eyes. "The white cliffs of Dover. We're almost home."

Weakened by blood loss, Allarde had spent most of the hours of the trip across the channel dozing with his head in Tory's lap, but now he was strong enough to push himself to a sitting position against the wheelhouse. Before them the famous white chalk cliffs stretched for miles in each direction, timeless and welcoming.

His hand tightened on Tory's. "For how many centuries have returning Englishmen rejoiced to see those cliffs?"

"Many." Tory wiped tears from her eyes with her other hand. The desultory conversations among the soldiers stopped as all gazes turned to the cliffs. "Since there first *were* Englishmen."

Since Allarde was no longer in danger after his healing, they'd decided not to flag down the hospital ship. He didn't need a doctor, and stopping to transfer a patient would make both vessels easy targets for the Luftwaffe and German submarines.

Captain Rainford took over the engine room so Polly could rest, but first she'd made a last batch of heavily sugared tea. Tory gulped hers thirstily, needing the warmth and energy after the huge drain of magical energy. She'd made Allarde drink a cup, too.

Even after the tea, Nick was swaying on his feet both from the fatigue of being up two days straight, plus the energy Tory had pulled from him. One of the passengers, a corporal from a Lackland fishing family, took over the wheel while Nick sprawled on the deck and slept like the dead, Polly curled up beside him.

With the cliffs in sight, Nick woke, yawned, and got to his feet. "I took *Annie's Dream* to Dunkirk, and I should be the one to bring her home."

The soldier nodded and relinquished the helm to Nick. Tory thought she recognized Lackland harbor. . . . Yes, Nick was heading straight for it.

As they approached the harbor at an angle, the passengers moved over to that side, gazes hungry. Nick called out, "Don't all rush to port! We don't want to capsize this close to home."

Some of the soldiers moved back to the other side, but all of the passengers were vibrating to get ashore. As they entered the small harbor, Tory was surprised to see a crowd of people waiting. Most of the berths were filled with boats, some with bullet holes matching their own. The sight was very different from when they left.

As *Annie's Dream* appeared and headed toward her pier, a great cheer rose, echoing from the cliffs. "Can you get to your feet for the triumphal homecoming?" Tory asked Allarde.

He gave her a crooked smile. "I can manage if you help."

She did, aided by one of the soldiers. Allarde was pale, but by leaning against the wheelhouse and wrapping his other arm around

Tory's shoulders, he managed to stay upright. The engine coughed and quit, but they were close enough to the pier to drift in.

Two soldiers tossed mooring lines to the pier and eager bystanders secured the vessel. The battered passengers began pouring off. With most of them from Lackland, there were cries of welcome and embraces. A soldier bent to kiss the pier, then was swooped into an embrace by a weeping woman who must have been his mother.

There was such a churning of excited villagers that Tory was grateful she and Allarde had their safe spot against the wheelhouse. Softly she said, "I'll never forget this if I live to be a hundred."

His arm tightened around her shoulders. "Nor shall I."

Tory's enjoyment of the scene was pierced by a sense of great anxiety, but it wasn't her own. The energy was familiar, and after a moment she realized she was sensing Mrs. Rainford.

A moment later Mrs. Rainford appeared, sliding through the crowd to reach the boat. As soon as she stepped onto the *Dream,* Nick and Polly engulfed her. She locked arms around them both, saying in a choked voice, "God be thanked, you're home safe!"

Yet even the joy of embracing her children couldn't silence her frantic mental calls of, "Tom? *Tom?*"

Captain Rainford climbed wearily onto the deck, dirty, damp, and with a beard that rivaled a hedgehog. "Nick and Polly, you planned perfectly. We just used up the last drop of fuel."

He stopped in his tracks when he saw his wife. *"Annie!"*

Blazing with joy, Anne Rainford broke away from her children and surged into her husband's embrace. Waves of emotion rolled in all directions as they wrapped their arms around each other as if they'd never let go.

Tory sensed that their love had layers she couldn't yet understand. The shared experiences, the joys and concerns of raising their children, the passion that usually was kept behind closed doors, but which now blazed like the sun at high noon.

Sadly, more separation lay ahead. Even a civilian like Tory knew wars were not won by retreats, even miraculous, heroic ones like the Dunkirk evacuation. Who knew what lay ahead for Britain? But for now, Anne and Tom Rainford were together, being watched with bemusement by Nick and approval by Polly.

As for Tory and her friends—they had done their part. Now they could go home.

CHAPTER 37

It was almost worth going to war in order to feel such peace. Tory lay in the sun, as lazy as Horace, who snoozed an arm's length away. The dog had kindly guided her to this quiet spot beside a lilac bush in a protected corner of the Rainford property.

If she opened her eyes, she would be able to look across the channel to Nazi-occupied France, but she preferred to ignore that, just as she chose to ignore the occasional distant rumble of war. Far, far better to let her mind drift along on currents of birdsong and sunshine and the exquisite scent of the lilacs blooming beside her.

Four days had passed since *Annie's Dream* had sailed into Lackland harbor, the last of the town's little ships to return. Another boat had arrived home just a little earlier, which was why there had been such a crowd.

The entire world had watched the evacuation, awed by the sight of all Britain working together to save their men. Operation Dynamo had officially ended on June 4, and the total number of men rescued had been almost 340,000. That had included the entire BEF, along with about 110,000 French troops.

Granted, tons of equipment had been abandoned across the Low Countries and northern France. But Britain's bravery and fierce refusal to surrender had paid off. The American president, Roosevelt, had announced that the United States would send tanks and ships and guns and anything else Britain needed to continue the fight against Hitler.

Not that any of the Irregulars knew that at first. They had all slept for days, getting up only to use the water closet and perhaps drink some tea before staggering back to bed or pallet. They'd all lost weight—the heavy use of magic had literally burned them up. Mrs. Rainford had confided to Tory that she was glad to have lost a few pounds, but Tory needed feeding up.

All of them had been awake by the time Prime Minister Churchill had given an amazing speech to Parliament the day before. The Rainford household had gathered in the kitchen to listen on the wireless.

In his magnificent deep voice, Churchill declaimed, "We shall defend our island, whatever the cost may be, we shall fight on the beaches, we shall fight on the landing grounds, we shall fight in the fields and in the streets, we shall fight in the hills; we shall never surrender . . . !"

Tory had wept openly, and Allarde's hand had tightened around hers. She suspected he was fighting back tears as well.

Today, the Irregulars would finally go home. It seemed a lifetime since Tory had led her friends through Merlin's mirror, though it had been less than a fortnight. She exhaled happily. Bliss was lacking only one more element.

A familiar deep power brushed her mind. Then a gossamer touch on her cheek, followed by another and another . . .

She opened her eyes to see lilac blossoms dancing in the sunshine above her. Swirling gently, they drifted onto her face and throat in a fragile, fragrant rain. Not that she needed to see lilacs dance to know that the last element of bliss was here.

Lazily, she turned her head to watch Allarde approach. Having lost so much blood, he'd been the tiredest of all, but that didn't make him any less splendid. Like Tory, he was wearing his own clothing from 1803 in preparation for the journey home. Call her prejudiced, but she thought the breeches, boots, and coats of her own time were far more flattering to the male figure than the shapeless garments of 1940.

"You look like a lovely little cat dozing in the sunshine." Allarde sat beside her on the grass and bent to give her a light, sweet kiss.

She savored the pleasure of his lips on hers. Even when they were apart, there was a thread of energy connecting them, and that intensified when they were together. Even more when they touched. She murmured, "I'm trying to absorb as much sunlight as I can before we return home to gray, wet autumn."

"Do you think we'll have any trouble going back to our own time?" he asked seriously. "The process seems rather uncontrolled."

"I can take us home by concentrating on our destination. I don't know why I was drawn here the first time, but since Nick knew to look for me, he came right to us. Just as we came here together without a problem." Tory rolled to her side and rested her head on his thigh, relaxed and happy. "I wouldn't like to try going to an unknown time, though."

He stroked her hair, tracing the edge of her ear in a way that made her want to purr like the cat he'd called her. "Strange to think that if all goes well, we'll be back at Lackland in a few hours," he murmured. "Mere students again."

"I'll be glad for it." She covered a lazy yawn. "It was an honor to be part of a great and noble undertaking, but I don't want to do it again! This isn't our war."

"Very true. We have a war of our own to worry about." Allarde rested his hand on Tory's shoulder. "Hitler and Napoleon both want to conquer the world. And in both eras, it's Britain that stands alone against the Continental monster."

"Perhaps that's why the mirror brought me here the first time," Tory said, interested enough to open her eyes. "The similarities between our times."

"I could wish for a different similarity than war," he said dryly. "I would prefer to die in my own time rather than in a different century."

Tory sighed, some of the brightness going out of the day. "Is your life still ruled by the certainty of your death?"

"Not like it was, Tory," he said thoughtfully. "I had my mortal wound, and you saved my life. Apparently Miss Wheaton was right when she said the future isn't fixed. Now I'm like anyone else. I'll die someday, but for now, I intend to live life to the fullest." He bent and kissed her again. "That means enjoying every moment I can with you, my Lady Victoria."

She slipped her hand around his neck, holding him close so the joyous kiss wouldn't end. "There is something very special between us," she whispered. "I'm glad it won't be wasted."

Gently he moved her head from his lap and stretched out on the grass beside her. "It won't." He smiled teasingly. "I'd be tempted to ruin you, but I'm weak as a kitten from losing so much blood. The doctor who bandaged that scratch on my arm said it would take weeks to get my strength back."

"Ruination is a wickedly tempting thought," Tory agreed mischievously. "But what seems possible in a time not our own will look different when we go home."

"You're right, of course." He took her hand, lacing his fingers with hers. "Ruination can wait. What matters is being together." He sighed. "I suspect it will be difficult to go back to being students in a school that exists to change us. People in this time may not believe in magic, but at least we're not condemned."

"That part I like," Tory agreed. "But I think that when we return to Lackland, we'll settle back into our usual routine quickly." She gestured toward France. "All this will seem like a mad dream."

"The headmasters may lock us all up separately so we'll never be able to go into the Labyrinth again." His fingers tightened on hers. "If that happens, we might not see each other for a long time."

Tory shivered at the thought. "I think I can get us back to the Labyrinth the same night we left. No one will know we've left, apart from the fact that we're all skinny and exhausted." Except Cynthia, who managed to appear pale and interesting instead of haggard. But she'd worked so hard on the weather magery that Tory couldn't even resent how beautiful her roommate always looked.

"That will be convenient!" he said, relieved. "Though it will only delay the time when I'm disinherited by my father. Since I'm his only son, he would be happy if he could overlook my magic so I can become Duke of Westover someday."

"Would he really disinherit you?" Tory asked curiously, thinking that the duke sounded more tolerant than her father had been.

"He won't if I behave like a proper young gentleman who never had any magic and Lackland was all just a big misunderstanding," Allarde said wryly. "But we still have a war to win against Napoleon, and I have a feeling that my magic will be needed. It's unlikely I'll ever be able to make you a duchess."

She rolled onto her back, helpless with laughter. "Do you know how many women in the world will never become duchesses? And most of them manage to survive and prosper very well."

"I want the best for you, Tory." He smiled into her eyes. "Have I mentioned that my given name is Justin?"

Justin. *Her* Justin. She savored the name in her mind. A just man. Perfect.

She leaned forward and kissed her foolish darling. "I already have the best."

AUTHOR'S NOTE

In 1803, Napoleon was assembling the Army of Boulogne on the French coast with the intention of invading England. Tunnels to house troops were excavated in the chalk cliffs under Dover Castle as a defense against the expected invasion.

Starting in 1938, the tunnels were extended and modernized and used for a naval headquarters. There were also living quarters and an underground hospital. It is now possible to tour many of the tunnels, but I understand that some are still closed to the public because they contain classified material.

The amazing armada of great and small ships that saved 340,000 men from Dunkirk is one of history's great stories. Usually the English Channel is rough and stormy in late spring, and the evacuation would not have been possible if not for the amazingly calm weather during those days.

In particular, on Tuesday, May 28, 1940, a storm heading in from the Atlantic miraculously swerved north between Ireland and Britain. (People ask where I get my story ideas. Believe me, history offers lots of great stories!)

There is no record of any teenage girls being part of the armada— but who knows?

Fish and chips were one of the few foods never rationed in Britain during or after World War II. If the attempt had been made, there might have been a revolt!

Turn the page for a sneak peek of

Dark Passage

coming in Fall 2011 from St. Martin's Griffin.

Copyright © 2011 by M. J. Putney

France, Autumn 1940

Tory had almost reached her destination when a machine gun blasted crazily from the farmhouse ahead. As Lady Victoria Mansfield in her own time, she'd been taught to dance and manage a household and embroider, rather badly. As a mageling and a member of Merlin's Irregulars, she'd learned to dive for cover when she heard gunfire.

She hit the ground hard and took refuge under the hedge on her left, grateful for the darkness. Clamping down on her shock, she peered through the dense branches.

The machine gun was being fired in bursts. Sparks spat from the muzzle that stuck out from a window on the upper floor. The weapon wasn't aimed in her direction, which was good. But damnably, it was aimed at the small barn that sheltered the people she'd promised to protect.

Another thing she'd learned in 1940 was swearing. She muttered some words that would have shocked her parents, the earl and countess of Fairmount, speechless.

She had to stop that rain of death, and quickly. But how? She was no warrior. She was an undersized sixteen-year-old girl dressed to look even younger. She wouldn't know what to do with a gun if it was handed to her fully loaded.

But she was a mageling, and she could draw on the magical power and talent of her friends. She studied the small stone house. It was old and simply constructed, two stories tall. Probably just two rooms downstairs and two on the upper floor.

The building was dark except for the room containing the machine gun. Likely the inhabitants of the place had fled when their home had been commandeered.

If she could get inside and come up behind the men with the gun, she should be able to do—something. Exactly what would depend on what she had to work with.

Cautiously she circled the farmhouse, glad she was carrying her stealth stone. It didn't make her invisible, but it would make the men less likely to notice her. Unfortunately, bullets were mindless and impossible to mislead.

Like most old houses, the windows were few and small. She tested the back door. Locked. Directly above it was a casement window large enough for her to climb through. In case it was locked, she selected a rock the size of a large man's fist from the stone border around a flower bed. Then she turned her mind inward to focus her magic.

Click! She began to rise, skimming her left hand along the stone wall until she hovered next to the window. She tried unsuccessfully to open it.

Could magic muffle the sound of breaking glass? She hadn't tried that before, but it should work. Doing magic was mostly a matter of focusing magical power on the desired result—and Tory had a great deal of power.

She concentrated on silencing the sound. For good measure, she waited until the next burst of machine-gun fire. Smashing the rock into the right-hand casement sent shards of glass flying, nicking her wrist.

The breaking glass made very little sound, but she still waited to hear if she'd been noticed. Coarse laughter came from the front of the house and a man spoke in French. So they were collaborators, perhaps police working with the Nazis. Their raucous words suggested that they were drunk and amusing themselves by shooting up the flimsy barn that sheltered helpless people.

One of them made a sneering remark about killing filthy Jews. For a red-rage moment, Tory wished she did have a gun and that she knew how to use it.

But magic was her weapon. She felt inside for the window latch. The latch was badly stuck, so she gave it a little blast of magic. The lock opened but her hovering bobbled as she diverted energy. She was using up power at an alarming rate.

She wrenched the casement open and glided inside the dark room. Then she cautiously created the dimmest possible mage light. The room was a simply furnished bedroom. The bed looked rumpled, as if the sleepers had left in a hurry. That would also explain why the door had been left ajar, enabling Tory to hear the voices.

As she'd guessed from outside, the primitive cottage would have been old in her own time. Gnarled beams ran full-length across the ceiling. Good.

Outside the room was a short corridor that led to the stairs and the front bedroom. That door was wide open, revealing three men in French police uniforms. All three held open bottles. As Tory watched, one took a deep swig and made some joke she couldn't understand. The deadly machine gun was mounted on a tripod and pointed out the window. Ammunition belts lay on the floor along with empty brass shell casings.

With only the barest of plans, she walked softly toward the front room. She had just reached the doorway when one of the policemen turned and looked right at her. He blinked uncertainly, but the stealth stone wasn't enough to conceal a direct stare.

"A little girl!" he exclaimed. "Must have hidden when the rest of the family ran."

A second man turned and smiled nastily. "*La belle petite* should have run, too."

He lurched toward Tory. Even from six feet away she smelled alcohol on his breath. Her rage flared again. Narrowing her focus to lethal intensity, she called on the power of her friends. Most of all, she drew on Allarde's special talent.

Their magic flowed into her, fierce and primal. She made a furious sweeping gesture that blasted her concentrated power at the ceiling beams. "*Enough!*"

. . . and she pulled the massive beams in the front half of the cottage down on the men and their horrible gun. Their angry shouts were cut off with lethal suddenness.

Tory instantly threw herself out the door in a rolling tumble. Even as she hit the floor, she heard the remaining roof beams begin to groan ominously.

Devil take it! The whole cottage was collapsing!

She scrambled to her feet and raced to the back bedroom, diving out the open window before the roof could crush her. Something hard struck her left arm. She barely managed to catch herself before smashing into the ground. With the last of her power, she turned her fall into a bumpy but safe landing. Damp earth had never felt so good.

Gasping for breath, she pulled her shattered nerves together before pushing herself to a sitting position. Her left arm hurt like Hades and blood saturated her sleeve, but at least she'd escaped. Worse was the pain and horror of knowing she'd just killed or maimed three men. They were brutes, but she hadn't wanted their lives on her conscience.

She drew a shuddering breath. She had *sworn* that she would never return to the future again. Why the devil was she here?

Because she had no choice.

Some risks must be taken.
And sometimes love lies
hidden in the
heart of danger.

Dark Passage

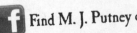

AVAILABLE SEPTEMBER 2011

In this exciting follow up to
DARK MIRROR,
Tory and her friends are called
upon once again to use their
powers to save a family in danger.

www.mjputney.com

Find M. J. Putney on Facebook

VISIT WORDSNSTUFF.NET
for chances to win your favorite books, sneak
peeks at upcoming titles, downloads, and much more!

St. Martin's Griffin